PRAISE FOR *MAGI*

"Wands weaves a thrilling and sometimes chilling tale that explores the predictive powers of the imagery found on tarot cards, connecting symbolism and legend through unique characters and extraordinary events."

✳ Lisa J. Yarde, author of *Order of the Dragon* and *Sultana's Legacy*

"Susan Wands's *Magician and Fool* tells the intriguing and little-known story of Pamela Colman Smith, creator of one of the most famous tarot decks in history. With meticulously researched period detail, Wands brings nineteenth-century London to life. From the secret chambers of the Golden Dawn society to private screenings of ancient Egyptian texts and artifacts, Wands takes the reader on a journey through not only history but also the compelling beauty and danger of the dark arts."

✳ Melodie Winawer, author of *Anticipation* and *The Scribe of Siena*

"*Magician and Fool* is a spellbinding story that combines history and fiction—author Susan Wands presents an enchanting picture of intriguing historical figures. This book will appeal to a wide range of readers interested in a glimpse into the Victorian theater and the mysterious occult group known as the Golden Dawn. I can't wait for the second book in the series."

✳ Sharonah Rapseik, host of the podcast *Magic Universe with Sharonah*

BOOK ONE, ARCANA ORACLE SERIES

MAGICIAN AND FOOL

SUSAN WANDS

Published by SparkPress, a BookSparks imprint,
A division of SparkPoint Studio, LLC
Phoenix, Arizona, USA, 85007
www.gosparkpress.com

Published 2023
Printed in the United States of America
Print ISBN: 978-1-68463-186-5
E-ISBN: 978-1-68463-187-2
Library of Congress Control Number: 2022920600

Interior Design by Tabitha Lahr

To Robert Petkoff, for believing

PART I

FINDING MAGIC

CHAPTER ONE

SEEKING THE CROWN OF BRUIN

A sudden clamor from out front startled seven-year-old Pamela Colman Smith. She ran to her bedroom window and squealed with delight as she looked below. In the road, a cluster of child-sized skeletons and scarecrows darted round a tall, fuzzy lion carrying a torch and a basket of turnips. In the dimming light, the masked guisers came up the walkway to her new house. While one of the skeletons knocked on her front door, a pirate with an eye patch set himself in the center of the yard and began a frenzied jig before the revelers.

"Oh, Maud, I want to go with them," Pamela said, hopping up and down. "I wish we knew people here who could take me."

Maud sat at the vanity, arranging her elaborate pile of dark, wavy hair. "Unfortunately, you're new to the neighborhood," she said. "And I'm too old to take you, my friend. So, there you are."

In the yard, skeletons and scarecrows armed themselves with turnips as the maid's voice rang out pleading for "no mischief." The pirate gyrated to cheers and clapping from the masked children, his palms open for payment.

Pamela stopped bouncing when she noticed a strange movement in the shrubbery. Luminescent figures, the size of a grown-up's hand, hovered in the hedge. Pamela's eyes adjusted to the twilight hues as the glowing, green beings flickered in the shrubbery. Several of them skittered up the fence and out into the street. They were too big for beetles, but too small for birds. Would there be butterflies here in Manchester in October?

"Maud, what are those?" Pamela asked, her voice rising as she pressed her face against the window glass.

"You mean, *who* are they. They are just noisy revelers with false faces on for All Hallow's Eve."

Pamela pointed to the small creatures milling behind the crowd of merrymakers. "No, Maud, come see. There's something odd in the garden."

Maud stood next to her holding the lamp, its light reflecting their mirror image in the window. Pamela was short and round compared to tall, willowy Maud. Her elegant friend at fifteen years of age was already six feet tall.

Maud dimmed her lamp. "I see them now."

At that moment, the trick-or-treaters noticed Maud and Pamela in the upstairs window and, in an attempt to frighten them, shrieked. Pamela watched Maud stretch open her mouth as though she were howling, then imitated her. For a few seconds, they silently screeched at the guisers. The scarecrows and ghosts jeered back at them, shaking their fists and waggling their bums. The maid called to them and they disappeared from Pamela's view as they raced up to the front door. They reappeared with biscuits in their hands and stampeded into Withington Road, bumping into one another in the murky dusk. A trail of blinking, greenish beings rose from the yard and flew after them in full pursuit in the twilight.

"The fairies are chasing the tricksters," Pamela said, straining to see the last of them fly off.

"Now, Miss Smith, we don't know that they're fairies," Maud said, returning to the vanity and turning up her lamp.

Pamela touched the cold window. The warmth of her finger left a ghostly imprint. In the glass, she watched Maud put finishing touches on her waves of curls. This was the first time the two girls had been alone since Maud and her father had arrived three days ago to visit with them. Pamela last saw Maud in London two years ago when she was on holiday from her boarding school in France, and had known her ever since she could remember. She was the older sister Pamela never had, and she relished her nickname, "fairy sister." Whenever Maud came to call, she always paid attention to Pamela and entertained her with tales of her travels and ghost stories.

She was different now; the years away had changed Maud. She no longer called Pamela "fairy sister" but Miss Smith. Maud wore a corset under her clothes and put her hair up, making her look like a taller version of her mother, who had just passed away.

Maud's father, Captain Gonne, was a scary man. Mother said he spoke six languages, none of them politely. Since he was a recent widower, Maud was expected to be her father's hostess at their new home in Paris. In the window, Pamela saw her own reflection: a stocky girl with flyaway hair and dark eyes. But someday she would have her own fancy dress and a tower of curls.

"I'll tell Father something odd was in the garden," Maud said. "Maybe something followed us from Ireland; they are rife with spirits there." Putting on her Irish accent, she continued, "Well, it's good to see Nera's fairies are still searching for those human murderers on Hallow Eve."

"Wait. I'm seeing Irish fairies in Manchester?" Pamela asked, bounding over to Maud.

"It's said that those with the gift can see the other world open up tonight, and maybe this part of the world needs opening up," Maud replied.

"What about the times when I see things that even you can't see?" Pamela asked.

"That's just your overactive imagination. Where was I? Oh yes, you know that on this evening, Nera comes out from the fairies' *síd* of Cruachan and tracks down the thieving murderers who stole the fairy crown of Bruin. Perhaps Nera thinks whoever stole it brought it here."

"Or maybe they're English fairies," Pamela said. She ran to Maud's bed and jumped on it. "Why are you talking like that?"

"I was given this accent by an Irish fairy, if you must know."

Pamela stopped jumping. "You did not. You learned it from your governess. Your father told us your Irish accent is why you had to go to school in France."

"Well, that was one of the reasons," Maud said, continuing the accent. "If I'm going to tell you Irish stories, I need to use the right voice. Just like Nera, you have to be a fool sometimes and find a different path, to speak a different way."

"Maud," Pamela said, "why did Nera even let the humans into the fairy kingdom? Tell me again."

Treads creaking on the stairs outside the bedroom meant buckets were being brought up for the bath.

"I said hot water, not tepid," Mother's voice rang from the bathroom down the hall.

The banging of the dining room door signaled the maid setting the table, while the front door slammed and Father announced he was home. He would be in the parlor, indisposed until supper. Pamela and Maud looked at one another.

"We only have time for a short story," Maud said, picking up her shawl from the back of the chair and throwing it over her shoulders. "Supper will be soon."

"I wish I could be at the table with you," Pamela said.

"All in good time. So, remember, the story starts with Nera, walking on Samhain with his little white dog on the mountain path near Cruachan. The wee dog was stopping and scratching at something, just as Nera was about to accidentally step off the cliff—"

On cue, Pamela stood on the bed with one foot, dangling the other over the edge, precariously balancing herself. "When he found a split path!" she said.

"And what have I told you about split paths?" Maud asked.

"They're thresholds for magic," Pamela answered, jumping down from her one-legged position and landing next to Maud.

"Correct. And it was at this split in the road that Nera almost fell off. But as his dog whined and scratched he showed Nera there was a fairy mound in the split. It was a fairy entrance, for the fairy mounds of Erin are always open on this day. Magic is all around us on All Hallow's Eve."

Pamela played with the fringe on Maud's shawl. "Those could have been magical bugs outside here tonight—" she murmured.

"Let me finish, Miss Smith. So, brave Nera followed the fairies, leaping from cliff to cliff, until he came to their king in the *síd*."

"What's a *síd*?" Pamela asked, rocking back and forth.

"The fairy underworld—how many times have I told ya? It's where he remained and married one of the fairy women. It was she who revealed to Nera the fairies' secret hiding place in the *síd*—the well. And it was there where the fairy king's crown was hidden."

"Why would the fairies hide a crown in a well?"

"Well, would you look for a crown there? On the following November Eve—Hallow's Eve—Nera was determined to go back to his human people to tell them of the sights he had seen in the fairy underworld.'

"'But who will believe that I've gone into the fairy world of *síd*?' he asked.

"'Take fruits of summer with thee to make proof of our world,' said his fairy wife. 'But come back to me.'

"So, he took wild garlic, primrose, and golden fern, then left the fairy world and his fairy wife. On the following November Eve when the *síd* of Cruachan opened again, Nera came back. But who do you think followed?"

"The greedy human men on this side," Pamela whispered.

"Yes, the hosts of greed heard Nera bragging about the riches of the *síd*, so the human traitors followed Nera and plundered the *síd*, taking away the crown of Bruin from the well. But the fairy king forced Nera to stay with his wife and the fairy world closed again. Nera is now captive in the fairy underworld and may only come out once a year."

Pamela rose from the cot and danced on one foot. "His fairy wife must have been angry with him—he goes away for a year and brings back humans? Just so he could prove he saw the other side? Did his dog go with him? How could the fairy crown be worn by anyone else? It would be too small, wouldn't it?"

Maud kissed the top of Pamela's head. "Enough questions. My family tells this tale each Hallow's Eve just once. For those of us with gifts of other sight, the other world opens up. Never forget that this feast of the dead came before the time of the church." Maud got up and lifted the dropper from a bottle. The scent of lilacs filled the room.

Pamela sat up. "All your stories come from before the time of the church. The Other Side, the Fairy Underworld, Flying Kings and Queens, Nera, the Fool. Wait—is Nera still stuck in the *síd*?"

"Last question. Sure he is. Every Halloween, when the *síd* of Cruachan opens up, Nera comes out to try to find the murderers who stole the crown of Bruin. It's the least he can do to make amends with his fairy family. He's out there looking for the crown now."

"I wish I could help him look or be with you at dinner instead of staying in my room," Pamela said.

In a short time, she would be having supper in the kitchen with the staff—out of the way of the night's festivities. Pamela was allowed to be around the adults only to perform her piece in the parlor before dinner. She rehearsed with the parlor maid yesterday and was anxious to show Mother and Father. During the month that they had been here in Manchester, Pamela had only spent time with her parents when they went to the Sweden-borgian church. As far as Pamela could tell, no one at the service came from Sweden, and it was all pretty dull except when they talked about visiting planets.

Maud motioned Pamela to sit at the vanity. "Let's see that you look your best tonight." Her Irish accent was replaced by a refined English pronunciation. "You look like you've been pulled through a bush backwards. Let's neaten you up before the Boggart sees you."

"Oh, you said that before," Pamela said as she sat with a thump. "I don't know why the Boggart is bothered just because I'm wearing my play clothes. Why would a spirit pinch you just because you wear the wrong blouse, or don't put your toys away?"

But Pamela did feel the Boggart pinch her, especially when she got paint on her dress or spilled tea on her shoes.

"Dress, now," Maud said, lightly tickling her side.

Pamela stood and took off her shift as Maud picked up the ironed white dress the maid had set out. Pamela lifted her arms as the starched smock slid down her body. She was facing the mirror and in the reflection she watched Maud fasten her buttons.

Maud unpinned her top curls so that a massive pile of ring-lets cascaded down her back like a waterfall. "Make my hair look like yours," Pamela begged. "I want to look like you for my performance."

Maud set the curling iron on the lamp to heat. "Well, I can use these tongs to make some curls. Maybe they will last until your performance."

Usually, Pamela's hair was styled in the simplest way—tied in braids and pinned on top, according to Mother's instruc-tions. When they lived in London, Pamela had to pass Mother's inspection in order to be allowed into the parlor. Pamela dreaded getting ready for parties here as the maid had not been very patient, tugging a comb through her hair and scrubbing roughly behind her ears. Tonight, having Maud's gentle touch was a treat.

"Did your governess teach you how to style hair?" Pamela asked as Maud twisted her hair around the heated tongs.

Maud snorted. "No, she only knew how to braid. I was the one who studied fashion plates. You can be sure I'll know how to do my hair when we live in Paris." She patted the fat sausage curls appearing on the back of Pamela's head. "There. This ought to please even your mother."

Pamela held a hand mirror up to see the back of her head. The three rows of pinned swatches were a far cry from Maud's plump swirls, but at least they were curls. Pamela sighed, then brightened.

"Shall we tell Mother we saw the fairies?" Pamela asked. "If magic is out tonight, she'll want to know."

"Magic is out every night, but tonight all mortals can touch it. And your mother finds enough magic with her religious friends. I only hope you don't become a Swedenborgian, Fairy Sister."

"Why not?" Pamela asked, wiggling with pleasure at her nickname. "The Swedenborgians believe they can fly."

"And they believe they can eat green cheese on Venus and Mars, which I highly doubt. If prayer led to miracles, we'd all have access to our own magic. But we don't." Maud smiled at her. "Except for tonight, when the spirits are roaming about, we can touch magic from the other side."

"Oh, Maud, can you teach me how to touch magic tonight?" Pamela asked.

Maud put the brush and tongs away. "Well, I'm not saying I can do magic, but we can imagine what magic is like."

"How?"

"Let's try to find it the way Nera did."

Maud stood on the edge of the bed and balanced herself, reenacting Pamela's mimic of Nera nearly stepping off the cliff, one foot dangling out. Pamela grabbed Maud's other foot, anchoring her, while Maud made whistling sounds as though she were flying through the air like a bird. Pamela pulled her back and they tussled, mussing her hair.

"My hair!" Maud squawked while laughing.

Pamela stood up and Maud held her by the foot as she pretended to step off the cliff.

A lump formed in Pamela's throat. She looked back at Maud and cried, "What if I really fall?"

Maud growled at her, "And what if you really fly?" She loosened her grip on Pamela's ankle. "Fly!"

Pamela fell off the bed onto the soft rug, both of them laughing as she landed. Pamela sat up, and a spasm coursed through her, making her head jerk. Behind her eyes an image froze—a blond young man. He looked up, a dog leaping at his heels as laughter echoed in the distance.

It was Nera. He had escaped from the fairy kingdom. He lifted a foot from the side of the path toward the cliff's edge as a strange music of harps and horns played.

Maud peered over the edge of the bed, eyeing her sharply. "What is it, child? What is happening?"

It hit Pamela in her mind first: the man—or was he a boy?—was standing sideways right before her. He turned to her and dissolved into tiny crystals, pouring behind her eyes, behind her skull, dripping into her blood. She felt the crystals dissolving in the countless tiny rivers of blood flowing through her veins. When she'd absorbed the image, her blood bold with pieces of him, the fool blossomed inside her. Half on a cliff, half off, waiting for the world to start.

Pamela raced to get back on top of her bed to fly again. Maud switched places and sat on the floor, watching her. Pamela raised both arms to balance herself and slowly lifted one foot off the bed. In her mind's eye, Nera again came to the spot on the mountain pathway. Maud lay down on her back, both hands behind her head as though she were watching clouds going by, whistling her flying sounds as Pamela teetered above her. Pamela looked up and saw the last rays of the sun as it dipped out of sight. The music in her head played even more loudly, and in time she felt herself lift her other foot off the bed. The blood inside her body was warm and churning. She reached toward the last rays of the sun with outstretched hands. Nera also lifted his other foot off the cliff. She moved forward.

Pamela cried out, "Look out, Nera, you Fool!"

Her body had no weight, no feeling.

Looking down, she saw she was floating in the air above Maud, whose mouth dropped open.

⁓

An hour later, Pamela sat on the hallway floor outside her mother's boudoir.

Urgent undertones from Maud and sighs from Mother burbled from within. As Pamela stared at the door handle, a feeling of blue-black chalk bubbled in her throat, almost choking her. When she tried to explain this kind of feeling to her parents (feeling colors, seeing smells, and tasting the minutes of the clock), she was reprimanded for being "too fanciful." But when the blue-black bubbles appeared, she usually saw something that she had never seen before. Above the bathroom door handle, the gold-plate inset around the keyhole darkened. Smoke drifted out of the keyhole, and something bat-like swooped out of the small opening and soared above Pamela. It fluttered down the hallway and disappeared.

Was it a bat spirit taking a bath with Mother? She scanned the hallway and ceiling. Nothing. Whatever had come out was now gone, nowhere to be seen. These sightings happened frequently. When she told Mother and Father, they always gave one another a mysterious look before dismissing her.

The door opened and Maud stood, her coiled hair now hanging in limp curls. Gesturing for Pamela to come near, she held her close, whispering, "I've told your mother about the appearance of the fairies and your episode of possible flying—"

"Possible!" Pamela hissed. "Maud, you saw me!"

"Yes, I did," Maud said, straightening Pamela's smock. Bending down further to murmur in her ear, she breathed, "Pamela, your mother might have a hard time believing you are as special as you are. She has problems of her own, and she's worried if people hear of this they might shun . . . you. But remember—I saw you fly." Maud stood up straight and said loudly, "Now, go in, she wants to talk to you."

Maud gave her a quick squeeze of the shoulder and guided her into the bathroom, closing the door behind her. Pamela could hear her walking to her room.

Lolling in the only bathtub in the house, Mother had a damp cloth over her eyes, her face coated with some sort of pink mud. Her opaque body was barely seen under the surface of the water; dried rosebuds, herbs, and orange blossoms covered the bathwater and perfumed the room.

"Mother, did Maud tell you—" Pamela started.

"She most certainly did," Mother said, snatching off the eye cloth, her rose-colored face mask cracking as she sat up. Her naturally wavy, light brown hair was tied up in rags for curls, and care had been taken to keep the clay mask away from her eyes and hair.

Pamela stared at Mother's oval face, the round circles of clay cracking over her cheeks and her small, pointed nose. She must have been taking her cough medicine again, as her blue eyes were filled with the little red lines she got when she took it. Mother stared back at her and shook her head.

"Why, Pamela, why?" she murmured. "Why do I see so little of myself in you?" Mother's knees went up to her chest, and she motioned for Pamela to take the pitcher off the stand next to the tub and rinse her back.

As bits of blossoms and buds washed away, Mother took handfuls of water to dissolve the mud on her face.

"How many times have I told you, Pamela, no one is to know about the fanciful scenes you think you see. Your visions would be considered odd by a few, strange to most, and terrifying to everyone else. Keep them to yourself."

Pamela stood with the empty pitcher next to her mother's back, unsure of what to do or say next. She sat on the stool and tried to keep from crying.

"Mother, you know how in church they say you can fly to planets?"

"Only blessed people who study the Swedenborgian religion can fly," Mother replied, taking a towel and standing. Streams of flowery water gushed down her legs. "And this is only after years of study. It is true that our founding father visited the moon, Mercury, Jupiter, and Mars, and spoke with the human angels there. But you didn't fly tonight, Pamela."

"Well," Pamela said, looking down as her mother changed into her robe. "Maybe I didn't fly. Maybe I only floated."

Mother came over and lifted Pamela's head up with her damp hands. "It is possible, Pamela, that your mind fell asleep for a minute in the world of the spirits. These are the spirits that help you to the afterlife. Maybe they are trying to help you find your heavenly path."

"What is Heaven like, Mother?" Pamela asked, trying to slow the release of Mother's hands on her face. It was no use. Mother's hands dropped and she sat before her mirror, putting a thick, gooey white cream on her face.

"Ah, Heaven!" Mother murmured. "Heaven will be a grand ball. I will dance my magic slippers off, so don't mourn for me!"

"Will all our relatives be in Heaven?" Pamela asked.

Mother held up a fingerful of cream. "Well, your father's father might not, as mighty as he was. He was not particularly good to us."

"Will you be there? Will Father and Maud?" Pamela asked, standing behind her mother, almost putting a hand on her shoulder.

"If we play our cards right, we will," Mother answered. "Speaking of Maud, I want you to do well with your piece tonight. Her father is a very important man, so don't disappoint us."

It hadn't occurred to Pamela that Captain Gonne would be there in the parlor.

Mother had said that Captain Gonne was more like a father to their family than their real ones. In fact, Pamela knew her first voyage as a baby was not to sail back to New York to meet the Smiths or Colmans of Brooklyn, but to visit Captain Gonne and his family in Paris.

"Is Captain Gonne going to be a mayor in Paris like Grandfather Smith was in Brooklyn?" Pamela asked.

"No, Captain Gonne is a military diplomat born to a fortune and speaks six languages. Your father's father spoke only one language—climbing out of poverty and remaining out of it."

"Is that bad?" Pamela asked, putting her finger in her mother's face cream jar.

"Not necessarily," Mother answered, dusting powder over her shoulders. "Cyrus Porter Smith was ambitious, I'll give him that. A lawyer, senator, builder of subways and ferries. And he finally got what he wanted to be: mayor of Brooklyn. But he didn't love art, and he certainly wasn't fond of me. Enough. Let's concentrate on tonight. You do know your lines?"

"Yes," Pamela said in a small voice. "Mother, what does 'adulterous' mean?"

Her mother's hand stilled the feather puff full of powder. "Why, it means being an adult."

"I thought so," Pamela said. "And who will be here tonight?"

"In addition to Maud and Captain Gonne, your father's employers, Mr. Nicholas and Mr. Culshaw, and some of their artists. Hopefully, one of them can accompany me on the piano. Now, go downstairs and have your supper. You'll be in the parlor at seven o'clock."

A roar of laughter from the guests inside the parlor made Pamela's heart thump. She stood in the hallway by the door awaiting her cue, the curls Maud had styled now sitting on her head like rolled lumps of felt. At least her dress was still clean after dinner. She gazed at the floor where she had set her toy theatre.

On her first visit to her father's store, Pamela had been given a welcome gift by the owners, Mr. Nicholas and Mr. Culshaw. Nicholas and Culshaw owned the most popular interior design shop in Manchester, and Father was their new accountant. Their gift was a toy theatre, a replica of the local playhouse, the Theatre Royal Manchester. Mr. Nicholas told her that twenty years ago, a famous London actor, Henry Irving, started out there. The gift included a paper doll of Mr. Irving, with a somewhat large nose and high forehead, and two other cutouts, one of a handsome young man and a beautiful young woman.

For tonight's entertainment, Pamela had decided to perform the play *The Cup*, using the three cutouts in her toy theatre.

The parlor door opened, she picked up the theatre, and Pamela's mother ushered her into the crowded room. Maud and her father sat on one couch, Mr. Nicholas and Mr. Culshaw on the other. The six designers who created the wallpaper and paint for the store sat in chairs around the room. One stood and brought Mother back to sit next to him. Father gave her a small wave as he bit his lip.

After putting the miniature theatre down on the table in the center of the floor, Pamela stood in front of the guests, her knees knocking together.

"A short play, *The Cup* by Alfred Tennyson."

She knelt down and from one wing of the miniature theatre, she extended a paper doll attached to a wooden stick.

"Here is the Galatian noblewoman, Camma," Pamela announced.

She then slid out the paper doll of the handsome man so that they stood side by side. "Here is her husband, Sinnatus."

In a voice that she hoped sounded like a noblewoman, Pamela recited:

Oh, Sinnatus, Let in the happy distance, and that all
But cloudless heaven which we have found together
In our three married years!

Leaving the two paper dolls to lean against one another center stage, Pamela slid out the third doll. This was the Henry Irving look-alike, which had a knife attached to his paper hand. The Sinnatus paper doll glided over to the intruder. In as low a voice as Pamela could muster as Sinnatus, she continued.

Synorix, Adulterous dog!

Mother groaned from her chair as Synorix, the Henry Irving doll, knocked Sinnatus down. Pamela mimicked stabbing sounds as Sinnatus turned over and over. Sounds of muffled laughter from the guests reached Pamela's ears, and her face burned but she carried on. Camma leaned over the fallen Sinnatus, and the paper doll shook with weeping. The murderer Synorix took center stage.

Camma for my bride—
The people love her—if I win her love,
They too will cleave to me, as one with her.
There then I rest, Rome's tributary king.
Marry me.

Pamela hooked a paper cup over Camma's hand.

I have no fears of this second marriage. Drink
From this wedding cup.

Pamela made drinking sounds.

It's poisoned.

Both dolls fell over dead.

The End.

The room exploded with sounds of applause. Mr. Nicholas and Mr. Culshaw made their way to her, patted her on the head, and then showed the other guests the theatre's detachable roof. Maud was by her side giving her a kiss on the cheek, and soon the rest of the designers lined up to congratulate her.

Captain Gonne, in his dark blue military uniform, came up to her and kissed her hand.

"Well done, Miss Smith. A lot can be told in a few lines," he said in a very proper English accent.

"Twelve lines," Pamela answered. "And I said them all correctly."

Mother rubbed her arm and Father smiled, and raised up his hands in applause. Before Pamela could ask to stay longer, the maid picked up her theatre and she was escorted to the door. The maid and the cook brought her up to her bedroom on the third floor, the cook leaving some of the biscuits handed out to the revelers earlier. As soon as she was helped into her night-dress, they both went downstairs.

Pamela lay in bed listening to Maud sing as the piano played along. She fell asleep for a while and woke up. Her bedroom was too dark, so she tiptoed to the door to prop it open. Light from the gas lamp in the hallway spilled in, and the room seemed warmer.

The toy theatre had been placed on her bedside table, and

she stopped to examine it before hopping back into bed. She took her fingers and traced the theatre's four gray pillars in front and the sloping windows on the side. *Good job, theatre. If you were a puppy, you'd be panting after your showing tonight,* thought Pamela. She reached out to pat it as another gale of laughter rose from downstairs. Tomorrow Maud would have to tell her everything that had gone on.

Pamela gazed out the window next to her bed. Wisps of clouds stretched past the pitted, pearl moon. *There seems to be so much magic on the other side trying to press itself in tonight.* There were no signs of flying spirits. Was Nera still out there looking for the thieves who'd stolen the crown of Bruin?

Maybe she could fly to meet him. She gathered her nightgown around her so that her legs were free and waddled to the end of the bed, facing the headboard. Dropping her nightgown's skirt, she held out her arms and lifted one foot off the bed's edge, circling it.

The clock struck two. She took a deep breath and started to lift her other foot. Instead of floating, she fell headfirst on her bed, her arm hitting the bedside table. The miniature theatre crashed to the floor. She rushed down to see it. In the half-light, she realized the toy had broken completely in half. The stage section lay one way, and the audience seats lay another. The roof had tumbled under her bed. She lay there stunned for a moment, and before she knew it, she was crying, holding the mangled roof and the two sections together. She gathered all the broken pieces and put them on her bed.

Placing the roof on her pillow and one section on either side of her, she cradled herself into the interior of her Theatre Royal Manchester.

I can sleep inside my own theatre. She curled up, holding both pieces of her theatre as tenderly as a broken doll. Sleep came to her as sweet notes of beige; it tasted of cream and soothed her hot tears. The scarlet seats from the miniature theatre purred like a cat, curling up beside her.

CHAPTER TWO

DARLING OF THE GALLERY GIRLS

"Don't you think, Guv'nor, a few rays of the moon might fall on me? Shines equally, you know, on the just and unjust." Terriss's voice rang loud and clear from a darkened section of the Lyceum Theatre Stage.

Standing in the spotlight center stage, Henry Irving, six-foot-two-inches tall in a shoulder-length black wig and black mustache, glared at the invisible person speaking to his right. Wearing black satin breeches with white silk stockings, an embroidered beige vest, a red jacket with black lapels, and a white fringed sash, Henry's costume seemed to radiate in the light. He lit the cigarette he held, then blew the smoke into his bright circle of limelight and extinguished the match. His face was set in a cold fury. Then he quickly burst out laughing. Directing his remarks to the limelight operator, he boomed, "We will share limelight. Refocus, please?"

The members of the theatre company sitting in the house started laughing. It was rare to see their leader react like this. Terriss was one of the few actors who could talk to the Great

Man that way; Irving loved his frankness. He always called him by his last name, Terriss, a sign he remembered him among the throng of his employees. Terriss was also one of the few men that Henry socialized with outside the theatre's walls.

The Corsican Brothers starred Henry, double-cast as the fair-minded twins, Fabien and Louis, while Terriss played Chateau-Renard, the villain. In this scene Louis was dueling with Chateau-Renard in the forest of Fontainebleau as a light snow fell on the ground. The single set piece was a huge tree. As the limelight widened out, Terriss slowly appeared in his Chateau-Renard costume: a blonde wig, elaborate cravat, lace-cuffed shirt, and handsome frock coat. He tapped the floor with his sword and gently began to parry with Henry, singing softly under his breath. The female extras in the company raced up to the highest gallery in the house, the "gods" as they called it, and squealed with delight as the sword fight began.

William Terriss, "Breezy Bill," was a wandering spirit who couldn't be held down to one profession or one partner. The "Darling of the Gallery Girls" had been a tea planter in Bengal, sheep farmer in the Falkland Islands, midshipman at sea, and horse breeder in Kentucky. Terriss was willing to chance all, living his life to the fullest. His luxuriant head of hair, tall athletic build, and sincere genial manner made him popular wherever he might go, and he might go at any moment. The girls in the gallery whispered to one another that he was a vanishing breed—a true adventurer.

"Remember that day he showed up at the theatre soaking wet?" one extra whispered. "Miss Terry teased him, 'Is it raining out there, Bill?' And he only smiled back at her and went on his way to prepare for the show. I found a few days later he had jumped into the Thames River to save a girl from drowning and had had no time to go home to change his clothes."

Another girl sighed. "Robin Hood, Romeo, that's what he should play here. He's my idea of a matinee idol."

But it was Henry Irving's company and Henry was the star. Henry had been under contract at the Lyceum Theatre for eight years with the American-born Hezekiah Bateman. In 1875, almost twenty years ago, Henry convinced Bateman to produce *The Bells*. With that play Henry won great acclaim, and soon after Bateman died, leaving Henry to buy out the widow to run and manage the Lyceum Theatre.

The Lyceum Theatre was a huge auditorium that had yet to turn a profit in decades and was in urgent need of renovations. Henry had to start from scratch and build his company from the ground up with actors like William Terriss and Ellen Terry, an actress Henry had been in love with for years. These actors were the magic of Henry Irving's Lyceum Theatre, with help from Henry's innovative ideas for stagecraft and lighting. And with Henry playing all the leads, of course.

A roar went up from the house as Terriss's sword cut through to brush the fringe of Henry's white sash. The sword fight choreography displayed both men's characteristic tendencies, as Terriss came out swinging. Terriss was all sunny disposition and a man's man, but Henry Irving, with his bowed legs and long face, had an exacting demeanor—a choirmaster whose moves resembled an attacking crab. Terriss's advances were like an unbridled dog, full of energy and attack. Henry's parries were more elegant and studied, with a sudden display of back and forth when his adversary turned his back.

Now the stage was properly lit, and the sword fight continued. Henry switched swords to his secret sword, the one the fight master had given him. This had a cavalry hilt, outfitted with an épée blade; it was solid, yet flexible enough for complicated moves. For a month, both men had been coached by the exacting Mr. Bertrand, an award-winning swordsman. Terriss had his own sword fashioned after the Armoury of the Council of Ten in Venice, a showy sword, its hilt designed to form a heart pierced by an arrow. But he didn't have a backup trick sword.

As Terriss's villain squared off with Henry's hero, both men kicked stage snow out of their way for this last parry. Chateau-Renard charged and then jumped up to grab a tree branch. Swinging from the limb, he kicked Louis's shoulder, propelling him into the prop snow pile. As he dropped down from the tree, Louis rose up from the snow and with a grand leap stabbed Chateau-Renard in the heart. As the death throes ebbed, he stood over Terriss's body and made a sign of the cross.

The company in the house broke into applause as Terriss playfully removed the sword embedded in his chest's padding and handed it to Henry. "Here. I know how you are about this sword."

Henry looked down at him. "Was that enough moonlight, Terriss?"

⟳

At the tavern afterwards, Terriss and Henry joined a group of odd-looking men sitting around the remains of the hearth's fire. It was the height of fashion for beards to resemble the Prince of Wales's own goatee. However, this group of men were mostly free of facial hair. Older men usually wore the old-fashioned "door knocker" beard of Charles Dickens, not the shorn chins of Oscar Wilde or Henry Irving.

This clique of men first met while having drinks at the Covent Garden Tavern after shows two years ago. They eventually evolved into the Freemasons of Jerusalem Lodge No. 197. The Masons' insistence on secrecy and lack of an official religion lured many members. They wanted to belong to a community where no one would repress them. The membership of the elite men's clubs was usually dependent on recommendations by fellow aristocrats. This was a gathering of men who wanted a spiritual yet not religious brotherhood, with no aristocrats clamoring to belong—at least, not yet.

And it was a refuge for the two actors who had interests outside the world of theatre. Here they met men who were writers, doctors, attorneys. (Women were not allowed, but as they didn't have the vote yet, some men did not feel their influence to be of much importance.) Besides, in this new era of the 1880s, the men wanted to cultivate literature and drama on "a tankard and a chop," and the delicate sex might impede the blunt talk they felt was a man's prerogative. William Terriss, David James, Walter Joyce, H.B. Farne, Henry Irving: all were up-and-coming men from the working class who were engaged in the arts or other intellectual labor. And in this group, William Terriss had been the lifeblood of this particular gathering from the beginning. Men who hadn't taken the risks to leave the country to try to make a fortune listened in awe to his stories of his many varied careers.

Surrounded by half a dozen men, "Breezy Bill" told of his disastrous adventure in the United States trying to breed racehorses. The remains of a chop or a pie lay in front of most of them as they smoked, listening in rapt attention, as Terriss stood in front of them with a glass of cheap beer.

"Yes, it was quite the 'vacation,'" Terriss drawled. "This American businessman had convinced me to move with my wife, and with our little Ellaline, just a year old. We made the voyage and settled in a place called Lexington. On my arrival, I thought about joining a Masonic lodge and it's a good thing I did, for after a while I found that I had spent every last dollar saved to start my business. I became quite good at working a rope, but I could not master the art of making money at this and after a while, I realized we were down to our last dollar, not even enough to get home in steerage. A Mr. Oliver at the Masonic lodge heard of my misfortunes and asked to see my skill at roping a horse. I went out to the paddock, and he picked out the most uncivilized horse of them all. I managed, however, to rope the beast and at that, Mr. Oliver gave me fare to travel steerage back with the words, 'Pay me back when you can, my boy. Godspeed and God bless you.'"

Walter Joyce teased, "And you never saw him again."

Terriss replied, "I haven't seen him yet, but you can be sure I will someday. I took the little money I had saved back here in England and sent all I borrowed from him within twenty hours on our arrival. What a man! That's a lesson learned, I tell you!"

Henry added, "And that is the best of brotherhood, to be of service to one another."

Walter Joyce joked, "Would that be a request for a good review for your *Corsican Brothers*, Mr. Irving?"

Henry winked at the newspaperman. "I've learned that salting the good and bad reviews together makes for a much livelier box office."

The men all laughed, as this was a strictly pro-Irving gathering, unlike those who found him old-fashioned or controversial. Meeting with people like this group of men outside the immediate circle of theatre was a breath of fresh air to Henry. And the purpose and aim of their newly founded group, to be of service and action to one another, was something he was trying to instill in the theatre community. Or so it was said. Friendships forged in the struggle of building a theatre sometimes did not flourish when the venture flourished. There were no unions, agents, or managers for the common worker, in theatre or not.

Big Ben struck the bells for two, and the men stretched and reached for their coats, hats, and walking sticks. Once out on the uneven cobblestone streets, they wobbled and laughed at one another.

As they staggered out of the tavern and looked up at the foggy, ink-yellow sky, the vegetable carts for Covent Garden rolled down the street. Children who tended the stalls perched on the loads, looking like sleepy owls, jostled by the swaying but remaining upright. The tipsy men watched as the convoy rambled along, the horses' clomping echoing into the night.

A rumble of thunder boomed.

All at once, a huge lightning bolt etched across the sky, splitting in half right above them, followed by a terrific clap of thunder. The horses whinnied, one rearing up and only just restrained by the driver. Dogs barked from all quarters. Out of the sky, from where the lightning had forked, a burnt ebony stick, shaped like a wand, fell at Henry Irving's feet.

CHAPTER THREE

INJURIOUS MAGIC

In a shaft of light, tiny sparkling crystals of snow floated down from a leaky skylight in the small, dark back room. Outside, the sounds of the back alley were muted, and in the window the glow of silent white missiles streaked past the glass. A stove hissed, its red coals throbbing, and the room's drafty and darkened corners seemed to shrink in the dim light. The smell of incense and burning coal filled the room. Dr. Westcott's study doubled as the office where he worked as a coroner. The tools of his trade, used to investigate the causes of both natural and unnatural deaths, were assembled on two counters against the wall. Saws, needles, vials, magnifiers, forceps, tweezers, they all seemed to belong to a doctor or a butcher. A single lamp on the counter illuminated a newspaper with the headline "Unknown Attacker Targeting Young Women in Brick Lane."

Westcott, in his early thirties, was known for his exquisite beard and mustache, and his elaborate vests of Italian brocade silk. A true "dandy" and man about town, he was genial and accustomed to being the center of attention. Seated next to him was another gentleman, and both watched in rapt attention the third man standing in front of them. Dressed in an unworldly shift with a large turquoise belt, Samuel Mathers was arranging twenty-two papers around him in a circle on the floor. He was in his late twenties, a nervous fidgeter, with brown hair sticking out like shingles on a roof, and dark circles smudged underneath his eyes. He was definitely not a "dandy." His blotch of a mustache quivered as he finished arranging the splayed-out papers.

Felkin, the third magician in the room, stood up next to Mathers and took out a small, worn book from his vest pocket. Dr. Felkin was a blond-haired man, with one eye that wandered off to the side behind his thick glasses. He was freakishly tall, at almost six foot four, and his shoulders sagged as though he didn't want to stand out any more than he did.

Mathers retrieved a smoldering staff that leaned over the stove. The staff was five feet long and was made of tektite, a stone said to have come from falling stars. The incense tied to its heated hilt snaked in a smoky path up to the open skylight. Mathers, carrying the staff, circled the splayed-out papers five times with intense concentration and then put the staff back near the stove.

"Gentlemen," Westcott announced, "we must pledge that these practices and these contents are for our knowledge alone. We know a great change is about to happen in the world, and we must ready ourselves to lead."

The three men all stood together and lifted their left hands, reciting, "I pledge." Westcott stepped forward and took a piece of paper from the circle, memorized it, then dropped the paper to the floor. He stood with both hands in front of him, palms up, and recited from memory:

"Isis, Egyptian goddess of magic and nature. Urania, Greek muse of astronomy. Guide us as we form this practice to advance our spirits."

Stone bricks appeared around his feet and quickly began to form a barrier around him. The bricks themselves were finely designed and seemed to have a transparent quality. They started to amass, making a clicking sound as they tapped together, almost like the sound of a typewriter. The doctor twisted his torso from side to side, the bricks building layer after layer around his feet. Just as it seemed the bricks would completely envelop him, Westcott clapped his hands wildly to break the spell. The stones continued to encase him. Mathers and Felkin came running and tried to wrest away the almost-living bricks, but to no avail. There was no means to penetrate them, as they seemed painted on the air but had real substance.

Westcott cried out, "Help! Help! Mathers, Felkin, what the deuce . . . I'm . . . ahhhhh!"

Mathers's hand was bloodied as a brick crushed his fingernail, its fellow bricks continuing their movement. Felkin circled the stones, trying to find a point of entry.

"Ow, ow, ow! Really, this needs to stop! Felkin, do something!" Westcott's muffled voice came from under the dome of bricks now stacking around his head.

Mathers quickly rifled through the papers on the floor, as the stones continued to encapsulate Westcott. Felkin tried to reach over the bricks to lift him out but couldn't get a grip on Westcott. Finally, Mathers found the desired page and over the clicking sounds started reciting something in a foreign language.

Felkin shouted, "Do something! This thing is going to seal over!"

Mathers repeated his last foreign phrase and looked up as the final stone totally entombed Westcott. There was complete silence. Then from inside the igloo-type encasement came a muffled oath.

After a moment, the entire formation of stone disappeared into the smoky air. Dr. Westcott sat on the floor, his hands over his eyes, rocking back and forth as he rubbed his head. Two small wounds on his forehead appeared where the stones had scraped Westcott's face. Mathers approached him with his bloody hand and helped him to his feet.

"It's a good thing you're a coroner," Felkin said. "You of all people would know how to keep yourself alive."

"Not necessarily," Westcott said, dabbing at his wounds with a handkerchief.

Felkin finished bandaging his own hand and sat. He barked, "Well, Mathers, let's see if you can't make a go of it."

Retrieving the staff from the stove, its end smoking with heat, Mathers stepped around the circle of papers five times and then placed the staff in its original spot. He placed his hands over his eyes and chanted, "W-w-we who believe in Enochian m-m-magic, command that our consciousness bend the material world and allow us transport."

At that, two sphinxes appeared at his feet and lifted him up, levitating him toward the open skylight. Felkin and Westcott held their breath as they watched Mathers floating twelve feet high in the room. The sphinxes were of different colors, one black, one white, and seemed to be wavering in the air. The snow shifted through the open skylight, and as it drifted down it passed right through the sphinxes.

Mathers trembled with excitement and tried to bend down to touch the headdress of one of the sphinxes. Suddenly the sphinxes began to disappear and he pitched over and fell, making a hard landing on the floor. "Ohmmmph! My eye. R-r-r . . . rotting hell!"

He clutched his eye and sat up. A clanging, rolling sound was heard. From under the piles of paper, a small golden cylinder rolled out from a satchel. Mathers dusted himself off and grabbed it. "Bloody hell."

The two others ran to him and examined his face, seeing the beginnings of a huge black eye. As they observed him contemplating the cylinder, a silence descended. Reluctantly, Mathers handed the tube over. Westcott and Felkin took turns examining it.

"W-w-what is that?" Mathers asked.

"I don't know at the moment," Felkin replied. "I thought it might be a container to return the papers to Count Apponyi.

But again, this could be a sign it is something else." He pocketed it and smiled at the other two.

"You can keep it for now," Westcott said. "But it belongs to the three of us."

Mathers stuttered, "Felkin, n-now you should command the next incantation."

Felkin stood, smoothing his beard and mustache, and put on a pair of thick work gloves from his pocket. Mathers pointed to a sheet of paper off to the side.

"Try this one," Mathers said.

Felkin stood above the paper, studying it. A few minutes later, Mathers handed him the staff, the tip glowing from heat, smoke streaming from it. Felkin stood in the center of the papers and looked up at the ceiling, closing his eyes. After a moment of silence, his eyes opened and he began to cautiously circle the papers.

With one hand, Felkin held the staff straight up and in a low voice intoned, "We are the stars in the sky. We are the fire of the sun. We command the light!"

A low rumble shook the floor, and a loud crackle tore through the room. A green-gold starburst erupted in Felkin's hands and the staff transformed into an effervescent bolt of lightning, its brilliance racing up to the open skylight and out into the night sky. Two seconds later there was an explosive boom, and everything outside was lit in a spectacular golden light. All was silent and still as the snow resumed floating down from the open skylight. Felkin looked down at his singed glove.

"Holy Mother of God!"

Felkin raced to the side table and peeled off his gloves as quickly as he could.

Mathers and Westcott jumped up at once and rushed to him. Westcott filled a basin of water and plunged Felkin's hand in. Mathers held the lamp as they examined his wound.

"Just a second-degree burn, very little blistering. Ointment should take care of it," Dr. Westcott said to Mathers.

The two men looked at one another as Felkin hugged himself. "Thrilling, just thrilling! At the moment, uncontrollable and could have been a real disaster, but thrilling!" he bubbled.

Mathers took up Felkin's hand and examined it closer. "Just a burn after all that? That was a lightning bolt!"

Felkin took his hand back and looked around the room. "But where is the staff?"

They looked in every corner, but there was no ebony staff.

"That was tektite, comet stone," Felkin said. "The rarest of magical stones."

"True," Westcott said. "It wouldn't have just melted!"

The fireplace let out a loud pop. All three men jumped and looked up to see a bolt of light streak into the night sky.

CHAPTER FOUR

CROWLEY BREWERY

~⌒⌒⌒⌒⌒⌒~

The brewery was a stone masterpiece on a side street in Leamington Spa, three stories high with an ornate entrance for horses and wagons. Workmen smoked cigarettes as they exited the factory, and jostled with one another on their way to the street. One man snapped a rag at another and a mock fistfight ensued. The men's horseplay echoed in the street. The Crowley Brewery was the main source of ale throughout the region; the brewmasters, barrel makers, wagon drivers, and porters were all proud of the Crowley name and of its owner, Edward Crowley. And at closing time, the wage earners were exuberant.

Inside the entranceway, Edward Crowley, a dignified man with gray mutton-chop whiskers, stood handing out coins with an accountant standing next to him checking off each man's wage. No one had ever seen Edward not in his starched conservative garb of a Plymouth Brethren preacher, contrasting sharply with his workmen's soiled aprons and grease-stained trousers. Some may have seen a contradiction that Edward Crowley, who preached of all things denial and judgment, had come to own and administer a brewing company. Others saw it as a watery salvation. The Plymouth Brethren Church Edward and his wife belonged to was a sort of Puritan offshoot, with severe clothes marking a severe judgment of vices, secular interests, and even emotions. At weekends, Edward would hitch up his own wagon and with his son attend country fairs where he would preach his "hell and damnation" sermons.

At the entranceway to the brewery, Edward paid the last of his employees and dismissed his accountant, who returned to the office. Edward watched the remaining workers mingle in the doorway of the wagon entrance. A few of the men acknowledged him, but the laughter and teasing among the men came to a halt.

Thirteen-year-old Aleister Crowley came running down the street to the brewery. Young and lanky with brown hair falling into his eyes, he bounded energetically up to his father. Aleister had suffered from ill health since he was seven and ever since that time had been tutored by a pious church secretary. At the end of each day, it was up to him to provide proof to his father of the daily lessons learned and of the morality in each subject covered.

Aleister came up to his father, and the two started the slow and steady walk home.

"Paracelsus was born in the 1490s in Switzerland."

"And then?"

"Paracelsus founded the study of toxicology, gave zinc its name, and was the first to see that some diseases are found in the mind's condition."

"And then?"

"*And then?*" was Edward Crowley's constant phrase, whether he was preaching, hearing the details of the brewery accounts, or listening to his son's latest studies. "And then?" was sure to be the first response he provided. Aleister never tired of hearing his father's "And then?" It was an invitation for the boy to pour out his day's accomplishments and questions.

"He tended to villagers during the time of the Plague."

"And then?"

As they continued to walk, Aleister jumped up and down from embankment to curb, like a young cub.

"He said some evil builds immunity to other evil."

Edward grabbed his son's arm, stopping him in his tracks. "What did you say?"

Aleister was taken aback by his father's intensity. It was rare that he lost his temper or was less than totally in control. "He said evil builds immunity to evil. 'To cure some diseases,' he said, 'let evil expel evil.'"

Edward took Aleister by both shoulders and bent down to look straight into his eyes. "Evil is the rejection of our Lord the Redeemer. There is never a cause to justify evil."

Aleister looked confused and could not bear to look his father in the eye. Edward sighed, slightly tousled his son's hair, and started to move on. Over his shoulder he softly called, "And then?"

With that, Aleister skipped forward, and to impress his father he continued to recite all the facts and knowledge he'd poured into his head earlier in the day.

"And then, Paracelsus was one of the first to unite medicine with chemistry using mercury, sulfur, and iron."

The two continued down the street, the younger bouncing and spinning in glee, the elder trudging along with a lingering gait.

❧

Five months later, on an early November morning, Aleister and his mother, Emily Crowley, dressed in the severe clothing of the Plymouth Brethren, stood together graveside. Mrs. Crowley had a bonnet of plain worsted wool that almost blocked out her entire face, and both she and her son wore plain high-collared black coats with mourning armbands on the left sleeve. Black-garbed men shoveled dirt into the grave while crows cried out to one another that their domain had been trespassed. The other dour members of their sect stood behind them, with no singing or preaching, each repeating the Lord's prayer to themselves.

Aleister tried to contain his tears, which rolled down his face and splattered on his clenched hands. The showing of emotion was not acceptable, and the soul's reuniting with its Savior was a long-wished-for event. All he could feel was the emptiness at the loss of the one person who delighted in his company and his thoughts, who now lay at the bottom of this yawning hole. In a terrible trick of fate, cancer of the tongue had prevented his father from being able to ask, "And then?" New tears raced down Aleister's face. He looked up and saw the fury in his mother's eyes, for he was making a spectacle of himself.

She pulled him sharply to her and hissed, "The condition of your father's soul was spotless. Stop this display at once."

Aleister tried to stifle his tears and looked skyward; a crow squawked. He felt as if a fist were squeezing his heart.

The Brethren School in Cambridge was one of those fine institutions where children were sent to learn for the betterment of their character and the improvement of their mind. Its splendid arches, beautiful courtyard, and full-length windows in the headmaster's office were full of sixteenth-century flourishes. In exchange for the beauty of this environment, any daily affirmation that the boarded student was loved or valued was beside the point. The beds were to be filled at top price, and if one needed the reassurances of a family bond, they were told to contemplate the Holy Family in one of the stained-glass windows.

Emily Crowley walked glumly inside the Brethren School hallway, still in deep mourning costume, as decorative as a nun's habit. As she approached the headmaster, she clutched her simple crucifix, staring at the slumped-over Aleister.

She turned to the headmaster with a sigh. "Well, Reverend Champney, I hope you have better luck than I have. He has at heart the desires of a beast and seems to remain outside the blessings of true faith."

It shocked Aleister to hear his mother say this to an outsider. At home, she made her feelings about the conditions of his soul very clear—he was a natural sinner and would continue to sin. His father's gentle rebukes to her were the only thing that reined in the continual damnation of his every infraction.

The Reverend H. d'Arcy Champney had a bald pate, his remaining hair in curls around his collar. His straight, aristocratic nose and piercing brown eyes gave him the air of a determined scholar and passionate disciplinarian. He wore a dark smock with the Brethren School's emblem over the heart. It depicted two lions flanking a shield with four towers on it and the inscription "*Turris Fortissima Est Nomen Jehova*," which translated to "The name of our Lord is our strongest tower." In addition to this medieval coat of arms, he sported an elaborate white scarf tucked into his coat. He had a high and crackly voice.

"Certainly, Widow Crowley, we will give young Crowley every consideration to make sure he stays on the straight and narrow."

"I give you permission to apply whatever methods necessary to improve the disposition of my child," she said.

Aleister looked up at his mother, and any thought of an embrace or even of talking to her completely disappeared. His mother was never pleased with him, and even when his father was alive and setting off to preach with Aleister, she complained bitterly that it was her place to go with him, not her son's. Every need of her son's was a sin: how much he ate, how much he slept. On the subject of what he wanted to read or what he wanted to talk about, these were all of an ungodly pursuit. His presence seemed to be the biggest sin of all.

How he longed for the quiet "And then?" from his father. His encouragement for conversation, for reflection on the folly of man and on sin, the discourse of ideas with respect and nurturing: all gone. The relationship with his mother was contentious and full of disapproval; she seemed to have resented him from the day he came home from the wet nurse at three years of age. His many illnesses seemed to further disgust her and he was no more than a beast to feed, one who was becoming bigger and surlier by the day.

Mrs. Crowley looked at her son and sighed. She took a pouch from under her arm and gave it to the Reverend Champney.

"Here is his funding. Don't spare the rod to spoil the child."

Mrs. Crowley looked at Aleister staring at the ground, and without another word she turned on her heel and headed for her carriage. He looked up for one final glance, but she was bustling out of sight. Aleister continued looking at her disappearing form as the Reverend Champney firmly took him by the elbow and led him into the school.

Two years later, in the high-ceilinged Brethren School classroom, Aleister sat staring out the window into the courtyard, studying the other boys racing and playing with one another. This place had not provided him with one friend. How could it? In the first months that he had been sent here, it was one round of solitary confinement after another, with bread and milk and sabotage as his only meals. Then there were the attacks from rivals who wanted his boots or his books. Showing up to class without boots because they were missing led to more punishment. His missing books caused him a real sense of loss, as they were his only companions.

After the first few months away, he had written to his mother, begging her to let him return home. Instead, her brother,

Tom Bishop, came from London to lecture him on the duty he owed if not to his mother, then to the memory of his father, to stay the course. His uncle shared his mother's lack of affection for Aleister, but the boy plotted a course to please him so that he might one day stay with him in London. In three years, when he was eighteen, he would come into the inheritance that his father had left him. Then he would attend university and escape from the censure he felt at home. Meanwhile, this school's very essence burned hot inside him; every day he felt stifled and found wanting.

Now in the classroom, Aleister had a pen and paper and several large books of chemistry in front of him. He tried several times to get back to his assignment, but he could not stop watching the others outside the window. The sounds of chapel bells started, and the boys drifted away from his sight.

The Reverend Champney came in with a crop in his hand and saw Aleister seated, surrounded by his books.

"Young Crowley, why are you not at chapel?"

Aleister busied himself with his paper and books. "Reverend Champney, I am studying a god who makes infinitely more sense than the one presented at chapel."

Charging into the room and drawing himself up before Aleister, the headmaster boomed, "What heresy are you speaking?"

Aleister tentatively stood and showed the Reverend a passage in his book. "Paracelsus said, 'Besides the stars that are established, there is yet another—Imagination—that begets a new star and a new heaven.'"

Reverend Champney moved threateningly toward Aleister, who retreated still holding his book. "Young man, I demand that you attend services at once, at your soul's peril!"

"You see, Reverend Champney, I am not so convinced that I *have* a soul, and if I do, I am beginning to realize that I must apply it to Paracelsus's motto 'Let evil expel evil.'"

Trying and failing to grab the book out of Aleister's hands, the headmaster began to chase him around his desk. "Devilish boy, you've totally misunderstood Paracelsus! He was referring to the cures he used in applying doses of illness to cure illness!"

"I totally understand Paracelsus! Chemistry of the body is chemistry of the brain. The evils the Church practices can only be cured by further evil!"

The Reverend Champney finally swatted the book out of Aleister's hands and pointed his crop at him.

"You cannot name one instance where evil cures evil."

Aleister pushed the crop away from his face and calmly stared at the Reverend. "The ingesting of small amounts of mercury to cure the pox one catches from young ladies in the local brothels. I hear you have made use of such remedies."

Reverend Champney lunged and grabbed him by the back of his neck and started to drag him out of the classroom. "Your mother will hear about your despicable behavior!"

Aleister tried to gather his notes and papers as he was being dragged out of the room, the Reverend swatting him fiercely with his crop. Finally, Aleister grabbed the crop out of his tormenter's hand and snapped it in two, his face red with ferocity.

"I will endure!"

As Champney dragged the boy down the hall to be whipped in front of the other students, the reverend was unaware that he too, faced a similar fate. In five years, the reverend would also be dragged down halls, only these halls would be in the Streatham Mental Institution for the Criminally Insane. One of his beatings would have an unfortunate, mortal effect on a younger student.

CHAPTER FIVE

The Thames

~~~⋙⋘~~~

"Of course you're an artist—you're a Colman!" Grandmother crowed.

While her parents obtained documents for travel at Her Majesty's passport office, Pamela and her grandmother sat in a hansom cab surrounded by a soft, yellow December fog. Ten-year-old Pamela grabbed the hand of her grandmother and laughed in response. As was the fashion in 1888, Grandmother Colman wore an elaborate porkpie hat, with red and white feathers tacked in the back. Pamela wore a smaller version with white ostrich feathers. The bay horses snorted and pawed the ground in exasperation. Suddenly the horses lurched forward and the cabbie quickly restrained them, but not before Pamela and her grandmother were jostled so roughly that their hats almost slid off their heads. Combined with the dangling, beaded fringe of her velvet cape, Grandmother Colman was a blur of beads swaying and feathers bobbing.

This was her first visit to London from New England to spend time with Pamela's family. She was a hearty woman, well-humored with a big laugh, and always interested in her granddaughter. She made her granddaughter's needs a topic of conversation every day. At breakfast she insisted on knowing, "Why are we leaving Pamela at home again?" "What are we going to do about Pamela's hair?" "When are we getting the child some decent clothes?" Thanks to her interference, Pamela now wore a pretty white dress under her blue wool coat. Unfortunately, her hair was no longer styled in the sausage curls the maid had so carefully set that morning. Pamela pushed some of the loose strands away from her mouth, moving the ribbons on her own miniature version of her grandmother's hat.

Grandmother Colman continued her story. "And when your mother was just thirteen, my first book, *Stories for Corinne*, was published and even named for her. But all my children are remarkable! Your aunt Pamela—your namesake—is a writer. Your mother acts, and your uncle Samuel is a world-famous painter. All the Colmans! It's in your blood, Pamela. You are destined to be renowned for your talent."

Pamela looked back from scanning the smudgy, foggy street and asked, "Grandmother, what's a Jesus?"

Grandmother laughed softly. "What you mean, child, is *who* is Jesus."

Pamela sat up straight in her seat and toyed with the jet beading on her grandmother's cape. "No, I heard someone say Mother is a Jesus."

With that, the older woman laughed and straightened Pamela's hat. "Pamela, your mother is a parlor actress, a *diseuse*, not Jesus. Oh look, here's Maud. I hope your parents straightened out her passport as well."

Maud approached the carriage wearing a new coat and freshly styled hair, her suitcase in hand. Pamela hadn't seen Maud since that Halloween, three years ago in Manchester, when she flew. She had never been able to fly again, no matter how many times she stood at the end of her bed, dangling one foot in front of her. Inevitably, there would be a thump as she hit the floor. The last time, not even a pile of blankets prevented her from bruising.

Eighteen years old and unusually statuesque, Maud stood out like a poppy in a field of dandelions. She had had so many marriage proposals! Even the Prince of Wales had expressed interest in marrying her after seeing her at a social event.

Her father had recently died, leaving her a fortune, but other family members had tried to cheat her out of it. Scheming uncles had informed her that her father had left her nothing, and that she would be adopted by an English aunt. Maud knew that this was a ploy to handle her inheritance, however. To stop the adoption, Maud determined to earn her own living, and became an actress, delaying her uncles' schemes until her father's will was probated that spring. She was now on her way back to Paris to live with the Comtesse de la Sizeranne, her celebrated aunt—with her fortune intact.

Maud put her suitcase down and reached a hand through the open carriage window to touch Pamela's face. It was time to say goodbye. Maud was now a grand debutante at eighteen, and Pamela was still a fanciful girl at ten years old. Grandmother waited patiently for their face patting to turn into tear wiping. Laughing and leaning forward in her seat, Grandmother Corinne slipped an envelope to Maud.

"Here's a little something for when you get to Paris, Miss Gonne. Not that you need it." Maud blushed a little and demurely accepted the envelope, stuffing it into her coat pocket.

"Ah, pickpockets, Miss Gonne! London is full of them. Best to put that in your case, my dear!"

Maud opened her suitcase and put the envelope on top. After closing it, she turned back to the carriage where she saw tears streaking down Pamela's face.

"Oh, come here, you!" Maud opened the door and Pamela flew out to embrace her. They stayed together for a short while, and then Maud lifted her up and planted her on the sidewalk. "Ah, now, is that any way for a sister of a fairy to behave?"

"It is."

Maud knelt before Pamela and tapped at her own heart, whispering, "You have me here and with your second sight, you can always see me. And remember, you can *fly*!"

Maud gave Pamela one more hug and turned her around to walk back to the carriage. She picked up her suitcase and walked away with a quick pace as Pamela's parents came out of the passport office.

As they approached the hansom cab, the horses jerked the carriage forward slightly once more, prompting Mr. Smith to call out, "To the Covent Garden Opera House by way of St. James's Park." He opened the door and helped his wife in next to her mother. As he climbed in, he sat next to Pamela, patting her hands. He had a pleasant face and was a man of slight stature. He wore a fine paisley cravat and a blue silk waistcoat from which he pulled his watch and looked at the time. Mrs. Corinne Smith was in her finest blue wool coat, and Pamela's coat was tailored in the same material. Mother's porkpie hat was styled with artificial cherries instead of feathers, and the cherries bounced on her forehead as the carriage jounced down the street.

Grandmother Colman helped adjust her daughter's skirts and addressed her son-in-law. "I'm glad you've helped to straighten out Maud's passport. God knows why she wants to live in France. Does she think she can reinvent herself there, as you hope to do in Jamaica?"

At this, both parents looked at Pamela with concern, prompting Mrs. Smith to have a coughing jag. Quickly, she opened her small purse and took out a handkerchief, as worried looks passed inside of the cab. As if the horses could hear the distress, they took off at a spirited trot.

Her grandmother looked sharply at Charles. "Well, all I

meant was, I hope this Jamaican weather helps my daughter's health and puts an end to this coughing."

Mr. Smith ignored his mother-in-law. "Now, Pamela, your friend will be perfectly all right. Miss Gonne has spent many years accompanying her father in his time as a diplomat. She is an experienced traveler."

Taking a deep breath and recovering from her coughing fit, her fingers tapping in time to the horses' hooves, Mrs. Smith added airily, "Yes, Pamela, your grandmother will see that you and Maud stay in touch. Not to worry."

Mr. Smith smiled warmly at his wife as the carriage entered St. James' Park and took her hand. "Well, enjoy the view through the fog. In a month's time, we will be in the bright sunshine of Jamaica."

Pamela peered out, seeing another horse and carriage vanish into the midday fog. "Will there be horses and carriages in Jamaica too?"

Her father cleared his throat and said, "Yes, there are carriages, but I will be helping them build the finest railroad system. Wouldn't you like that?"

Pamela sat back. "I don't know if I would like that. I know I will miss Maud and our Irish fairy tales. And flying."

At this her mother started another coughing fit.

"And I would like for Mother to stop coughing."

For over a year now, Pamela's mother had developed a cough that had crept into her everyday conversation, and no amount of rest cures or bathing trips seemed to help. The life they were living in Manchester was not the success that Charles had hoped. His American accent marked him as an outsider to all he did business with, creating an obstacle to any real accomplishments. The pressure of Grandfather Cyrus Smith's many successes had weighed on him heavily. Charles would finally "live up to his potential" leading the West India Improvement Company, and the Jamaican climate would do away with Mother's cough. The backers were old friends of Cyrus who had contributed to the success of the Brooklyn Railway, and they had scoured the world seeking where trains were needed. Pamela was not told all the reasons for the move, only that they would be starting a new life in Jamaica.

In the cab, Pamela rocked back and forth, enjoying the security of sitting next to her father. She closed her eyes. Then the music in her head started, with Maud saying, "What if you really *do* fly?" over and over.

The carriage arrived at Covent Garden, where the singsong hawking and calling of wares deafened even inside of the cab. "Violets, pansies, gardenias," one young girl sang while baskets of crops and trays of iced fish were laid out on tables under gas-lit canopies, which were necessary even at noon due to the fog. A man wearing a fez sold slippers from Arabia, and a tea station was set up next to a bonfire. Everywhere, young children with no shoes and threadbare clothes scampered around, begging from passersby. A fashionably dressed, determined-looking middle-aged woman carried pieces of paper that she thrust into the hands of anyone she could. As the carriage drew alongside her, she drove a sheaf into Grandmother's lap through the open window.

Grandmother picked it up and read, "Discover the Lord Jesus. He is your only redeemer and savior."

Handing the paper to Pamela, she muttered, "Here is your Jesus, Pamela. Perhaps you can give this paper some value by putting some of your excellent artwork on the back."

Mr. Smith chortled. "Now, Mother Colman, it's a fine message she's promoting."

His mother-in-law shot back, "If she were handing out fish and bread to the starving children instead of paying for printed paper, it would be a much finer message."

Pamela looked out the window thinking about this "finer message." She watched the frenzied street with its calls and shouts of buying and selling, the children running after the carriage asking for "Jest a coin, Guv'nor." As they passed the fishmongers and their wares on ice, an elderly woman bent over next to a booth, staring intensely at the cobblestones in the street. Suddenly, she stood straight up and stared into their carriage as it paused, allowing a family to cross in front of them. She wore a gray wool blanket over her head and a dingy apron over her brown, plain dress, and she seemed like a mourner rigidly standing there. Just then, the blanket slid down her shoulders, revealing a mass of long white hair, loose and flying free. The large black eyes in her lined face were shining and fixed, staring straight at Pamela. She lifted a finger, pointing right at the girl, and began to speak.

Frightened, Pamela shrank in her seat, looking at her parents. Her grandmother was still talking about fish and bread. Pamela ducked her head even further under the windowsill, her parents giving her annoyed looks.

Her mother tapped her knee. "Goodness, Pamela, whatever are you carrying on for?"

Pamela hesitantly motioned out the window. Her parents twisted their heads to look out and then looked back at her questioningly. She raised her head to see the terrifying woman. No one was there but the children running alongside the carriage and the fishmongers calling out for buyers for their eels and eel pie.

Mrs. Smith turned to her mother. "You see, she takes after me when it comes to dramatics."

The carriage suddenly took off at a short trot but then lurched to a stop. Mr. Smith opened his door and hopped down to pay the driver. He helped his wife, daughter, and mother-in-law out of the carriage and took them to the Bow Street entrance of the Covent Garden Opera House. As she made her way out of the carriage, Pamela looked all around her, but the old woman was nowhere to be seen. The girl took a deep breath and followed the quickly disappearing forms of her parents up the steps at the side of the building. The opera house was impressive, with large columns and oversized windows. Mr. Smith took his wife's arm as they made their way to the stage door. An impressive Sergeant Barry was posted at the entrance, reading a newspaper at a little desk, his long legs stretched out in front of him.

He eyed them up and down. "What can I do ya for?" he asked in a strong Irish accent.

Mrs. Smith came forward with a spirited step. "Miss Ellen Terry has invited us to see the stage canvases being painted in the paint room. She said she would leave word. We are the Smith family."

The sergeant rose to his great height of six foot five, and his tone changed instantly.

"Ah, *the* Miss Terry. Now she's the love of the town, ain't she? She said ya might be here. Ya see those stairs right there? Just follow 'em up one flight, and there's the paint room. Mr. Craven and such are in there now, and they like a bit of silence while they work. Keep that in mind, or they'll toss ya out."

Pamela's eyes widened. Sergeant Barry gave her a wink and she almost laughed, but her grandmother grabbed her elbow and guided her up the flight of stairs. At the top, they made their way past a dressing room with sections of seating, and then a reception room. Next, they came into a room of enormous height, open and airy, with a lean-to roof and three skylights shored up by trussed rafters.

In the diffused light of the muted fog outside, the motes of dust fell in the air, and the quiet of the whole room gave the hush of a cathedral. Two fifty-foot canvases were propped up while ceramic pots of paint lay on the floor next to three large tables, covered with a drawing of a castle and moat. Four men worked in silence, painting different sections of the castle on a hill. Carpenters entered carrying pieces of canvas, already smeared with a prime coat, waiting for the painters.

One man had a long pole with a brush at the end, and he painted the trees surrounding the castle. He wore a white shirt with a dark waistcoat, and small globs of paint traveled down the pole toward his hands. At the far end, a man in a three-piece suit stood before a table, surveying the sketched-in stones on the canvas; he picked up brush after brush, seemingly lost in the choices. Before the middle canvas stood a very large man with a bandana tied around his head, looking like a pirate. He wore a suit with a watch chain that dangled far down and swayed back and forth as he weaved to and fro, daubing bits of paint in the castle's window. He kept one hand in his pocket, and often refilled his brush on a large palette smeared with small blobs of paint.

Pamela and her family stood to the side, watching as the hiss of the small strip of gaslights on the walls emitted a faint sour scent. The man examining the paintbrushes finally picked one up.

The pirate painter exclaimed, "So, Harker, did ye find the magic brush yet?"

The other men in the room smiled and grimaced, and went on with their work. Harker blew on the bristles and shouted back, "Ah, Craven, we don't all have your talent for going to Germany to see the castles firsthand."

Pamela tugged on her grandmother's arm. "He's been to Germany to see real castles!" she whispered in her ear.

The pirate turned and saw them. He took a wiping cloth from the table, cleaned the brush, then strode toward the group.

The other painters stopped their work; one of them groaned.

"A tight deadline and dilettantes in the paint room," someone muttered.

"And who's this, disturbing us?" the pirate demanded in a loud voice.

Charles Smith stepped forward and extended his hand. "Mr. Craven, Mr. Smith and family. So very sorry to disturb you. Miss Ellen Terry said we might stop by and see your magnificent work. We are leaving the country, and wanted one last chance to see your artistry."

Mr. Craven stopped before the group, thumbs hooked on his waistcoat pockets. He caught Pamela's eye, tilted his head sideways, and smiled. Pamela smiled back.

Pamela walked past him to the giant canvas and held her hands on either side of her face, transfixed.

Craven watched her, then addressed her parents. "So, Mr. Smith and family, which of you is the artist here?"

Before anyone else could answer, Pamela, still enraptured with the canvas, said, "Mr. Craven, I make miniature theatres and am told I have a promising career."

The group chuckled at her announcement. Craven came over to Pamela. "Ah, promising career. What is your name?"

"I was christened Corinne Pamela Colman Smith, but you may call me Pamela."

"Well, Pamela, would you like to come closer and see some of your contemporaries' work?"

"Oh, yes! Please! It's all we talk of in Manchester!"

The laughter only grew at that. Craven nodded to her family as he guided her to stand in the center of the activity.

Pamela stepped forward to devour the huge landscape with its hundreds of flowers, trees, castle walls, and windows.

As she stood totally captured by the canvas, her head started to slightly sway. She moved her finger along the castle walls and banners. Behind her closed eyes, she saw them: the four figures that were to be on the banner of King Arthur. She opened her eyes and they were still there, floating in space before her, moving to the music in her head. She knew the magic was here, waiting to be set in motion.

Craven looked at her for a minute. "Are you seeing the secrets in the castle?" he asked her kindly.

Pamela smiled at him and edged closer to the canvas. "I'm hearing the colors. But the secrets need something. I'll show you what it needs."

"You'll show me what the scene design for *King Arthur* needs?"

Pamela quickly moved to a sketch pad on the floor. She picked up a piece of charcoal and started sketching. Mr. Smith and the others came over to protest her use of his materials, but Craven lifted his hand. Pamela drew first an oblong flag, then started to fill in the corners. "Yes, the banners need a tetramorph."

Craven hung over her, watching her sketch. "Do you even know what a tetramorph is?"

Pamela continued sketching. "Yes. We need a man, lion, ox, and eagle in the four corners. And they shall all have wings. There! That's the sketch. Shall I paint it in?" She gestured toward his palette.

The other painters in the room stopped what they were doing and came over to watch.

Craven looked at her, astonished. "You want to paint on the banner that I've started?"

"Yes, please, sir. I know what to put there."

As the others whistled at her comment, Craven handed her a palette from the table and a brush from behind his ear. He then placed a small ladder near the canvas and motioned for her to climb up. Pamela swiftly scaled the rungs and painted a man with wings. She painted quickly, roughing out the shape, then moved on to paint the ox, eagle, and lion, all with wings. She bobbed and weaved, responding to a music only she could hear.

Harker walked over and put his glasses on to watch what she was doing. "Be careful, Craven—she may be replacing you!"

The men all laughed as everyone stood a little closer to the canvas. Pamela was unaware that the room had now gathered around her, observing her work, while some of the construction workers made signs of derision and snickering.

Mr. Smith moved closer to Mr. Craven. "You must forgive my daughter, Mr. Craven. We've always given her free rein."

Craven contemplated the parents, registering the fact that while they were probably not artistic themselves, they were proud of their daughter. He sighed. "Well, if I end up painting over it, at least I know it was over free rein."

Pamela reached the higher section of the canvas and sketched a banner with different objects in the middle: swords, cups, stars, and wands. A slight, startled murmur went through the room as the men saw what she was painting.

Craven stepped forward to see what she was doing. "What are you adding in there?"

Pamela turned and looked at him—they were around the same height, with her on the ladder—while continuing to paint. "The magician will have his tools: swords, cups, stars, and wands in the middle. May I?"

The whole room stood at attention. Mrs. Smith coughed slightly.

"How did you know to put those in? Those are the secret symbols Henry Irving has us put in every scene design!"

The painters laughed among themselves. Craven crossed over to Harker. "All right, Harker, you've had your joke. You arranged this, didn't you?"

"I assure you, Craven, I've never seen this child before."

Craven looked at her in amazement. Pamela smiled and continued painting as conversation among the others grew. The music inside her head helped her to find the next image. Her brushstrokes became bolder, and the smell of paint, linseed oil, and turpentine swirled in her nostrils as her flying hand moved with a life of its own.

A bearded, broad-shouldered, red-haired man wearing a three-piece suit entered the room, looking at his pocket watch.

Craven looked up and called, "Bram, we've found the artist to create the artwork for the Lyceum tour!"

Bram Stoker squinted and made his way over to the young girl, painting away on one of the canvases, surrounded by adults. He pulled himself up when he saw the symbols she was painting: the tetramorph as seen in the Sola-Busca tarot deck. *The Golden Dawn should see this*! he thought.

"Sure, this could be talent here," Bram said, his Irish accent showing through with hard *r*'s and upward inflections.

⟨✧⟩

Bram escorted the Smith family across Strand Street; they were keen to see Waterloo Bridge, the finest stone bridge in the world, while there was still light. Bram wanted to see who this Smith family might be. He walked with Mr. Smith as they trailed behind Pamela, flanked by her mother and grandmother. As they crossed the Embankment and neared the bridge, Pamela gasped and pointed at every horse-drawn car and woman with a hat, wondering how she would paint them. They approached the riverbank of the Thames in the lowering light. Waterloo Bridge looked majestic and powerful; the Cornish granite gleamed through the swirling fog, its nine arches hunched over the outgoing tide.

Pamela ran to the nearest railing and leaned over the balustrade's edge, looking at Somerset House.

"They've cut Somerset House off from the river! Where is the water gate?" cried Pamela.

As the group lined up against the rail to take in the sight, Mr. Smith gave Bram a slight smile. "You see, Mr. Stoker, we only had outdated art prints of Somerset House to school our daughter."

"But the barges would sail right into the palace, wouldn't they, Mr. Stoker?" Pamela mimicked brushstrokes in the air with her finger, filling in the missing arches.

"That's right, Miss Smith," Bram answered. "It was a palace on the river."

As Pamela painted the missing palace entrance in the air, hearing music only she could hear, the adults turned to take in the view on the other side of the bridge. The sun had begun its descent behind the skyline; they crossed the road through a gap in the traffic to take in the stunning sunset.

Grabbing the bridge's railing, Pamela looked down at the water, seeing the double Doric stone columns rising up from the river's mouth. "Look, Mother!" she called, leaning over the railing. "These columns are like the ones in my Manchester Theatre!" She extended out still further into the gathering dusk, twisting her head to look at the bridge's underbelly. Her hat strings slid off her upside-down cheeks, and Pamela saw the inside of her hat float downward into the darkening water of the Thames.

"My hat!" she blurted out, reaching for the disappearing strings. She felt herself pitch forward.

Bram turned just in time to see a flash of Pamela's petticoat disappear over the sides of the parapet. He thought he might have imagined it, but the screams of the women let him know this was a parent's worst nightmare, a tragic accident in the making. The group reached the side of the railing in time to see Pamela's face bobbing in the whirling waters forty feet below.

Suddenly, a man ran next to them, tore off his wool coat, climbed over the railing, and dived into the water. The dive was effortless and seemed to go on and on. Later, Bram would reflect that he and the rest of the people on the bridge were paralyzed while the diver seemed to be floating, free and unencumbered.

A splash of water broke the spell. In the thick mist around the surface of the water, the man's blonde hair stood out like a beacon. The wailing and cries of the women drowned out any hope of hearing what was passing between the man and Pamela.

The man approached the struggling girl in the black water, held up one hand to motion for her to be still, and disappeared. He resurfaced with the girl clinging to his back. When she flailed about, he removed her clutching hands from his shirt and secured them around his neck, then churned through the brackish water. His arms sliced through the water as he swam, his head slowing down its beat from side to side as he strained against the current.

Pamela's eyes burned, and she tried to keep the terrible water out of her mouth, her hands clasped around the man's neck. Every time his head dunked underneath the surface, she had to arch her head back. Over her rescuer's head she saw the dim outline of St. Paul's Cathedral. The golden dome's glint was quickly draining away, a palette of grays and blacks replacing it.

Victoria Embankment's wall soon loomed in front of them, and he managed to aim for a ladder embedded into the wall. When the strong current of the cold water lessened for a moment, he reached around and lifted Pamela out in front of him.

"Reach!" his deep voice commanded.

Pamela obeyed and grabbed the rung above her, her cold legs trying to steady themselves on the wall so that she could pull herself up. She struggled with the weight of her wet coat but soon she felt herself hoisted from below as the man gave her an added push. When the second rung was firmly in her grasp, she turned her head to see the man treading water below her. She scrambled up another rung and he lunged from the water to follow her. The entire ladder shook as he landed on the rung. Soon he was shimming up with her.

Mother, Father, Grandmother, and Bram were still a block away, running down the Embankment, as Pamela reached the top and collapsed on the ground. The man steadied himself at the top of the ladder, heaving as water dripped from his clothes, and pulled himself onto the Embankment. He stood, took a deep breath, and bent down to examine the girl. Pamela's head was flopped over, her hair covering her face. Her small body jerked with short, spasmodic motions. He pushed her hair back and lifted her chin. Her head was still limp, but her eyes opened wide and focused on him. Life came back into her arms and she beat at him with her fists.

"We're alive?" she cried.

He clasped her fists with both of his hands and looked straight into her eyes. "So alive," he said softly. Pamela sighed and closed her eyes.

Bram ran up, carrying the coat the man had dropped on the bridge, and crouched down to the child. "Mother of God, she's alive!" He wrapped the coat around Pamela.

"Hello, Miss," Bram said.

Pamela's eyelids fluttered but remained closed as she mouthed "hello."

Relieved, Bram stood and steadied the wobbling, drenched man. "Terriss, you devil! That was no stage jump!"

Terriss reached down and picked Pamela up from the ground, holding her in front of him.

"Enough heroics," Bram said. "We need to get you both to a doctor."

The Smith family finally caught up to them. The mother and grandmother clamored over the girl, the father looked pale and helpless, and the girl's eyes remained closed.

Terriss turned around and took in his surroundings.

He motioned to the stunned-looking father. "There's Bow Street, I know a street doctor there. We can try him," Terriss said. Carrying Pamela, he rushed ahead, and the group struggled to keep up.

Pamela's head swirled. She opened her eyes and fixed them on the man who rescued her.

From behind them she heard the red-haired man from the paint shop grunt, "He's a damn fool."

CHAPTER SIX

Woodman and the British Museum

With a bounce in his step, the large man paced in front of the crate on the floor of the British Museum's private viewing room. At sixty, Dr. William Woodman looked like a large bird of prey stalking a victim, his beard flowing over the collar of his black manteau, his hands behind his back. Three other would-be magicians, Dr. Westcott, Dr. Felkin, and Mr. Mathers, watched the workmen opening a large wooden box.

Woodman's eyebrows leapt up and down as the two workmen applied their hammers, releasing the lid of the dusty, battered crate. Finally, the last nail screeched at the exact moment a man wearing a fez entered carrying a wooden box.

Dr. Woodman nodded at the new arrival. "Kamal," he acknowledged.

Samuel Mathers spoke up. "Dr. W-w-woodman, we are honored to be here."

Dr. Woodman smiled and addressed the speaker. "Gentlemen, you have the best timing in the world to visit me today. Henry Kennard's mummy from Egypt has just arrived."

"This would be the young princess he's been boasting of?" Dr. Westcott asked as he stepped forward.

The workmen each took an end of the lid and lifted it off. Dr. Woodman knelt, placing a hand on the crate to steady himself. The workmen watched the large man lift a strand of gauze from the mummy as he muttered, "The colored resin on the linen wrappings does seem to confirm that she was a princess. Her shroud is in good shape, but her mask has been twisted."

Dr. Felkin stood behind the kneeling form of Woodman and grasped his shoulders. "Good show! So many of them come here jostled to bits, but not this one. Kennard will be unbearable now."

Mr. Mathers edged to the front and looked into the crate. "Just fantastic. From another era. Fantastic," he whispered in an accent that almost sounded Scottish.

"Well now," Dr. Woodman said, touching the fragments of the linen shroud. "It's in better shape than I thought it would be. Help me up."

Dr. Woodman stood up with help from Dr. Westcott.

"Doctor, I believe your arthritis has gotten worse," Westcott said as the stocky man righted himself.

"Ah, true! From a career tending to others," Dr. Woodman replied. "But, gentlemen, as pleasant as it is to share this moment, I have a feeling you didn't come here to watch the unpacking of Kennard's latest find."

Dr. Westcott held up his leather carrying case. "I believe, my fellow good doctor, that we have found a prophecy from Egypt that will change the course of mankind."

Dr. Woodman chuckled and led the way to the door. "Well, chaps, let's consult with the expert here, Mr. Kamal. We will see if it's destined to change life as we know it."

Ahmed Pasha Kamal, the Egyptian antiquities expert, who wore the same muslin overcoat as Woodman, lifted an eyebrow. In his midforties, Ahmed's goatee already had streaks of gray, its close-cut style distinguishing it from the Englishmen's bushy beards. He motioned to the rack of curator smocks for the others to wear.

Ahmed's position was with the Department of Antiquities at the Palace of Ismail Pasha in Giza, Egypt. His current project entailed preserving five thousand boxes of artifacts being prepared for the move to the bigger Egyptian museum being built in Cairo near the British barracks. Tracking down some of the artifacts that had gone to the Louvre or the British Museum by "mistake" was one of his first assignments. He had worked alongside Sir Earnest Wallis Budge in the preservation of the mummies and tried to give Egypt a voice in the decisions that were being made by the French, Italian, and English "conservationists."

Working at the British Museum to identify his country's artifacts could be trying. It amused him that Sir Earnest, when visiting the museum in Giza, told the vacation team that the mummies there "seemed sad." It had everything to do with the gaudy room the French had painted: blue, gold, and orange with a mural on the ceiling depicting Venus and Cupid. It was not Egyptian scenes that "seemed sad" to Budge, but rather Roman gods painted by French occupiers looking down on Egyptian mummies. It was a typical misidentification by foreign experts.

What was sad to Ahmed was that his country's artifacts were being removed by the thousands and shipped off to various officials and foreigners as bribes and tokens. He was intensely proud of his country's small, local Egyptian museums and campaigned to keep artifacts in the areas where they were uncovered, to keep Egypt's history in Egypt. But in this time of English and French rule, that seemed impossible.

The doctors Woodman, Westcott, and Felkin, and Mr. Mathers, put on the muslin overcoats and stood around the table. Dr. Westcott removed a cylinder from his leather case and placed it before them.

Ahmed opened his wooden tool kit, pulled out a pair of archival gloves and put them on. "There are two distinct items here. Let us take a look at this first one." Ahmed's English had a French accent, learnt from Auguste Mariette, the late French Egyptologist. As the leading expert in translating Egyptian Coptic manuscripts, papyrus artifacts, stelae, and altars, Ahmed's French and English helped put him at the forefront in France and England's museums. He was the link to those who had helped themselves to his country's antiquities. He removed a rolled-up section of parchment from within the cylinder.

"This does not look Egyptian; it is modern-day paper." Ahmed looked at it more closely. "Yes, modern-day paper, but the inscription is in code. Let's see, this is the Trithemius Polygraphiae code for the Hermetic and Rosicrucian lineages and refers to a cipher . . ." He started to read the text written in Arabic.

Mathers asked him in Arabic, "How old is the cipher?"

Startled to hear Mathers speak Arabic, Ahmed answered nonetheless, "From the fourth or fifth dynasties."

Dr. Westcott fish-eyed him. "Speak English, please, Mr. Kamal."

Ahmed continued, "Ah, well . . . English, then. These codes suggest something about fourteenth-century magic and indicate there is an item from the fourth or fifth dynasty in Alexandria." He put down the paper and looked back inside the cylinder. "And there it is!"

He sat at the table and used a pair of tweezers from his toolkit to reach inside the cylinder again. From its interior walls, he gently pried out a rolled-up linen sheet. It was fixed shut with a wax seal. His eyebrows twitched. "I see the scarab seal has been broken and reattached," he said as he held the rolled papyrus up to the light.

"Ah, the sands of the desert have been good to this papyrus." He unrolled the linen sheet. Affixed to it was a grainy, yellowish-gray papyrus textile, very fragile, with some pieces of fiber broken off. "The English fog will not keep this black iron gall ink from fading, so write these characters down imme-diately." With that, he laid the delicate tube down on the white table as the four other men inched forward, Mathers taking notes. Ahmed took a small sharp knife and pried the seal off the side of the scroll. It fell to the table with a dull sound.

The men crowded around him to examine it.

As he pulled four smooth stones from his tool kit, Ahmed said ironically, "Thanks to Napoleon invading my country and locating the Rosetta Stone, we may be able to decipher this text." Using the stones, he gently anchored the corners of the scroll. Picking up a magnifying glass and looking through it, he moved a finger above the symbols and squiggles on the ancient papyrus as he read.

"Ah, the Demotic language, mostly used for religious and court decrees." He looked at Woodman. "It is a prophecy."

Dr. Woodman grabbed the magnifying glass from Ahmed and examined the scroll. Dr. Felkin hurriedly put on a pair of archival gloves and walked back over to the papyrus, muttering slightly to himself. He saw the others staring at him and he stopped. "Mr. Kamal, I still do not grasp the sense of this," Dr. Felkin said.

"Well, Dr. Felkin, I am using the 1832 Champollion trans-lations of the Egyptian language . . ."

The viewing room door opened, and Bram Stoker came in, hurriedly putting on a protective muslin coat. He rushed to the table. "Sorry I'm late, gentlemen. Mr. Kamal, please go on. I just got word at the theatre that you may be able to translate this."

Ahmed took a moment and looked at the five men. Part of him was loath to give these men the secrets to the antiquities that had made their way from his father's country to this English museum. He thought of Dr. Woodman as an old-guard plunderer. And this Dr. Westcott, there was something nefarious about his interest in gods and goddesses of ancient Egypt. The same with the very tall doctor, Felkin. What was it about these English doctors that they wanted to study and own all the esoteric artifacts from other countries? Mathers, with his elementary Arabic, seemed a harmless scholar; it was only Bram Stoker whom Ahmed genuinely liked, as he was Irish and would let slip the rare comment that indicated he was not fond of the English. But Bram worked for the very English Henry Irving and brought him to meet Ahmed so that he might study the Egyptian hieroglyphics while on his world tours. What these men were up to in their enthusiasm and excitement over these Egyptian scrolls troubled him, but he kept a level head and translated as much as he thought was appropriate.

"Good day, Mr. Stoker. Yes, these are the ideograms. You see this bird, snake, beetle, and lion?" The men passed the magnifying glass around. "These images reflect an idea and give meaning to the phonograms." Ahmed then pointed to a seated man, birds, and a pair of walking legs. "These are the determinatives, image signs that are less concrete." Pointing to one set of images he said, "Here is the genius of perception, and this is a girl giving birth. Over here is an emblem of divinity, to unite, and this last set is the symbol for the genius of creative utterance."

Dr. Woodman grunted, inhaled, and pronounced, "A girl giving birth is divine and unites the genius of creative utterance?"

"Ah, Dr. Woodman, this foretells much more," Ahmed said. "The essence is that each human will become a god or goddess with all aspects of magical properties. Once the entire race of these superior beings is created and fulfills its destiny, the fate of the world will be tested in one last conflict, and the result will be survival or destruction."

Dr. Westcott unfolded his arms and said dismissively, "Are you sure it's a *girl*?"

Ahmed smiled and looked up at the smug Englishman. "Yes, we have a tradition of women as rulers."

Dr. Woodman looked up and out the window. "My dear chap, isn't this a reference to the Virgin Mary and the birth of Christ?"

Ahmed shook his head and, biting his tongue, went back to the table. "Chap" was the word that Woodman used instead of "idiot."

"No, this is not a prediction of the birth of your Christ and the disciples," Ahmed said, standing. "This is a girl who has the means to communicate to all without language. It says that this sequence of gods and goddesses will incarnate and that there will be a universal language. Or, universal destruction."

Dr. Woodman chuckled and put his hands in his pockets, then smiled deferentially. "Of course, one could say that our good book, the Bible, infers that by following Christianity, a superior race of people will be produced."

"Ah, Dr. Woodman," Ahmed replied, "even your Shake-speare says, 'There are more things in heaven and earth, Horatio, than are dreamt of in your philosophy.' These symbols are much more complex than what is found in your King James Bible. And there are many other languages than those your Bible encompasses."

Dr. Woodman looked and pointed to one section of the script, and then touched it, making Ahmed flinch. "But what of all these symbols here?"

"Doctor, don't forget your gloves," Ahmed said. "These are not easily understood; we are only in the early days of deciphering. It seems to suggest five beliefs, twenty-two worlds, and then four different armies, or continents, I'm not sure. I will investigate them here." With that he let out a yelp. "Oh no! The air is erasing the writing!"

The writing on the ancient page turned pale and started to fade. Ahmed moaned as more of the ink dissipated into the air. Woodman's touch must have started a reaction. He took the tweezers and lifted the papyrus into a box. He quickly sealed it and wrapped it in a heavy cloth.

"What is happening?" Dr. Westcott asked.

"The damp air here is destroying the compound of the ink," Ahmed said. "Only by putting it in an airtight container can we hope to salvage any of it."

"Does this mean we can't take it with us?" Dr. Felkin asked.

"Not presently," Ahmed answered. "But please feel free to take the newer writing with you."

"Well, Mr. Kamal, thank you for letting us take our own property with us," Dr. Woodman said. "I hope you will be able to preserve the ancient text so we can view it later."

Ahmed stared at Woodman. "If it survives," he replied.

"Let us know," Dr. Woodman said, wiping his hands.

The Savage Club at the Savoy Hotel had just opened, and the men sat in leather tufted club chairs in the elaborate dining room. The staff finished clearing the empty glasses from their first round of drinks. Mathers tugged at his collar, overwhelmed by cigar smoke, as Bram chose his next cigar from the humidor.

Dr. Woodman settled back in his chair. "Well, Dr. Westcott, it's a shame we had to leave the papyrus at the museum with Mr. Kamal, but at least we were able to take the modern paper about fourteenth-century magic with us."

"How did you know it was fourteenth-century magic?" Dr. Westcott asked.

"Why, the manuscript looked like those from that time in the museum," Mathers said in a faint Scottish accent.

"Now, Mathers, do we call you McGregor now?" Dr. Woodman asked. "We've all heard this Scottish accent you've been putting on."

As Mathers squirmed in his chair, Dr. Westcott joined in the teasing. "Come on now, McGregor? Mathers, you're born in England and you've become Scottish all of a sudden? For what reason?"

Mathers almost looked as if he were going to bolt from the room.

"Here, take a cigar. It will help settle you," Dr. Woodman said, reaching for another cigar.

"Well, I may not have been born in Scotland," Mathers said, "but I do believe I have just f-f-f-found I may have Scottish family and I live in hopes of an inheritance, so . . ."

"So, you're Scottish for a little money!" Dr. Westcott joked. "Not a good trade, if you ask me. What do you think, Doctor?"

Dr. Woodman settled in. "Well, I think we have to talk about what this fourteenth-century manuscript foretells and how we are going to publish the results."

With that, Dr. Westcott called over a waiter and curtly ordered, "Five whiskeys."

When the men were alone, Dr. Westcott leaned toward the center of the table and quietly said, "We are not going to publish these results. We are going to create a tarot deck that will instruct our higher levels in the ways of magic."

"We'll need a committee for this phase," Dr. Woodman said. "I'll see to the organization of it."

"Dr. Woodman, as the man with the connections and money to make this group viable, we appreciate your consideration," Dr. Westcott said, as the other men fidgeted.

The three doctors talked amongst themselves. That left Bram and the deflated Mathers to talk together. For the next half hour, two separate conversations sputtered along.

Dr. Woodman choked slightly on his cigar and looked at his pocket watch. "Twelve thirty? How did this happen? I'm too old for this nonsense. Now I must hire a hansom to go home."

Mathers fondly looked at the table and sighed, "Best meal I've had in a f-f-fortnight."

"Not much work for a translator these days, eh?" grunted Dr. Woodman.

Mathers put his head in his hands and closed his eyes. "No, and I was so hoping I would be able to translate those symbols on the papyrus, but that ancient Egyptian language is one I don't know. Now Mr. Kamal will have all the glory of b-b-bringing its meaning to the world."

Slapping Mathers on the knee, Dr. Felkin said, "You recognized that first scroll. Quite an accomplishment. Where did you say you found them, Westcott?"

Dr. Westcott looked calmly over his cigar smoke. "They came into my hands through a friend, and I have heard it mentioned that Count Apponyi has some important artifacts going back to the time of the Library of Alexandria. I thought these might be those."

"You think these scrolls could be part of the Count Apponyi p-p-papers?" Mathers stuttered.

"They might be," Dr. Felkin answered tersely. He signaled the waiter to pour another round of brandy, and teasingly pushed a snifter toward Mathers. "Well, Mathers, if you are to be a Scottish McGregor, what is your family motto?"

Dreamily, Mathers leaned back in his chair and in his best Scottish accent intoned, "Royal is my race."

This prompted everyone to spasms of laughter, with Bram laughing loudest.

Dr. Woodman then cocked his head toward Mathers. "As a polyglot, into how many languages can you translate 'Royal is my race'?"

Dr. Felkin joined in, "Here's our drinking game: for every translation that you do, Dr. Woodman must down a brandy." With that he snapped his fingers and the waiter appeared with a decanter. "For each translation, pour! French for 'Royal is my race'!"

"Too easy! *Royal est mon sang!*" Mathers preened as he answered and the waiter poured Dr. Woodman a refill which he downed in a single gulp.

Dr. Felkin sat bolt upright. "Hebrew!"

Mathers shot back, "ילש עזגה איה לאיור."

Another drink was poured and with a little more effort, Dr. Woodman downed another glass.

"Latin?"

"*Regalis sanguis meus!*"

The waiter looked at Dr. Felkin questioningly while he bellowed, "Pour, man! Gaelic?"

"*Is ríoga mo chuid fola!*"

Dr. Woodman leaned toward Bram. "What do you think, man? Was that a good enough approximation of your native tongue?"

Bram laughed again and replied, "Not bad for an Englishman."

Dr. Woodman looked imploringly at Felkin and said, "Really, my good fellow doctor, you know our motto, 'First, do no harm.' A fifth brandy might be pushing it."

Dr. Felkin chided him, "We need to see if Mathers is up to this translating job!" And to Mathers, he said, "Let's hear your Arabic! Besides, it's the most curious thing that you, Mathers, don't stutter in other languages."

Trembling, Mathers hunched over the table. "The Count Apponyi Hungarian Hermetic and Rosicrucian lineage p-p-papers? You would hire me to translate those?"

Dr. Woodman laughed and, taking a sip of water, tapped Mathers's arm. "My dear fellow, if we can acquire the rest of the papers, and if you can translate your motto into Arabic, we will give you the job."

Steadying his hands on the table and closing his eyes, Mathers intoned, "الملكي وه سباق لي."

With that, the waiters and amused men applauded as Mathers sat down, flushed and happy.

❦

Doctors Woodman and Westcott sat swaying across from one another in the hansom in the early morning enshrouded by yellow London fog as the horse made its tired clip-clop echo through the empty brick streets to Dr. Woodman's apartment in Belgravia. Dr. Westcott looked at Mathers's small pencil notes on the translation of the papyrus, which he had written at the museum.

Dr. Woodman tilted his head back and rubbed his eyes. "Dr. Westcott, next time Felkin decides that a drinking game is the way to interview a fellow on his translation skills, count me out."

Dr. Westcott chuckled and gazed out the carriage window into the pea-soup air. "Yes, but Mathers is now on board, and he's poor as a church mouse, so we won't have to pay him all that much. And those Count Apponyi papers will take at least a year to decipher."

"You think a year's living is what I should provide for Mathers, then?"

Dr. Westcott coughed into his handkerchief and slowly said, "Yes, I think a year should be enough. Would we make the arrangements with your bank?"

Dr. Woodman exhaled and gestured for the notebook, taking the pencil from Westcott's hand. "Yes, let's get all this in order. I haven't been feeling well, and we might as well sign the trust to be set up for this position. Now, I will insist on being the main chief here, Doctor; as you can see, there is a lot to manage. Once Mathers translates the Count's papers, I want to take our time before we create a tarot deck. You know, due diligence and all that."

Dr. Westcott looked out the window and thought, *Yes, and all that. Here it is! He will take the papers for whatever magical instruction and bloody sit on them for years to come while he shows them to his inside group at his Junior Athenaeum Club instead of to the Golden Dawn.*

Because Woodman had been a military doctor in India and Egypt, he belonged to the Junior Athenaeum Club, the one club Dr. Westcott was not officially qualified to join. Although it had been suggested that Woodman might sponsor him, which he wanted dearly and had pursued since they met at the former Duke of Newcastle's home, so far it was only a promise of an endorsement. Dr. Woodman had previously insisted there would not be enough votes to get him through the vetting process.

Dr. Westcott could imagine Woodman saying: "Ah, Westcott, let's face it, man, you are a coroner. These are gentlemen connected with literature, science, and art. It would be a stretch for you to feel at home there."

On a blank page in Mathers's notebook, Dr. Woodman scribbled a few lines. "There. This is the directive for a living for Mathers for a year. Take it to the bank on Monday."

Dr. Westcott looked it over and nodded his approval, casually adding, "Oh, and Woodman, you might want to make it official and transfer the funds you were going to dedicate to starting a research group to study the findings of these esoteric manuscripts."

Dr. Woodman looked sharply at him. "Mathers hasn't even started translating those papers. Do you think that we need to start financing a group to research something not yet translated? How will it be known that this research is my property?"

"My dear fellow doctor," Dr. Westcott replied, "from my time in Austria, I can tell you the findings from the Count Apponyi papers will have worldwide effect. And to please you, we will call this research position the 'Dr. Woodman Fund.' But, in order to keep the results to ourselves, we should start our group as soon as possible, for others are sure to be on this trail of discovery."

Dr. Woodman assented. "You are probably right. I'll just sign a note that you are to enter into discussions with my solicitor and my banker to start the Woodman Fund. Here's the account number and my signature. Then I'll have a paper drawn up declaring that I am the legal owner of the paper's findings."

Just then, Dr. Woodman brought his right hand up to his heart and groaned, "Oh dear, that's a major one. Ah, zounds! That really stabs, good God!"

"What is it, Woodman? Is it your heart?"

"Yes, let's just hurry home. I have medication there." Dr. Woodman began to take off his overcoat. "It's so bloody hot in here! Tell the driver to get a move on!"

"No need, old man, I have what you need here. A physician must always be ready. Let's get you sorted out."

With that Dr. Westcott rapped on the top of the cab and shouted to the driver, "Pull up here! I need to administer aid!"

As the coach slowed down, Woodman, groaning louder, slid against the side of the carriage. Dr. Westcott, springing into action, found his small medical kit and took out a syringe and a small vial. He finished removing Woodman's coat and rolled back his shirtsleeves.

"This sedative should help your racing heart. Woodman, do you know what I think these fourteenth-century papers are all about?"

"No," groaned Woodman, as the needle sailed into his arm.

"They are manuscripts that empower a soul to reach, by magical means, earth to heaven. When the new order begins, I shall be the conduit from earth to heaven. Goodbye, Woodman."

Gasping for air, Dr. Woodman clutched his chest. "Good God, what have you given me?"

"Why, it's some heavenly cocaine, Dr. Woodman."

Dr. Westcott watched as Dr. Woodman died with his eyes finally wide open.

CHAPTER SEVEN

Corsican Brothers' Magic

Waiting to seat the Smith family for the production of *The Corsican Brothers,* Bram had a strange sense of foreboding. Terriss's rescue of Pamela had been the talk of the town, and the fact that both of them had escaped with only bruises was miraculous. And in Bram's experience, trouble usually came in pairs.

Henry Irving's private seats in the Governor's box were still empty just as the electrical light in the lobby signaled that the show was about to start. The head usher suddenly appeared with the group, and Bram quickly led the four guests to the beautiful tiered seats. The box seats were framed with a red velvet curtain that hid a secret pass door to the backstage platform. This door led to the area where the stage managers called the show.

Bram saw the child, Pamela, standing before a stall seat as she craned her neck to take in every nook and cranny of the Lyceum auditorium. Instead of the customary white dress for a young girl, she wore a black dress, a version of her mother's attire. As Pamela turned her head, Bram noted she still had traces of a black eye and a bruise on her cheek, the result of her fall from the bridge. She smiled through her injuries. She would be a serious and well-behaved audience member. Watching her parents and grandmother settle in beside Pamela, he positioned himself behind them, his six-foot-two frame just barely visible from the auditorium as he stood near the pass door. *With her funeral-like dress and bruises, this child certainly doesn't look like our typical Lyceum Theatre patron*, Bram thought. And she didn't look like either parent; her coloring was darker and her moon face was unlike her mother's pinched oval visage, nor did she have her father's low hairline.

How odd that she should be drawing the tetramorph just when we were discussing its potent power at the Golden Dawn. And that a young girl should be the one to recognize the symbols.

Just then the overture began, played by some thirty black-clad men in the orchestra who followed the baton of Sir Arthur Sullivan, conducting his own melodramatic score. Pamela turned in her seat and whispered to him, "Mr. Stoker, you know I make miniature theatres. But in my life, I have only ever been in the Theatre Royal Manchester."

Bram looked at her parents and grandmother and offered, "I'll take her backstage before the masked ball scene, then, to take a look around?"

Mrs. Colman and Mr. Smith nodded appreciatively while the mother pleaded with her eyes, setting Bram to chuckling, "Well then, there might be two of you?"

Pamela squeezed her mother's hand as the house lights dimmed, and they turned back in their seats to watch the show as Bram made his way back to his office through the stall's secret door. The story of the twin Corsican brothers, Fabien and Louis, began to unfold as the great velvet curtains swept back, revealing the great hall in the castle of the Corsican twin, Fabien. The audience broke into applause at the sight of the elaborate set.

Bram was pleased with the audience's reaction. Keeping the curtains closed until the show began and dimming the house lights were all Henry's innovations.

Henry Irving was playing both twins, with his understudy performing the shadow play roles when the brothers were on stage at the same time. Williams Terriss, with his expertise in a swash-buckling style of swordplay, was the evil seducer Chateau-Renard. For a month, he and Henry had practiced the swordplay at the *salle d'armes* under the tutelage of a weapons expert from the army.

Bram couldn't wait to get into his office. It was his den, where he hired and fired, and bestowed favors requested, whether it was to hire the old woman who could no longer sew to watch over the other three old women who fed the theatre cats, or to set up auditions for the Great Man to look for new company members. It was a middle-sized room with an actual window facing Exeter Street. Down the hall was the theatre's private entrance where Sergeant Barry kept guard. Barry was good about keeping out anyone without an appointment and understanding that all appointments came from Bram. The desk was of decent size, with three good club chairs, a lovely rug from one of Henry's besotted patrons that was too "bright" for him, a spittoon, a good cigar case, and a small hidden bar. Tonight, outside Bram's office, was a rack with the specialty act clothes, shepherded by the officer, for too many had turned up missing lately.

Lovejoy, one of the stage managers, stopped him the minute he got in the door. Bram held up his hand and turned his head to hear the gasps and cries from the audience.

"Ah, good—the Corsican Trap worked well tonight."

The trap, named after the play, was the only one of its kind. It was a sort of floating platform that Henry's understudy would stand on while a series of drums and shafts operated by a winch system would drag him sideways and upwards. A specially designed moving floor, called a Scruto, would travel in the same direction at the same speed, allowing him to move at a gradual rise. If the pullers did their job smoothly, it was a seamless and graceful way to make the spectral apparition "float" from one side of the stage to the other, as if coming out of the floor.

Lovejoy motioned to the rack of clothing outside Bram's door and quietly reported, "We have those nine clowns from the regions filling in tonight during the reveling in the masked ball. Sullivan knows to add the extra phrases for their routine."

The rack was down to just a few costumes now; the dominoes (capes worn for masked balls with slender-pointed hoods and wide sleeves) and the masks and slouch hats had all been picked over. Lovejoy could see the clowns had been there, suiting up into their costumes. The difficult part was getting it back from them. Usually, their pay was dependent on their handing over their costumes. There was a tradition that novelty acts, if they were available and were permitted in advance, could be a part of the entertainment during the masked ball segment of *The Corsican Brothers*. Sometimes they succeeded in making it on stage, and sometimes, due to time or other matters, they didn't. The performers would only be paid if they were able to get past or "break" the black curtains that masked the backstage area, known as the "legs." Thus, the tradition of wishing a performer luck by saying "break a leg" referred to their being paid, not to their fracturing a femur.

But clowns were unpredictable and raucous, sometimes spilling into the elegant dining scene, where they could help themselves to the sponge cake and bread that was used for an elegant Dumas period feast. At other times, they would bring boxes on stage, which they would jump from and somersault over. These boxes would block the dancers and extras in the backstage area from being able to enter onstage, leading to their not being able to "break a leg." It was up to Lovejoy to monitor who was on that night and to see that proper attention was paid to the provided attire, as the colored robes were given out according to height with the darkest cloaks given to the tallest.

Bram saw that there were still four or five revelers' outfits left on the rack and thought that Pamela and her mother might make good extras, if they stood out of the way and understood it was a voluntary position, not a paid one. Checking on the number that the usher boy in his Eton suit had just delivered from the front of house, he saw that attendance at tonight's performance was excellent and went to fetch the Smiths as it was nearly time for the masked ball scene. It would be good publicity to give Mrs. Smith, obviously a hungry actress, a walk-on. She would talk endlessly about it in the future, and the fact that they were moving from London meant international word of mouth.

He walked by the prompter, a military veteran who had served in India, "Jimmy" Allen. Jimmy was following along in his prompt book, ready to hiss out the lines that were temporarily forgotten while turning the cluster of potatoes he had piled up against the hot water pipe that ran next to his chair. It was said that he knew if the show was running long at any given performance if his potatoes were overcooked. Using his key, Bram opened the pass door slightly so that he could see the focused faces of Pamela and her group. Of course, it was the mother who eagerly caught his eye and who motioned to Pamela to quietly stand while they stepped through the open door to the backstage area. Bram lifted his finger to his lips to silence them and motioned for them to follow him as they made their way past the cloaked members for the upcoming masked ball scene. He walked briskly down the hall to his office and in a *sotto voce* aside presented the rack with the few costumes on it.

"You can be part of the masked ball scene if you put these on."

"Oh! Can we?" Pamela whispered fiercely.

"It's a voluntary position. That all right with you, Mrs. Smith?" Bram said, looking at her overwrought face and knowing the answer.

"Yes, yes, oh, yes, yes!"

"You are to stand next to Mademoiselle Fornay, who will keep you in place. Do not do anything more than stand next to her, and do not take off any part of this costume."

He showed them the rack's selection. Mrs. Smith excitedly dressed herself first, then put a large hat with a chinstrap on Pamela and a black mask that tied in the back. They both donned dark purple capes so they were almost unrecognizable, and they trotted down the hall after Bram. He ushered them to a darkened area of the backstage where five lines of actors in black and purple capes stood ready to go on. He tapped a short purple-caped form and whispered in her ear. Mademoiselle Fornay turned and acknowledged the duo. Bram knew they would be in good hands with Mademoiselle. She quickly pulled Pamela and her mother to either side of her and put their hands on her shoulders, signaling that they were to stay there and only there.

There was a pause in the music, and then a loud whistle shot out from above. Pamela tried to look up to see where the whistle was coming from, and then another two-toned whistle rang out. A huge, beautiful mirror was being lowered on ropes until it filled the main space upstage. Two actors came on stage and with lit tapers ignited the candles affixed to either side of the mirror as the swarm of cloaked dancers surged onstage. Mademoiselle Fornay led them to the right of the mirror and glanced out of the side of her mask with a threatening look to remind Pamela and her mother to stay glued to her sides. Now the *coryphées*, the dancers of the musical interlude, took their places and performed an elaborate and elegant dance. Pamela looked at her mother, and through the very small opening in her mother's mask she saw tears in her mother's eyes as she was finally living her dream of being on stage at the Lyceum Theatre.

Suddenly the dancers glided off in a swirling line, and from every angle backstage, black-caped men ran into the middle of the stage, performing their own grotesque, demonic type of dance. With amazing kicks and lifts, they spun in a circle, and when the tallest turned his head sharply, he saw Pamela, and with a jerk of his head he signaled to the others. Fearing their wrath, Pamela instinctively took her hand off Mademoiselle Fornay's shoulder, and before she knew it, it was grabbed by the tall dancing demon. The tall hats, cloaks, and masks made them all unrecognizable as men: they seemed to be whirling dervishes. They seized her by the shoulders and drew her into the middle of the circle. They spun her and tossed her, throwing her forward from one black swirling cape to another, rushing backward and forward in exact time, twirling her so insistently that she was breathless. She watched the theatre audience spin in the reflection in the candlelit mirror before her. Her mask slipped sideways, and she found herself turned around facing the audience, glancing at her father and grandmother seated in the stall. One more spin, and she was tossed into the arms of Mademoiselle Fornay, who seemed to have expected her, as she braced her side against Pamela's hurled body. Pamela was now in exactly the same position she had been in before she was drawn into the demon dance.

She was dizzy and euphoric, trying to regain her balance next to the candlelit mirror when the scene of the ball now settled down to a series of promenades and bows. A phrase of music picked up in tempo, and Mademoiselle Fornay placed her hands on the small of Pamela's and her mother's backs and marched them offstage. The music dimmed, two more whistles were heard above, and the group of extras came to a halt. Pamela tore off her mask to see Henry Irving standing alone on stage before a great mirror with a pair of double-candled scones.

In his elaborate Fabien costume of breeches, brocade vest, and frock coat, surrounded by smoke, Henry looked quite debonair as he regarded his reflection. The great glass mirror swayed as it was gently hoisted up. Fabien was waiting for his opponent to arrive and answer his challenge to a duel. The music paused slightly and there was another sharp whistle from above in the flies. Pamela caught the motion of a black cloak as someone ran above on the catwalk. At the same time, one of the ropes holding the mirror snapped free, resembling a crudely cut serpent's throat. The cut rope flew around as the great mirror swung back and forth on its only tether. The bottom part of the mirror's frame broke off and fell, almost hitting Henry, causing great gasps in the audience and backstage. The exposed blade-like edge of the mirror dangled back and forth like a great guillotine above Henry. He ducked quickly to keep its sharp edge from decapitating him.

All at once, a tall, athletic man rushed past Pamela and her mother and leapt through the air, tackling the crouching Henry under the path of the mirror and rolling downstage with him. Immediately the other rope snapped, and the mirror, on the upswing, floated for a moment in midair. Then the entire mirror dropped flat on the stage floor, exploding into shards.

But the sound! The sound of the mirror smashing was brilliantly clear, pinging out against the back wall of the auditorium. Slivers of glass skidded to the front of the stage and pinged against the covered limelights lining the orchestra pit. Great scratches appeared on the stage floor, reaching out from the mound of broken glass like the claw marks of a monster.

Some in the audience rose; others let out cries and shouts. The two figures at the lip of the stage near the orchestra pit picked themselves up and stood heaving, brushing off glass. Then Henry suddenly turned to the audience, and with a flourish, lifted his arm up and bowed as though this was simply a tremendous effect they had created for the audience's benefit. They erupted with rapturous applause, clapping and stamping their feet. Now, both Henry Irving and William Terriss bowed to the audience and then to one another. They then signaled that they should carry on their fight as Fabien and the evil Chateau-Renard. On cue, the orchestra music picked up once again, and the men went through the motions of a fistfight. During the improvised fisticuffs, their boots crunched on the shards of broken glass. They carried on the fight as they exited stage left.

Back in Bram's office, Pamela and her mother were seated in club chairs while Henry and Terriss went over a list of costume assignments. Pamela had told Bram of the figure in the cloak she had seen in the flies right before the accident. Pamela was mesmerized. She watched Terriss's every movement, while her mother watched Henry. The men were going over a list which had assigned the eight black cloaks, only seven of which were now thrown on Bram's desk. Mr. Lovejoy and Bram counted once more the number of cloaks. One was definitely missing.

Finally, Bram came over to the mother and daughter and said, "Well, it was more than you bargained for, I'm sure, and since you don't know any more about it than what you've told us, we'll be letting you leave now."

Mrs. Smith was just about to ask if she could be introduced to Henry Irving, but Bram anticipated this. He saw it all the time, and he started to kindly usher them out. "Thanks for your participation and we'll keep in touch, won't we, Miss Smith?"

He looked down at the girl, whose spirits were far from crushed by this goodbye. She was still in a euphoric haze from watching the show and being near her hero, Terriss. She rose from the club chair across from her mother, her eyes taking in everyone in the room.

She looked at Bram. "Yes, sir, I will write to you from Jamaica."

"Ah, Jamaica, that's right. You're leaving your motherland. Yes, when you come back from Jamaica and if you've kept up with your artwork and have something to offer us, come look me up."

"Yes, Mr. Stoker. Goodbye, Mr. Terriss."

Terriss looked up and saw her earnest face. "Goodbye, Miss Smith." He came to her and politely shook her hand. "Until we meet again."

With that, Bram gave a short wave and tried to pass them out to the hallway to the policeman guarding the door to be escorted outside. Just before she left the room, Pamela offered her hand to Bram, who bemusedly shook it, as her eyes were still totally trained on Terriss. *So smitten*, he thought.

Mrs. Smith tried her best to smile at the Great Man, but Henry was totally consumed with Terriss and the missing cloak. Defeated, she turned and, with her hand on her daughter's shoulders, allowed them to be led out of the room.

Pamela turned one last time to see Terriss and then walked down the hallway, spreading out both of her hands at her sides as though she were flying and feeling the very air of the theatre on her way out. She let out a yelp and ran, turned the corner, and was gone.

Harvey, the main carpenter, came into Bram's office and threw a short piece of rope on the desk.

"It's been cut. And here is a note left in this prop from *The Cup* by the sandbags."

He showed them a large, elaborate chalice with a folded piece of paper in it. *The Cup* was a melodrama that Henry and Ellen had starred in, which resulted in much success years ago. The plot involved a Galatian lord who lusts after a neighbor's wife; he kills the husband only to learn that she loathes him. She murders him on their wedding day by putting poison in the cup that they drink from at the wedding feast. The chalice used in the production had been the subject of much artistic debate between Henry and the designers. Its final incarnation was a large gold bell cup with a long, squarish stem.

Henry looked at the prop that Harvey was holding and snatched the note from it, reading, "Just as Dedi hypnotized a lion and was found to be only an entertainer, so are you. We unite to stop your trespass."

Bram and Henry looked at one another as Lovejoy picked it up and read it, then exclaimed, "What the hell does that mean? What lion? Who is Dedi?"

Henry then remembered, "There was an extra whistle right before the mirror fell."

Whistles backstage were the signals the stage crew gave one another to cue the rigging; most of the men at one time or another had worked as seamen, and that was the method by which they signaled one another and the reason why whistling was forbidden backstage by anyone but flymen.

Harvey folded his arms. "Weren't any of my men. We don't know who got up on the catwalk, but it seems sure they did."

Henry took in Harvey's defensive stance and calmly replied, "Mr. Harvey, what was different about security tonight? How could someone have climbed the flies or gotten to the catwalk?"

Harvey immediately shot back, "Same procedure as always, Mr. Irving."

Lovejoy looked down and Henry, seeing this, asked the stage manager, "Well, sir, what happened?"

Lovejoy lifted his eyes and then confessed, "Well, you see, Guv'nor, the food during the feast in the ball has led to quite the riot. They'd just race to the table and start shovin' in the sponge cake and bread, so we backstage decided to teach 'em some manners. The fancy food tonight was papier-mâché. Ya know, to show 'em they shouldn't just race up to the table and start shovin' it into their gobs."

Bram tapped his foot. "And how did that lead to a breach in security?"

Lovejoy continued, "We were all mostly watching the mob try to chew on papier-mâché instead of sponge cake when we shoulda been manning our stations for the mirror preset."

Bram, William, and Henry all looked at Harvey. Henry finally lifted his hand and said, "Very well, Mr. Lovejoy, Mr. Harvey. We must all be more diligent. And we may well be at a loss for a mirror. That was a gift from my patroness, Baroness Burdett-Coutts."

"We can at least console ourselves that whoever broke that mirror has seven years' bad luck, right, Guv'nor?" Lovejoy asked.

Harvey shrugged his shoulders. "I'm very sorry, Guv'nor. It won't happen again. We will be doing our job." He shot a look at Lovejoy but he left with his head bowed. Bram looked at Lovejoy and motioned for him to leave too.

"Most sorry, sir. Ya know my men didn't do that extra whistle." With that, Bram closed the door behind him and the three men exhaled. Bram sat behind his desk while Henry and Terriss each plopped down into a club chair.

Terriss took the oversized cup from Bram. "First it was a wand, now it's a mirror and a message in a cup. Something's brewing here."

Bram looked at Henry. "A wand? I've not been updated on a wand."

Terriss replied, "Well, Bram, I'm not sure the wand should be something that your Golden Dawn knows anything about."

Bram bristled. "Listen, Terriss, I've never claimed to be a part of the Golden Dawn's inner circle. I study their teachings the same way you do the Freemasons, for my own development, not to climb some obscure hierarchy. I've heard there is just as much magic in the Freemasons as there is in the Golden Dawn. I think I know what is safe and not safe to share with my group!"

Henry looked at the quarreling men. "Gentlemen, please. If this is an opening salvo fired in a war of magic, squabbling amongst ourselves won't help. I'm a Freemason and belong to several other orders; the Golden Dawn is not in my orbit but in Bram's. Let us keep these bizarre happenings amongst ourselves and leave the Freemasons and Golden Dawn to flourish without knowledge of whatever mischief or manifestations may be visiting us."

Bram and Terriss glared at one another and then both burst out laughing. Terriss clutched Bram's coat. "Oh please, if there's going to be any more magically appearing things, I'll put in for a decent pipe. You, Bram, what will you be wanting?"

Bram regained his composure and looked at the two men. "For protection? A decent crucifix."

Out on the street, Pamela felt tears prick at the back of her eyes as her father guided her through the milling crowd. Her mother was talking to someone with Grandmother, and her father parked them next to the pillars outside the entrance of the Lyceum Theatre. She hopped up and down on one foot, then the other. *My magic will find a way here. Why must we leave?*

"A penny for your thoughts," her father said, the warmth of his hand coming through his gloves as he took her hand in his.

"I have no thoughts," she answered. "Only feelings that I belong here."

CHAPTER EIGHT

DEDI, FIRST MAGICIAN

Ahmed sat back in his chair and looked at the gathering of gentlemen clustered at his open door. "So, you want to know all about Dedi, the first of all magicians."

The men answered in gruff affirmations.

Ahmed motioned to wooden chairs. "Well, gentlemen, seat yourselves and we'll begin."

This bearded coroner, Dr. Westcott, took the nearest chair to Ahmed. He had come several times to the British Museum since William Woodman's death. During his first visit there, Ahmed noticed that the contents of Woodman's desk had been of much more interest to Westcott than the deceased's personal locker.

Three other Golden Dawn members vied for the chairs along the wall. They also had made previous visits here: the stutterer who spoke Arabic, Samuel Mathers; the man who lectured when he talked, Mr. Waite; and the blond giant, Dr. Felkin.

But it was the presence of Henry Irving and Bram Stoker that surprised Ahmed the most. Ten o'clock in the morning for a meeting with theatre people was unheard of. Ahmed waved to chairs before his desk. "Mr. Irving, Mr. Stoker, please sit."

"Yes, we've come to learn about Dedi, who is mentioned in the Westcar papyrus," Dr. Westcott said.

Here is my chance, Ahmed thought. "The Westcar papyrus? The artifact that belongs in Cairo?" Ahmed asked.

Dr. Westcott's head snapped forward. "It belongs to the world," he answered.

Dr. Felkin tapped his heels as he sat. "Come, Mr. Kamal, we have all had a proper education. We know about the Westcar papyrus—that may well be the very first depiction of a magician in recorded history—an Egyptian! But it belongs to the world, not to Egypt."

The Westcar papyrus had been taken out of Egypt in 1824 by Englishman Henry Westcar. Somehow, through a series of exchanges, it now lived at the Museum of Berlin. The papyrus was created in three segments, depicting five stories of magicians and priests in the fourth dynasty, Ahmed's specialty. The dates of its origin were thought to be during the time of King Khufu (known to the English as King Cheops), who built the great pyramid of Giza. That pyramid and its artifacts were Ahmed's first grand passion.

After some under-the-breath grumbling by the Golden Dawn members, Ahmed addressed the most agitated. "Dr. Westcott, why don't you tell me what you've heard of Dedi."

"Well, it's covered in the Westcar papyrus that Dedi was the first magician," Dr. Westcott snapped.

Henry leaned forward from his seat and placed a palm on Ahmed's desk almost as if to soothe it. "Mr. Kamal, even our Bible gives credence to magicians in Exodus: 'Then Pharaoh also called the wise men and the sorcerers: now the magicians of Egypt, they also did in like manner with their enchantments. For they cast down every man his rod and they became serpents: but Aaron's rod swallowed up their rods.'"

He is an actor. Of course, he has memorized many lines. He smiled at Henry. "Yes, your Bible claims that Christian Aaron's rod swallowed up our Egyptian serpents, Mr. Irving. It seems reductive to reduce magicians to a tale of a competition between snake swallowers."

Henry crossed his long legs, making Mr. Stoker move his feet out of the way. "Indeed, Mr. Kamal, and it may very well be a Christian rewrite of history. Perhaps, Aaron's rod was actually defeated by the magicians' serpents. However, we would dearly love for you to share your knowledge on this first magician, Dedi."

Ahmed had seen *The Corsican Brothers* and knew Henry Irving was good at sleight of hand and onstage tricks. There was some talk that his ability to conjure things out of air was not a stage trick, but that he really was a magician.

The men all turned toward Ahmed in expectation. Why were all these men deferring to Henry, who had no university experience as far as Ahmed could tell? University attendance was a credit usually brought up within minutes of introduction to an Englishman. "He's a graduate of Oxford or a fellow at Cambridge." Ahmed had taught at the Egyptian University in Cairo, so he knew the prestige an academic title could bestow. But during his brief London stay, there was very little weight given to Ahmed's scholarly expertise on Egyptology, the study of Egypt's language, history, culture. But if he were to say the word "antiquities," there was a clamor for expertise to authenticate every trinket "discovered" in Egyptian soil.

Ahmed addressed Mr. Stoker, with whom he felt the most comfortable. "Mr. Stoker, I know you are writing a play, *The Undead*? Is this Dedi magician material for your play?"

Ahmed saw Henry look away at the mention of the play. Mr. Stoker cleared his throat and sat back in his chair. "Ah, Mr. Kamal, my play is now called *Dracula*, and Dedi has nothing to do with it."

Seeing this was a sore subject for Mr. Stoker, Ahmed gently asked, "So why are you all here to ask about Dedi?" As much as he liked this Irishman, he knew it was best to know why they wanted his information before he shared it with them.

"Someone tried to kill Mr. Irving at the theatre last night and left this note with Dedi mentioned in it." Mr. Stoker took a note out of his coat pocket and put it before Ahmed.

Ahmed picked up and read the typewritten message. "Just as Dedi hypnotized a lion and was found only to be an entertainer, so are you. We unite to stop your trespass." He looked back at the strange, long face of Mr. Irving. It occurred to him that they were both dressed almost identically, like proper English gentlemen: the black frock coat, the pince-nez sitting on the bridge of the nose. Except for the tall fez on Ahmed's head, they could have come from the same fashion plate.

"And just how did someone try to kill Mr. Irving?" Ahmed asked.

Mr. Stoker's brogue came out even stronger. "You know that scene in *The Corsican Brothers* with the mirror? The mirror's rope was cut; it fell onstage and almost decapitated Mr. Irving."

Ahmed raised his eyebrows. "Well. Gentlemen, let us talk about Dedi. But I must warn you: I will expect some help in a different matter in exchange for this information."

"We will do whatever we can," Dr. Felkin answered, brushing lint off his trousers.

"Of course, we will be glad to assist you," Henry said. "As we are grateful for your most knowledgeable opinion."

"Very well," Ahmed said, meeting the blank stare of Dr. Westcott. "For this information I am about to give you, I would like your word that you will help me start a correspondence with Herr Erman, in charge of the antiquities department at the Museum of Berlin. I want to learn how Henry Westcar happened to take this papyrus out of Egypt sixty years ago."

Mathers began to sputter, "A-a-a-dolf Erman donated Westcar's papyrus 'Tale of King Cheops and the Magicians' to the Museum of Berlin just two years ago. I can help you, as I have been in correspondence with him."

Perhaps Mathers's connection with the Museum of Berlin was bona fide. One of the methods used to make antiquities "disappear" was to retitle and misinterpret kings of origin. Ahmed had written to this Herr Erman earlier, to no avail. The fact that Mathers knew the papyrus's title had been renamed with King Cheops instead of Pharaoh Khufu was a good sign.

"I see," Ahmed said. "If you will help me establish a relationship with the Museum of Berlin, we can discuss Dedi and this note."

"D-d-done," Mr. Mathers said, as Waite pulled out a small notebook from his pocket and began taking notes.

"Dedi is said to be the first documented magician, as noted in the Westcar papyrus," Ahmed said, the rhythm of lecturing to a class coming back to him. "King Khufu—or 'Cheops' to you Englishmen—was building his Great Pyramid in Giza. For your calendar it would be the twenty-sixth century before the birth of your Christ, in the fourth dynasty. When building his great pyramid, he searched for the formula for the correct number of rooms. They were to be the same number that the great god Thoth had built in *his* pyramid. To Egyptians, the number of rooms within a pyramid bestows a special, magical quality. The secret chambers with crystals and mirror reflectors aid the priests and magicians to listen to the Universe and obtain wisdom which culminates in intercourse with the gods."

The men sat blinking at one another. Ahmed breathed a sigh of relief. *Well, this is good. They are not protesting with their tiresome morality, as some here at the museum have.*

"Pharaoh Khufu heard of this magician, Dedi, who was said to be 110 years old," Ahmed continued. "He was capable of eating five hundred loaves of bread and a whole shoulder of beef, and drinking hundreds of jugs of beer every day. He was able to restore decapitated heads and hypnotize wild beasts, making one lion so tame it followed him like a pet. The pharaoh ordered this famed magician brought to his court, where he commanded him to sever and reattach the head of a criminal. Dedi refused, but instead chose one of the pharaoh's geese at random. With one hand, he pulled off the goose's head, extending it in his hand to show that it was truly decapitated. He laid the lifeless goose's headless body on the floor and walked away. After everyone assembled saw that the goose was dead, he put the body under his arm and slowly pushed the lifeless head back onto the body. The goose suddenly squawked and came back to life, running around the room. He did the same with a pelican and an ox."

"There's a trick for your Lyceum stage," Dr. Felkin whispered to Henry, whose brow creased in response.

Ahmed continued. "Khufu then asked Dedi to tell him how many rooms there were in the temple of Thoth, but Dedi replied, 'Please forgive me, I do not know their number, but I know the place where the answer is . . . There is a box made of flint in the room called 'Inventory' at Heliopolis. In that box you will find what you seek.'"

"Did he find the flint box?" Dr. Westcott asked.

Of course, you only think of finding a flint box. Ahmed continued, "The king pressed Dedi about the location of the box, but Dedi could only tell him he would give birth to three pharaohs and they would have access to the box and its contents."

Henry picked up the story. "And so, King Khufu's son, Khafre, built another pyramid and the Great Sphinx, and *his* son, Menkauna, built the third Great Pyramid of Giza."

"Very good, Mr. Irving," Ahmed responded, pleased that the Englishman seemed to know the lineage of Egyptian kings. "Yes, they were the kings of his prophecy."

There was a silence while Waite continued to scratch away at his notebook. Mr. Stoker finally broke the silence. "So, Dedi decapitated animals and brought them back to life."

"Yes," Ahmed said. "And Dedi was determined to be the lowest form of physician. There are three: the regular physician of the body, the priest physician, and finally, the conjurer, or entertainment magician."

"Hear that, Mr. Stoker," Henry said. "I'm in the category for the lowest form of doctor."

"Yes, Mr. Irving," Ahmed said. "Tears and laughter are said to have healing properties, so you could be a doctor of sorts. The fact that the mirror was used to try to kill Mr. Irving is most interesting. Mirrors were used in channeling Thoth in his pyramid. Perhaps they thought you considered yourself a god by using a mirror during the conjuring scene. Personally, I found the floating head of the ghost in the play to be more evocative of ritual magic apparitions."

Waite spoke for the first time. "Why would people unite to kill Mr. Irving because of a mirror trick?"

Ahmed stood and sat on the edge of his desk. "It is possible that the trick in *The Corsican Brothers* of the head floating and reattaching itself to a body mimics the story of Dedi's trick enough to offend someone or something. There may be energies attracted by this feat, energies that have manifested in someone conjuring the spirit of Thoth. Perhaps they are trying to get Thoth's attention, attempting to find a suitable channel to bring his power to them."

Dr. Westcott clapped his hands together. "Who would be channeling the powers of Thoth?"

Ahmed looked at him and knew it was Dr. Westcott. He must have been engaging in ancient incantations and somehow summoned the great god's energies and was trying to blame the stage play. This was why he had heard the Golden Dawn group had been obsessing over papyrus and instructions. Thoth had come to take revenge on their playing with his light and fire.

Looking straight into Dr. Westcott's eyes, he warned, "Like all living things, all dead things do not obey according to every morality."

Dr. Westcott turned away without blinking, licking his lips. *Like a snake.*

Henry asked, "Mr. Kamal, is it because Thoth is not pleased with the stage trick in *The Corsican Brothers*? Someone knows he is offended and left the threat at the theatre?"

Ahmed smiled. "The stage trick of the head being reattached and the mirror used in ritual are reminiscent of the Thoth ceremonies. In London, there may be followers of Thoth, or perhaps an incarnation of Thoth himself, who want to make themselves or himself known. They may be making a sacrifice to have some lost power restored."

"Yes! Dedi was the performer for the king," Dr. Felkin said, jumping up. "They may be asking for a sacrifice for Thoth, just as Dedi did with the decapitated animals. Someone thinks you have magic, Mr. Irving. Maybe it is because there is a rumor that you are to be knighted as the first actor, Sir Henry?"

Henry flinched on "Sir Henry." Bram had advised Ahmed to call him Mr. Irving, not Sir Henry. Not yet, at least. How did these Golden Dawn men not know this?

"If I could truly perform magic, Mr. Felkin, I would conjure a full house every night," Henry responded.

"Back to this note," Ahmed said, picking it up again. "'Just as Dedi hypnotized a lion and was found only to be an entertainer, so are you. We unite to stop your trespass.' This is a warning from someone claiming to represent a group who has discovered a fraud. Perhaps it is a fanatic who claims to have channeled Thoth and feels the god has been disrespected by the show. Perhaps the mirror scene or the floating head scene is mimicking a ceremonial ritual of Thoth's. The claim of magical trespassing of the show itself is vague; it seems more to do with Dedi's or Mr. Irving's popularity as an entertainer."

"We can't get a replacement for the mirror for weeks," Mr. Stoker said. "Should we even replace it? And what about the

Corsican Trap used to create the floating head trick? Is that to be sabotaged next?"

"What does your Scotland Yard say about this note?" Ahmed asked.

"They have offered to provide new extras in our crowd scenes by bringing in detectives from the main office," Mr. Stoker said. "At least they would be off our payroll while they provide protection."

"Scotland Yard should investigate any leads on any new, clandestine magicians' gatherings," Ahmed said. He looked at Dr. Felkin, who dropped his eyes. "And the Lyceum Theatre should leave *The Corsican Brothers* off the repertoire for the time being."

Henry exhaled and patted Mr. Stoker's hand on the armchair. "Time to dust off the Scottish play." Mr. Stoker groaned. "It will be for the best. But now, Mr. Kamal, one last question: Why do you think Dedi could have been the first professional magician?"

"Why, Mr. Irving, for this simple reason," Ahmed answered. "It is known that Dedi was the first to be paid for his magic—and he was paid in beer."

CHAPTER NINE

SÉANCES OF JAMAICA

In her cousin Marian Colman's cold guest bedroom, Pamela sat in front of a box full of her clothes. The wool coats, silk stockings, and velvet dresses were all exactly folded into the same square shape. Mother had told her at breakfast that her winter outfits would be donated to the deserving poor; there would be no room to spare on their ship to St. Andrew. So many of the fancier outfits were smaller versions of her mother's clothes. When they went to church, they were a matched pair. She picked up the hat on top of the pile. It was Pamela's silk bonnet, her first grown-up hat. It was cherry red with a ruched panel of fluted pieces that framed her whole face, anchored by green string-fringed ties. Pamela loved to pin flowers or pine cones to the brim until her mother forbade her to add one more "stick, bone, or weed." The hat was to be left in England; the strong Jamaican sun would ruin it, Mother said.

The sun would be different in Jamaica; the beaches there were lined with sand instead of rocks. Father said there was almost no fog and that there was a rain that gushed sideways and, he said, the air was thick with flowers. She couldn't wait to see that, air thick with flowers. But she tried to imagine how she would be living with her parents in St. Andrew, and her mind had no images. She was told that she would have a nanny who would be from the island, one of the freed Black Jamaicans who understood the ways of a British household. Pamela wasn't sure what that meant. *Maybe my nanny and I will have tea together, like the grown-up people.*

She put her bonnet on one last time and looked at herself in the mirror. The hat was a little tight. It didn't tie in a big bow under her chin anymore, and the two flaps with the fringe barely went past her ears. She pursed her lips together and mimed picking up a teacup, her pinky finger crooked as she had seen her mother do. The doorbell downstairs dinged and she ran to the window to look out. A carriage had pulled up to her mother's cousin's house. The horse had a feathered plume on its bridle and Pamela watched her mother and mother's cousin, Marian, come out the front door.

"Look, Mother, look!" she called to the two figures hurrying to the cab. She leaned the top of her head against the window and pointed to her red bonnet smashed up against the glass. By the time she straightened up, they were gone.

Father had not been in all day. He was out giving a speech. Marian's husband would be shut up in the library, and their children were all older and terribly uninterested in entertaining their ten-year-old cousin, even though she had told them she'd fallen off Waterloo Bridge and had been in the performance on the Lyceum stage when the mirror broke. No one seemed to believe either story, or to care. It was another afternoon all to herself, despite a house full of family.

Pamela pushed aside the curtains to let in what little light there was and skipped about the room. The bleak rays barely penetrated the glass and all the colors bled out into inky forms, the corners of the bedroom particularly murky and cold. She opened the door and peered down the hallway. It was dark there too. When she had asked her art tutor in Manchester why colors disappeared when it was dark, he said something about light waves and rods and cones in the eyes. She didn't follow what he had said at all. She did understand colors had waves with different weights: the bounce of blue, the yawn of yellow, the wiry racing of red. And sometimes the darker shades of the same colors were slower, thicker, the purples, and greens. She was still learning how light could make a color weigh less and how the weight of a shadow could darken something to a different hue. Where was her painting kit?

She went over to the trunk her grandmother had packed for her. It was crammed with light cotton shifts and her artist's supplies, for Grandmother Colman had determined that if Pamela was going to the tropics, her artwork and drawing studies would not suffer. Grandmother had bought her drawing pads, a portable easel, brushes, a watercolor kit, pencils, and an instructional drawing set from the art academy. When Grandmother gave her the supplies, her mother said, "This will give Pamela hours of pleasure, Mother. And give us hours of not being bothered. Thank you."

The pencil sharpener was lying on top. She took one of the pencils from the art kit and sharpened the end quickly, smelling the sweet, woody, burnt smell of the curling leaf spiraling from the end and twisting in a crescent shaving. Preparing the brushes and pencils was hard to remember to do at first. In Manchester, her tutor allowed her to use the pencil or brush only when she proved that she knew how to prepare and care for them. Now that she was alone, she could just grab whatever she wanted and wait for the music to tell her what to draw.

These days she rarely heard the music that once played in her head. It had stopped almost entirely since she fell off the bridge. Her head felt heavy and without the company of the many thoughts that would jostle to come out.

Someday, I'll have kings, and queens, and knights all around me. And strange people too. People like me.

She opened a drawing pad and sat on the floor with her sharpened pencil. *Who is here to keep me company?*

⌒⁀⁄⁀⌒

Mr. Charles Smith strode into the hotel on Jermyn Street and was greeted by the hotelier, William Cox.

"Glad to see the man of the hour is here," Cox said. "Wouldn't be much of a séance if you didn't make it. This speaker is said to be quite the wizard." Cox escorted Charles over to the small group of men chatting nearby as they handed off their coats. They stood near a placard in the center of the lobby which announced:

Society for Psychical Research presents
Mystic D. D. Home
All Soul's Day, November 2nd
4 p.m., by Invitation Only

It was quite an illustrious group gathered for this event: James Wilkinson, famed Swedenborgian; Robert Browning, Elizabeth Barrett Browning's boisterous young husband; William Butler Yeats; David James, the Freemason; Sir Arthur Conan Doyle; and Sir Oliver Lodge. A few other guests arrived, surrendering their great top hats and coats to the concierge.

The hotelier had arranged for the American D. D. Home to hold a séance for Mr. Charles Smith before his move to St. Andrew. Smith had been looking for investors from England to finish a railway system in Jamaica. There had been talk that Mr. Smith's late father had successfully introduced a rail system in Brooklyn, New York, and his son might provide a good opportunity to invest with the East India Company's latest venture. But Charles Smith was leaving for a Caribbean island reputed to be full of voodoo magic and residents who were former slaves, not at all anxious to work for former "owners."

"Come on, Charles," Cox said, slapping him on the back. "Aren't you hoping to hear that your father on the other side gives his blessing for your investment opportunity?"

Corinne had told him he had to attend this event, or for the next few years together in Jamaica their life would be untenable. She insisted he make every effort to make a psychic connection with his father during this séance.

"This will be all in good fun," Charles said as cheerfully as he could. "If not, it's good to find out if there is a malingering spirit attached to the project."

James Wilkinson, a neighbor who came down from Manchester, approached and shook Charles's hand with a firm grip.

"Good to be here. I'm here as part of the 'Census of Hallucinations,'" James said. "I have permission to document the Society for Psychical Research's séance. It will be fascinating to see possible entities present themselves, and Charles is a perfect candidate to reach out to."

Charles knew he was only perfect because the investors wanted a sure thing. The group was ushered into a private dining room with a large round table. Sir Oliver Lodge pointed out where they should sit, and the ten men settled down.

Sir Oliver blustered, "There will be no covering up of the goings-on! Just to show there will be no crookery here tonight!"

Charles sat next to James; he was a fellow Swedenborgian, and not known to make a spectacle of himself during the services they had attended together. Charles hoped someone else would volunteer to have a visitation. A man entered the room and made a beeline to take the empty seat next to Charles. This must be D. D. Home, the featured guest. He had red curly hair and a walrus mustache; with his wild mane and bushy facial hair, he seemed a Scottish version of the American writer Mark Twain.

"To be sure, an excellent thing, an excellent thing that you are here to be a part of history!" he exclaimed, shaking Charles's hand before he sat. Turning his attention to the other men seated at the table, he said, "Ah, let's have Mr. Smith sit across from me so that you can be sure no tricks may happen."

Reluctantly, Charles moved to the other side of the table so that Mr. Home could have his chair.

What have I gotten myself into? Charles wondered.

The room had only one candelabrum on the round table, and the shadows of the seated men danced on the back wall. Home's head tilted back, his eyes closed. He jerked his head forward, stared at Charles, and with increasing urgency moaned in an other-worldly voice, "I shall not be dead when 'tis thought I am! I shall not be dead when 'tis thought I am!"

Mr. Browning shouted out, "Who are you?" to shushes and reprimands around the table.

"No, no, 'tis fair to ask. I am your ancestor, Philip Smith, in the time of the witch hunt in the Americas." Home's mouth opened wide as if he were gasping for breath. His head flopped from side to side. "I am cursed by the witch, the wretched woman in town who has sent cares my way. Now she is still tormenting me, stabbing me with an awl, sending the Devil to shake me, empty my medicine, and force me to live between this world and the next with no refuge."

Browning interrupted again, "Why, why would this woman try to torture you so?"

Home's head pulled straight up, levitating out of his body, it seemed, and looked at Browning. "For the trial. For the trial in Boston of Mary Webster."

Conan Doyle leaned forward. "Is she the witch that cast this spell of dead-while-living?"

Home dropped his head on his chest and whimpered, "Yes. Yes. We tried to kill her, we hanged her and left her in the snow, but she lived. Lived to curse me and all who follow me. ALL YOUR WOMEN ARE CURSED!"

Charles stood, tried to open his mouth to say something, and fainted dead away.

On the other side of London in Hackney, Corinne sat in a small dingy parlor waiting for a psychic. She was not allowed to go to the séance Charles was attending that night, even though she pleaded. No women allowed. She was determined to have her own mystical experience.

Her cousin was willing to leave Pimlico to accompany her, even if it meant going to a disreputable part of London. Corinne had tracked down someone said to be one of the best at fortune-telling, and at a good price, but it was in the Northeast section of town. She was glad Marian waited for her in the outer room. There were rumors of robbery and kidnapping in this neighborhood, so it was a relief to know they could return to the safety of the carriage just outside the door.

The main question Corinne wanted to ask was about their upcoming move to Jamaica. Would it be a success? Moving away from England for the next few years was a huge disappointment. But they must follow Charles, in whatever work he could get, as the design firm in Manchester had fallen on hard times and he was out of work. One of his relations in Manchester had started work on the railway line in Jamaica decades earlier, and it was decided that Charles was qualified to assist this new venture. How they determined this was a mystery to Corinne. Charles had already proved he was no accountant. But they were to move so that this East India Company could complete a total railroad system around Jamaica.

She heard footsteps near the back room and the curtains were pushed aside, revealing an older woman in a neat brown dress with a mass of white hair piled on her head. Her dark eyes reflected the candle she was carrying. She set her candle next to the lamp and shook Corinne's hand.

"Mrs. Smith? I'm Margery."

From her other hand, Margery produced a small mirror, placed it underneath the candle on the table and leaned forward, looking into Corinne's eyes. Corinne had done up her hair and complexion with just the right amount of care in the hopes of showing she was a woman of some standing.

"Ah, Madam," Margery purred. "You said you are a married woman."

"Yes, I've had my wedding ring for many years."

"Yes, Madam. And it would be many, many years. Shall we talk of that?"

Corinne nervously coughed into her handkerchief and nodded.

"Ah, I see you've kept a great secret from your husband. Your first husband was killed in a war. You've kept your years a secret, didn't you?"

"Ah, yes, but it is not that great a difference between us."

"Isn't it? Your husband thinks you have forty years of age? And you be in your fifty-fourth year, isn't that it?"

Corinne gasped. "How did you know?"

Margery smoothed out the main lines in Corinne's palm. "Oh, there's a great deal here in these lines. Your daughter. Your daughter you had ten years ago. You made a bargain to have her, didn't you?"

"I did give up a promising career to have a child, if that's what you mean."

"Ah, Mrs. Smith, that's not the bargain I see here." Margery looked into the candle flame and continued, "Mary Webster, she has cursed your female line. You will need powerful magic to help your daughter in the new place."

"This move, will it work out? Will Charles earn money from this post?"

"I see that it will work for a short while. But the girl, your daughter, she will need the stories and the magic there to protect her."

"But will my name live on? Will we Colmans have a legacy?"

"Ah, your name. Your daughter will have many offspring and your name will be part of it. But you will lose something in return—you will not be whole."

Corinne's eyes sprung wide and a coughing began. The spasm continued to such a pitch that Marian came into the room to find her.

James helped Charles to the lobby, William Cox insisting on ordering one of his hotel carriages to take Charles home. Charles sat on a couch while James scouted to see when the cab pulled up front.

"That was quite the scene in there, wasn't it?" Charles said apologetically. "Do you think Home is authentic?"

"Well, he didn't take off his slippers and wave his foot around with a cloth saying it was relative paying a visit, as I've heard he is wont to do," James answered.

"Oh. I hadn't heard that story."

"Yes," James replied, watching Charles wobble to a standing position. "This voice that showed up, is there really a Philip Smith in your family tree?"

"Well, there's a story of witchcraft handed down by my father's mother, but my father told me not to put any store in it." Charles took a deep breath and smoothed his rumpled coat.

"It's quite a story," James said. "Any chance Home heard of it when he was traveling in America?"

"I don't believe he was ever anywhere near Brooklyn, where my father was mayor. We never talked of this story outside the family."

"I see. Perhaps you could join the fellowship of Freemasons in Jamaica? They might be a good antidote against believers of curses and such. The Freemasons would be jolly company for you."

Charles looked at James. He seemed like a nice chap but did not grasp the seriousness of the railway project. Or how important it was that this project turned their fortune around.

"If I didn't have such a responsibility to bring this railway project off, it might be tempting," Charles replied coolly. "But Jamaica has one of the most difficult terrains in the world to build railways on; its mountains are legendary for how steep they are. Also, the local population is considered quite dangerous. But, just as there is the parable of the fool stepping off the mountain to attain great wealth, I have no doubt I will succeed."

"And why is there an interest in building a railway system there?" James insisted. "With the emancipation of the slaves some forty years ago, you will have no free labor."

Charles saw the carriage rumbling down the street, not a moment too soon. "That is true, but we think their recent wave of Chinese immigrants will provide the labor."

"Excuse me, Mr. Smith, but what is in Jamaica that can justify building a railway system in a jungle?" James said as they walked outside.

"Sugar, rum, bananas, and bauxite. It all must be brought to the ships," Charles said, his hands shaking as he put on his gloves.

"Ships that held human traffic not that long ago. You might not be welcome to work there. Our church workers have heard tales of strong voodoo magic on the island."

The carriage pulled up in front of them and Charles made a small bow.

"Well, enough of this sort of talk. Thank you, Mr. James, for your assistance."

"Well, Brother Charles, I hope your venture is not doomed, but I fear for your well-being."

"Nonsense," Charles said, getting into the cab.

When Charles returned to the house of his wife's relation, he found Corinne in the front parlor with a glass of sherry.

"Oh, darling, I am so glad you are home," Corinne said, uncharacteristically embracing him. "I had a feeling something happened to you. Did your father come through and speak to you?"

"Posh, this séance was just a sham, a chance for a voice to be put on by this Mr. Home," Charles said, pouring himself a bigger glass of sherry than Corinne's. "This voice claimed the women of the Smith family are cursed."

Pamela heard her parents' voices and raced down the stairway and hid in a crook to watch them in the parlor.

Her father spotted her and motioned for her to come down. She ran to embrace both her parents. Awkwardly, they hugged one another in a huddle. It was the first time in her life she remembered the three of them holding on to one another like that.

"Father, we're cursed?" Pamela asked, her face crushed against his waist.

"Don't be frightened, Miss Smith," her father said, laughing. "And if we are cursed, we are cursed with too much opportunity."

CHAPTER TEN

Ellen Terry's Curse

In the early morning light, a carriage rumbled down Tite Street in London. The rare sunshine broke between the clouds and shined inside; the shimmer of hundreds of glimmering green beetle wings reflected the appearance of the soft sunlight that appeared in its window. The iridescent jeweled beetle wings were sewn into the court dress of the thirteenth-century Scottish queen, Lady Macbeth. Ellen Terry, the most famous actress of her day, was on her way to John Singer Sargent's studio to have her portrait painted. Oscar Wilde, living on Tite Street, happened at that moment to part the curtains of his bay window and saw this astounding sight—a four-wheel carriage conveying the Scottish queen to his neighbor's studio. Wilde later wrote of this moment, "The street, that on a wet and dreary morning has vouchsafed the vision of Lady Macbeth in full regalia magnificently seated in a four-wheeler, can never again be as other streets; it must always be full of wonderful possibilities."

Ellen herself sat twirling one of her long braids and laughed in response to a comment made by the burly Bram Stoker sitting across from her. She was at the height of her beauty and fame and still had the classic Pre-Raphaelite face that painters had clamored to capture since she was sixteen years old. Since she was twenty-nine, she was known as the face of the Victorian Age. The Edwardian Age still considered her youthful, due to her face and figure, but she was over forty. Sargent's idea was that she pose as Lady Macbeth crowning herself, "filled top full of direst cruelty," a scene not in the play. Ellen thought it one of the more interesting requests she had received.

Her crown of plated gold was a large, simple band with a Celtic symbol in the center. The dress had huge bell-shaped sleeves with cuffs, bordered in a Celtic design worked out in costume rubies and diamonds. A velvet cloak in heather tones, with two great griffons embroidered in flame-colored metallic thread, lay behind her on a stack of cushions. Her own deep-red hair was augmented with false hair and braided into two plaits entwined with gold ribbon that hung to her knees. A sash with Celtic symbols was strewn across her waist, and a low-lying girdle sash hung across her hips. But it was the thousands of iridescent beetle wings, jewels of the smallest sort sewn into the fabric of the dress, which caught the eye. As she moved in her seat, they sparkled in the low light like early morning phantoms that had yet to disperse.

Bram Stoker tried to keep his scowl as he conversed with Miss Ellen Terry, but her merry ways continued to amuse him. He had close-set eyes and a grave and somewhat fashionable look to him. It was important to him as second-in-command at the theatre that he be taken seriously. Today, his job was to escort the leading lady of the Lyceum Theatre to Sargent's studio. Bram was devoted to Henry Irving and would perform any number of personal requests that the great and renowned actor demanded of him. Today, Henry had asked Bram to accompany Ellen, for this was to be a "big day."

At this moment, Ellen Terry was teasingly flaying him with her braid wig-piece over his mention of a rumor that their current production of *Macbeth* was using real black magic.

Ellen leaned back in her seat, still playfully batting Bram with her braid, and laughed riotously. "When, oh, when is this supposed black magic to take place onstage in our 'Scottish Play'? When I'm washing the grape juice from my hands, or sleepwalking?"

Bram, his large boxer's frame shifting uncomfortably in his seat, coolly replied with his slight Irish accent, "Miss Terry, it is said that some believers feel Shakespeare used a real black magic recipe during the witches' incantation around the cauldron in Act I, Scene 3."

She dropped her braid and laughed softly. "During the cooking scene? Oh, Brammy, will wonders never cease?"

He smiled patiently at the Lyceum Theatre's leading lady. "Sometimes, Miss Terry, the believers of magic don't mind tainting your fame with tales of black magic just to stir things up."

Ellen put her hand on her chin, leaned forward, and gazed wonderingly at him. "My fame. My fame as a fallen woman or as a famous actress?"

"You don't seem unduly affected by your fame in either case," he replied kindly.

"Oh! One's pretty lively when one's ruined," she said in good humor.

"I don't think you are ruined, Miss Terry, and I don't think Mr. Irving does either. But these stories of black magic could stir up the regular churchgoers of the Christian faith, and we have just now started to get them to come to the theatre. We'd hate to antagonize the Church now, wouldn't we?" Bram quietly asked.

The statement hung in the air.

After a disastrous marriage at seventeen, Ellen had borne two children out of wedlock and was now employed as leading lady to Henry Irving. He was separated from his own wife and estranged from his two sons. It was a miracle that the Church hadn't condemned Ellen and Henry, and they were treading on thin ice to think that the pulpit wouldn't soon be sermonizing about the Lyceum Theatre depicting the Devil's work on stage.

"Ah, Bram, the Church. It is so sweet of you to be thinking of my reputation . . ."

Here it is, Miss Ellen's catch-all phrase, "so sweet of you," the cue to butt out.

". . . I will deny any and all reports that I am a witch. But my reputation is better off left alone."

She sat back and for just a moment tears came to her eyes, as she softly said in her beautiful low voice, "But I admit it to you . . ." For a moment that voice faltered. ". . . in private, that I would resort to witchcraft to be with Henry. I only wish I knew he felt the same."

"So, my Miss Terry, why wouldn't he love you? You know he's trying to make an agreement with the wife to separate. But I hope you won't consider marriage with that new rascal you've begun to see? It's not like he's the father to your children."

Ellen had begun to be courted by former cavalry officer Charles Kelly, who had a short temper and craved regular drink. Henry had said he needed time to work out a proper divorce from his wife, Florence O'Callaghan, daughter of an upper-class army surgeon general. He had provided for his wife and two sons but refused to see her in person, as she despised his career. For these past two years, Henry had insisted that Ellen and he not be seen together so that there would not be cause for a trial with slanderous accounts in the newspapers. And there had been hints lately from Henry that the negotiations were starting to move ahead toward a formal divorce. Meanwhile, Charles Kelly sent Ellen gifts and thought that he would like to give acting a try, in the hope that he would be paired with the Lyceum's popular romantic lead. But Henry Irving had worked too hard to hand out work to amateur rivals for Ellen's affection.

Ellen had no trouble getting started in the theatre world, as her parents, Benjamin and Sarah Terry, were established comic actors in a touring company with their eleven children, five of whom became actors. Ellen and her sister Kate would play the provinces with her parents, performing in sketches and plays. Their family was close and self-schooled; on the road they had only each other for companionship and education. At seventeen she had married a forty-six-year-old artist, Mr. Watts, after posing for his celebrated portraits of her: *Choosing, Ophelia,* and *The Watchman,* among others. That marriage lasted only ten months, and she went back to acting, to great acclaim and a ruined reputation. Then, outside the realm of marriage, she had two children with an architect, with whom she lived in the countryside for six years but came back to "tread the boards" when that relationship failed as well. But because she had made her reputation as a child star in Shakespeare, her career was not totally destroyed.

Henry Irving was envious of Ellen's pedigree and career. The internationally recognized interpreter of Shakespeare, Charles Keen, had employed eight-year-old Ellen in both male and female roles, and she was considered theatre royalty, even if she had had an unfortunate marriage. Ellen had performed in some of the great theatres in London while Henry was an apprentice actor at the Theatre Royal Manchester. While in Manchester, Henry played all the great roles, having committed to memory in his lifetime between 350 and 400 roles. He eventually gained control of the Lyceum Theatre, and after meeting Bram Stoker on tour in Dublin, invited him to come to London as his acting manager. Bram was only too happy to make the move to London and work with his idol, whom the Irishman had reviewed most favorably as a theatre critic. Together, they created the Lyceum Theatre Company and produced over forty plays, averaging two new productions a year.

In 1878, in the London suburb of Pimlico, Henry went to hire Ellen Terry for his theatre season. He arrived at her well-appointed house with his fox terrier, Fussie. He was nervous and eager to hire Miss Terry, who was the legitimate actress he needed for his company, despite her illegitimate children. In her elegant parlor with his dog by his side, Henry's manner stiff and rigid, he proposed that she be his leading lady. The dog sensed his master's anxiety, and when he had finished, the dog reacted by defecating on the rug. Henry's mortification overcame his formal bearing, and he was all apologies and solicitude. He burst out laughing when Ellen gaily responded, "Your dog thinks very little of your employing me!"

The year that he hired Ellen Terry and opened his Lyceum Theatre Company, he played Hamlet to her Ophelia, which propelled them into a level of fame unheard of for actors in their day. Now that the theatre was an ongoing success, Henry had to socialize with the upper crust of society and demanding society women. While he had dedicated his life to making the career of an actor respectable, the prejudice against actors was only just now dwindling. It wasn't until recently that actors could rent or buy homes, mingle in society, and be recognized as more than "strolling kings" bellowing for tossed coins.

The carriage pulled up to Sargent's studio, the rain paused for the time being, and Bram sprang out of his seat. Gathering her beetle dress around her, Ellen prepared to leave the carriage when out of the front door of the studio a familiar tall form made his way quickly to the carriage.

Henry Irving, in his black frock coat and top hat, was elegantly dressed for ten in the morning, but he was always a formal dresser even on the slightest social occasion. He bowed to Ellen and then in his deep tones asked, "Might I have a word with you here, m'lady?"

A delighted laugh rang out, and Henry seated himself in the carriage across from Ellen as Bram made his way inside the townhouse to wait for the two stars to align.

Henry took Ellen's bejeweled hands and kissed them. Ellen turned and lowered the blinds on the inside of the carriage so they might have some privacy. When she turned back, Henry, who had taken off his hat, was still holding her hand, and he leaned back in his seat. His dark eyes softened as he took her in.

"Miss Terry, you look like a queen. Mr. Sargent should be honored to paint you."

"Yes, Henry, I am bedecked in our 'bug special.' It brings back such memories, doesn't it?"

When Henry and Ellen vacationed together in a break from the Lyceum Theatre, they stayed with Ellen's dresser, Alice, near River Rother. It was an ancient house and they stayed two weeks, living the pastoral life. They had both said it was their Garden of Eden. The memory of twilight at Alice's country house, called Smallhythe, suddenly came back to her: she and Alice in their white nightgowns chasing and leaping after the beetles at dusk, Henry and company sitting on the bricked portico, sipping their drinks, laughing at the women as they comically tried to capture the hapless insects for immortality on a stage costume. The shrieks when they caught the insects, and the laughter when they didn't, all played in her head.

"You mean the summer you spent capturing bug beetles at Alice's to put on this dress?"

"Yes, Henry, but don't forget these iridescent beetle wings are the whole reason Mr. Sargent wants to paint me."

"Ah, Miss Terry, not the only reason."

"Henry, thank you for arranging this."

Henry cleared his throat and seemed overcome before he began speaking again. He held Ellen's hands even tighter.

"Miss Terry, you know I have loved you since we were cast as Romeo and Juliet. Both of us have had . . . other relationships . . ."

Ellen laughed, "And marriages! We are both old hands at that."

Henry grimaced. "True. But I have never told you why my marriage has been over these many years. Florence, eight months pregnant with our second son, and I were in a carriage heading to a reception after the opening night of *The Bells*. After all the standing ovations and praise, I felt I had finally arrived. *That* was the moment when she demanded of me, "Are you going to go on making a fool of yourself like this all your life?" I stepped out of the carriage and have never seen her since. I have continued to provide well for my family and now, years later, I have a relationship with my sons. But I refuse to see Florence, although she always accepts my offer of tickets to opening nights."

Ellen could hear the bitterness in his voice as he pulled his hands away and lowered the window of the carriage to see the rain come down in a deluge. The pounding on the top of the carriage from the rain echoed in the cab, the horse moved slightly forward, and the cabbie settled the animal down quickly.

Henry took a deep breath and continued. "I've heard that Kelly wants to marry you and give your children a legitimate last name. I was hoping that I would be able to do so myself. But Mrs. Irving has heard word of this and informed me via her attorney that if there is to be any change in the status quo of our relationship, she will pursue you as the alienator of my affections in court."

Closing the carriage window, Ellen looked out to see the rain bouncing off the cobbled street. Unexpected tears sprang in her eyes and she blinked them back. "I see, Henry. I'm sorry that it has come to this. Of course, you can't risk the reputation you have built for yourself or for your theatre."

Henry pulled Ellen to him and kissed her passionately; they remained entwined for more than a few minutes and then realized that the blinds were still drawn up. Henry tried to lower them and they broke off in his hand, breaking the mood as well.

Ellen looked around and said, "I suppose she has hired detectives to follow me?"

"Yes. Dicksby and Dicksby."

"An apt name. So, she knows about Captain Kelly's intent to marry me? And his intention to adopt Edy and Gordon?"

Henry sighed. "I'm sorry *I* could not provide that for them."

"Yes, they both adore you, Henry. You are the most generous and kind man we have ever known."

"Ellen, I am in talks to purchase Smallhythe."

"Alice's house in the country?"

"Well, actually, I bought it."

"You bought our bug palace? Why?"

"Someone I love very dearly will need a place to live in the country. Even if I cannot be there with her." He reached into his frock coat pocket and drew out a docket of papers. "Here is the deed; it is in your name. You are to say that you bought this with your Australian tour money."

Ellen grabbed the papers and went through them until she found the deed. Laughing, she read, "Smallhythe, a six-teenth-century timber-framed estate has fifteen acres, four fireplaces, a brick terrace, wishing well, nuttery, fruit trees, roses, a pond, and a barn. It doesn't mention the bluebells. Or the ghost."

Henry smiled for the first time. "I don't believe the ghost would care to be bought. Who was it again?"

"Sir Robert Brigandyne, clerk of ships for Henry VIII," Ellen continued, holding the deed closer to read. "The window frame on the first floor, from the stern of a galleon, the last ship Sir Robert made, *The Great Gallyon*, is to be considered a national treasure."

"Well, Miss Terry, it is only right that one national treasure lives with another."

Ellen looked at Henry and softly said, "Ah. If only that meant that I would be living with you."

There was silence between the two while the rain slowed to an occasional ping.

"Smallhythe will be your small landing place, even if I cannot be there. That summer we hired the small rig and came upon Alice's magnificent empty house, being used just to store fleece. And the ancient shepherd inside—"

Ellen interrupted, "He didn't live there. I think he lived down the lane."

Henry continued, "—opened the door and when I asked, 'Is this a nice house?' he simply answered, 'No.'"

"So, you, of course, bought it. For me."

"Yes, and you are to say it was bought with your Australian tour money."

Ellen began to kiss Henry, and he returned the affection until he realized that the broken blind in the carriage made them easy to spot. He pulled away from her. Ellen tried to compose herself.

"Oh, Henry, I wouldn't mind having a child with you outside marriage. Wouldn't you like to have a little girl?"

Henry's dark eyes flashed and he hit his hand into his fist. "Of course, I would. But Florence would make your life, my life, and the child's life, hell. My hands are tied, Ellen. Live in Smallhythe, love every moment of it. Marry Kelly if you must. But under no circumstances let his name be on the deed."

"Yes, Henry."

"Promise me. Now that there is this Married Women's Property Act, you can own it outside of marriage."

"I promise."

"Very well then. Miss Terry, I wish I had happier news, but now I must take my leave. You know you have my undying love and devotion."

"Yes, Henry. And you have mine."

She leaned in to kiss him one last time and he gently stopped her and placed his hands on his heart, then cupped her face. Without another word, he opened the carriage door, put on his top hat, and strode down the glistening street.

Bram came out of the townhouse and called out, "Right. Here I am." He went up to settle with the driver, and Ellen wrapped her cloak around the docket to protect it against the rain.

A small band of chimney sweeps and women with tea push carts started to pass the carriage on the street. A wave of laughter went up as some of the workmen peered inside and saw Ellen sitting there in all her regalia. She nodded and smiled through her tears.

Suddenly, an older woman climbed on the running board and stuck her face into the carriage. She could have been one of the witches from *Macbeth*: her lined face, the few teeth remaining, wild gray hair escaping from its moorings atop her head. A gray blanket was her cape against the rain, and her terrible, bloodshot gray eyes took Ellen in. Ellen shrank back in her seat and froze momentarily.

The crone eyed her and said, "Your new daughter will need the strength of an empress."

The old woman disappeared from view.

PART II

BATTLING THE CURSE

CHAPTER ELEVEN

Aleister and Martha

Aleister stood over the small Christmas tree on the corner lot, a sleet-snow mixture coming down on the ratty little boy guarding the last few trees.

Perhaps, he mused to himself, *I can bring a little joy into my mother's life.* Since the death of her husband, his mother had two activities, churchgoing and tormenting her household staff. *Or a little joy to the unfortunates who live and work for her.* He paid the sad ragamuffin vendor and hoisted the pathetic evergreen onto his shoulder.

As he entered his mother's house, the contrast to where he had come from could not be more pointed. Herbert Pollitt's family was a boisterous and excitable group; there had been noise and song nonstop from his many sisters, brothers, and cousins. Here only the sound of the ticking grandfather clock in the parlor greeted him. At Herbert's house in Chelsea, the Christmas decorations were excessive and garish: paper chain garlands, glass baubles, hanging ornaments not only on the tree but on the fireplace mantel, the windows, the staircase. There was no sign of a Christian cheer here.

Aleister now regretted leaving the celebrations at Herbert's house. Herbert was his one friend at Cambridge, and arriving at the sterile Crowley home foretold a miserable holiday. This house was the new residence for the Crowley widow, bought so his mother could live around the corner from her brother, the dour Thomas Bishop. With the money from the Crowley Brewery now in their hands, they both lived in big, cold, empty houses.

A middle-aged woman with a maid's cap and apron stood at the end of the hallway. She had a full figure and a wild mop of black hair she anchored on top of her head with two large pins. Seeing him, she put her finger to her lips to signal silence and motioned him to the kitchen.

Putting the soggy tree down softly, Aleister approached the closed parlor door, boards squeaking as he glided down the hallway. Inside the parlor, he could now hear his uncle Tom droning on about the Plymouth Brethren and knew that he could safely reach the kitchen undetected. His uncle's hearing was almost gone, and his mother would be paying rapt attention.

Once inside the kitchen, the smell of gingerbread and cinnamon hit him like a warm cloud. He tore off his coat and sat at the servants' table.

"You're the new cook or the maid?" Aleister asked, eyeing the plates of cookies on the counter.

"I'm Martha Tabram, the current kitchen maid," the woman said. "Which means I cook and clean. And bake. Here . . ."

Martha giggled as she set a large plate of rolls and gingerbread biscuits in front of him. She sat down across from him as he ate in ecstasy. Martha grinned as she watched Aleister wolf down his food.

He picked up a biscuit shaped like a wreath with a hard candy in the center.

"Does Mother know that you are making heathen biscuits?" he asked sarcastically.

"No, and she's not about to, since I see you will be eating all the evidence."

They both laughed and she picked up one of them and took a bite.

"Did you have a good time at your friend's house, Mr. Crowley?"

"It's Aleister to you, Martha, and how did you know where I was?"

"Your mother complained that you stayed with a friend before coming to see her, Aleister. What an unusual name."

"It's Irish for Edward, my father's name."

He looked up and saw Martha's kindly face and thought for the first time about his father. He wondered what he would think of his attending Cambridge and studying the classics that they had talked about during his lessons.

"I was given the name Edward but at a young age I asked to change it to Aleister."

"Yer father must have not liked that!"

Aleister mulled this over and now reached for a cinnamon roll on the plate. The food at university was better than at his mother's, but treats like rolls and biscuits were never served at the university dining hall, or for that matter at his mother's house. This was a new occurrence and it gave a strange coziness to the bleak kitchen. Not that his mother had ever cooked; there had always been a cook as well as a kitchen maid who served the food—gray food. Gray meat, gray vegetables, gray bread. These desserts were colorful and full of flavor.

"I think he liked being the only Edward."

"I'm sorry for ya' that he's gone, Mr. Aleister."

"Well, I don't think he'll be coming back."

"Well, that's a probable thing. Why would you think otherwise?"

He thought of the cat that hung around the brewery. The workmen were always saying that the cat had nine lives, something that Aleister obsessed over in the days after his father's death. He would retrace the steps where he and his father had done their daily walks, reciting and talking, and where the cat would sometimes follow them.

The first time he walked down the street by himself after the funeral, there was the cat sitting on the corner next to the brewery, blinking at him. If the cat had nine lives, perhaps so did his father. But since uniting with his Savior was the ultimate goal of his father's faith, his father might not be swayed by the lure of seeing his son again. Or maybe he was trying to find ways to come through to Aleister from the other side. As a young boy he had heard of other religions that believed in reincarnation, where you could come back as other people or as an animal.

Maybe that was why he killed the cat, to see if it could come back as his father.

But when he watched the cat's lifeless body for a whole day, he saw it was just a cat. And it didn't come back to life.

"Aleister?!"

His mother's voice rang out from the parlor, and Martha involuntarily jerked herself up in alarm. Aleister smiled to see he was not the only one with that reaction. He wiped his mouth and trod down the hall, picking up the tree on his way to the parlor.

In front of the fireplace, Aleister held his small Christmas tree out to his mother and uncle. His uncle came up to him and took the tree as though it were a strange scientific experiment gone dreadfully wrong. He turned to his sister, shaking the tiny fir violently, needles flying everywhere.

"Nephew, what heathen practice is that school teaching you?" Uncle Thomas shouted. "Our Brethren have taught you that these pagan symbols are forbidden!"

Seeing his mother narrow her eyes, he took the tree from his uncle's weak grip. "Here's what my education has taught me, an enlightened idea to introduce a new tradition," he said. Seeing their frowns, he gently added, "Our very own Queen Victoria and her family follow the German tradition of staging a Christmas tree."

Mrs. Crowley rose and pointed out the needles now spread over the plain wool carpet.

"It is a heathen German practice! The only celebration we will honor is the sacred event of Christ's birth."

"Mother, you must allow—"

"I knew when you came from university you would be full of yourself!" his mother screamed. "Enough! You are the Beast 666. I've always known since you were little that you are inherently bad."

Aleister stared at his mother, who had turned away from him and was fussing with the back of her chair. His uncle had a hand cupped over his good ear and still seemed unsure as to what he had heard.

"Well, Mother, since my excellent father was perfect, I can only assume any evil I have, I inherited from you!"

Mrs. Crowley shrieked, took the tree, and kicked it toward the door.

"Take your pagan tree out with you! You are a godless child!"

Aleister scooped up the shedding tree and hurried to the door, turning to his mother. "And you, Mother, are a brainless bigot of the most narrow, illogical, and inhuman type!"

Taking what was left of the tree, he threw open the door and slammed it on his way out. He ran out the front door and down the stoop, hurling the tree to the curbside. Then, he waltzed down the street shouting, "Happy Christmas! Happy Christmas!" at the top of his lungs. Tom Bishop and Mrs. Crowley looked out the window as the snow turned into sleet.

❧

Having nowhere else to go, Aleister returned home late that evening and offered his mother a terse apology at her bedroom door. The next afternoon, Christmas Day, Aleister came out of his bedroom, intoxicated from brandy he had smuggled into his mother's house. Uncle and Mother were at the interminable Christmas service. No worries they would come back early; that lifeless celebration would last hours. He staggered down the hallway to the kitchen and stood, unsure what to do. Martha came in from her small bedroom off the kitchen, her hair loose and falling down her back. As she spotted his swaying, she sat him at the table and began to fix them both a cup of tea.

"Ah, let me guess," Martha said. "The bum tightener let you have it over the tree."

"Yes, Martha, but which one is the bum tightener? The tree didn't stand a chance."

"It were a mangy tree, anyhow. I spent an hour cleaning the needles up, Mr. Aleister. Weren't even my job."

"We're all mangy creatures, Martha."

Martha chuckled slightly. "Well, one of us is a little mangier than the other."

"You have family, Martha?"

"Not to speak of."

"So, if you were to die like some vile creature, would anyone miss you?"

She shakily lifted her teacup and hoarsely replied, "About the same as you, I think."

He stood, knocking his teacup to the floor, swaying back and forth, and finally stumbled toward her. She stood and comforted him as he broke into sobs that almost sounded like coughing. She held him for a few minutes, and then Aleister started to kiss and fondle her. After a few moments, Martha responded and they fumbled their way out of the kitchen. He broke off from her and took her hand, running up the servants' staircase to the second floor.

They paused in the doorway of Mrs. Crowley's neat, sterile bedroom. Martha laughed and pulled his hand to continue down the hallway. He dragged her into his mother's room and onto his mother's prim bed, where they began to enjoy each other with abandonment.

Aleister straddled Martha and awakened her from a post-coital slumber.

"You are a magnificent trunk of a woman."

"Em, I'm supposed to say thank you to that?" Martha snorted.

"Yes, you are not some delicate twig."

Martha started to laugh. Aleister touched her hair spread out on the pillow. He pulled her to him, and as she was unbalanced, she fell on top of him, pushing him backwards onto the bed. He kept a firm grasp on both her arms, staring at her intently, and then looked away in disgust. Then he looked back at her with a malicious smile. "And then?"

"Sorry?"

He released an arm, then propped himself up on one elbow. "And then?"

Martha extricated herself from his grasp and covered herself with the sheet, smiling. "And then what? More satisfaction?"

He turned her over and whispered in her ear, "I'm never satisfied."

She pulled away from him and laughed, "That's not much of a compliment to me."

They tussled on the bed, laughing and batting one another with a pillow. He pinned her down again and examined her in a new way.

"All this staring at me, it's making me feel most uncomfortable. Am I your first, then?"

"Oh, you are a first for me in many ways, Martha."

She swatted him away. "But I have a feeling I won't be your last."

They both laughed, and there was a moment that was almost tender between them.

"No, my mangy cur, most probably not."

Martha turned to him and pulled his face to hers. "Well, let's make this memorable, shall we?"

"Do what thou wilt."

They resumed just as a scream pierced the room. It was Aleister's mother standing in the doorway.

If there had been angst over a Christmas tree, then the mating on his mother's bed raised his mother's level of hysteria to a fevered pitch. At the height of her screams and wailing, neighbors coming home from church heard the noise and inquired if the police were needed. Mrs. Crowley seemed more traumatized by watching Martha collect her discarded clothing off her bedroom floor than by anything else, and when Mrs. Crowley felt faint, it gave both Aleister and Martha time to flee.

Aleister escaped to his bedroom.

Aleister heard a knock on his door; his uncle's voice rang out, "I insist you open this door immediately."

"Oh, but Uncle, I've been bad and I'm atoning for my sins." He lay on his bed still pleasuring himself.

"Nephew, I have come to tell you that you have grieved your mother to the core."

"Ah, to the core, Uncle, to the core."

At that Aleister had finished and was in the process of cleaning up when the rapping at the door started again. "Coming, Uncle, coming," he said, and at that he started to laugh uncontrollably while the rapping at the door was in earnest now. He heard the front door slam and went to his window just in time to see Martha trudging up the street with her one suitcase. As he watched her disappear, he thought, *I wonder who else can make those desserts?*

CHAPTER TWELVE

PITCHY-PATCH

~᳁~

A blur of bright colors ran past Pamela and Miss Jones in front of the Victoria Market Fountain. Pamela felt the comfort of Miss Jones's hand on her shoulder. In the strong Jamaican sunlight, Pitchy-Patch's costume was the most colorful one in the parade: strips of hibiscus red, sun yellow, parrot green, and ocean blue fluttered like a whirling rainbow. His ebony face was outlined with a white chalk skull, and he held up his whip to those who wouldn't move out of his way. Pamela squealed with delight as he approached them, his head tilting as he came closer to her. Pitchy-Patch reached out a hand to her just as a masked man with horns—the Devil—ran over to them. The Devil grabbed Pamela's other hand, and the characters used her in a game of tug-of-war as the crowd howled with laughter. Pitchy-Patch yanked her back and almost toppled her as the Devil pulled her to him until she was almost on top of him.

Miss Jones, laughing her big, beautiful laugh, pushed her way between them and shooed them off, lifting Pamela from their grip. They ran behind Miss Jones and Pamela as the two started down the sidewalk, swatting Miss Jones on her bottom. She turned on them, her face filled with furious fun, and they shrieked, running back to join the last of the parade. The heat of the afternoon sun made their disappearing forms waver as they blended in with the crowd that snaked down the street.

Thirteen-year-old Pamela clung to Miss Jones's slim waist, who remained fixed on the retreating figures of the Devil and Pitchy-Patch. Pamela looked up at her lustrous dark face framed by a ruby-red headscarf, two large hoops dangling from her ears. Miss Jones's holiday dress was made of a fine English calico print with large, ruffled sleeves accented with a yellow suede belt. Pamela begged to have a quadrille dress made for her too, but Miss Jones refused.

"This is a Jamaica thing, not of your knowing," was all Miss Jones said, in her lilting island accent.

Pamela had been with Miss Jones for three years since they arrived from England, and she loved her. She was allowed to accompany her on some errands to the local stores. On those days, the horse and wagon would be hitched up and they would travel from their suburb of St. Andrew to the big oak tree in Kingston, which was Miss Jones's main meeting place. Pamela would play with children—mostly English offspring of other railroad employees—while her caregiver gossiped with friends. Sometimes a group of children and their minders would go to the wharf to watch the tall ships sailing into port.

Pamela's biggest treat was when Miss Jones told her stories around a bonfire on the beach. There was Annancy, the clever spider who eluded many perils, Laurita, who danced with a king, and Death, who hunted children. Miss Jones would tell a collection of frightening, wonderful stories over and over again. There were tales of magic, monsters, and Maroons, the slaves who escaped from the Spanish and lived in the mountains. When Pamela told her of falling off a bridge in London and how a big mirror shattered onstage, Miss Jones said there was powerful magic around her and that someday, Pamela would find that Terriss man again.

The parade ended with the sight of two tall masked figures: the Queen and King. A crowd of children ran after them, taunting the royal figures with a song that dared them to prove how rich they were. The hot sun baked the street's surface dry as bones, and kicked-up dust rose like low-lying clouds. Around the fountain, women dipped their handkerchiefs into the water to dab at their faces. The noise of the crowds dimmed as they wandered down the street. Miss Jones firmly took Pamela's hand and walked to the post office. Pamela loved the feel of Miss Jones's hand wrapped around her own.

The windows of the merchant shops were decorated with Christmas garlands and festive gift boxes stacked as displays. In the street, some of the delivery horses wore large orchid wreaths and banana leaves around their heads. Christmas in Jamaica was nothing like the holidays in London or Manchester.

Today, Miss Jones promised they would go to the post office to see if there was any mail. Sometimes there were letters from Grandmother Colman in Brooklyn, or from Maud in France. Maud's last postcard announced that she was "out" in society, meeting *beaucoup de personnes merveilleuses.* Maud had also written Pamela's parents a letter that, no matter how many times she begged, Pamela was not allowed to read. "Maud has fallen in love with someone. He has a mustache," was all her mother would tell her.

Mother was often sick, and bedridden during most of the day. Her cough had definitely not improved; she spent many hours in a darkened bedroom. A rum medicine would be fetched when her hacking kept her from sleeping. Sometimes days would go by before Miss Jones told her to make herself presentable, Mother wanted to see her. Most times when they entered her bedroom Mother would have already fallen asleep again. Quietly, they would tiptoe out and hear a moan behind the shut door.

But today, thoughts of her invalid mother were brushed away when they entered the post office. The British clerk behind the counter called out, "Ah, the illustrious Miss Smith, another letter has arrived for you."

Miss Jones brought Pamela up to the window, and the smartly dressed older man in a pressed uniform handed a battered envelope to Pamela. She examined the handwriting on the front and recognized the canceled stamp. Maud's handwriting and a stamp from Paris! Pamela did a little dance to the door and burst out to race to the pony and carriage that waited for them.

Miss Jones called after her, "You sit there and behave while I get tonight's meal makings."

The groom from the market next door had been charged with tending to their pony, and he helped Pamela up into the carriage seat. The white pony stamped its feet and twitched its ears, ready to go. Pamela loved riding with Miss Jones. She'd been promised that someday she would drive the cart by herself. She tore open the French envelope and inside was a postcard for her and a letter for her father sealed with wax. She inspected the wax imprint at the center of the seal: *MG*. The seal was affixed so firmly there was no way to pry it off without being detected. She turned to her postcard, which was a watercolor view of the Seine with booksellers and flowers along the sidewalk next to the bridge. *Darling girl, I had a dream about you. Do not be afraid. I will be there, even if you cannot see me. And we will fly. All my love, Maud.*

Pamela sat back in her seat and fanned herself with the postcard. The clamor from the parade had settled down, and now a promenade of people, Black and white, city and mountain people, meandered along the dirt sidewalk. The sultry air felt heavy on Pamela's eyelids and she let out a large sigh, hoping to see Miss Jones arrive with the errand boy soon.

Down the street, in the haze of the churned-up dust, she barely made out a bird buzzing low over the street. *How odd,* she thought. *I've never seen one fly like that before.*

The pony nickered and whinnied as the groom let go of its bridle and it bolted into the market. The pony, still lashed to the rail, cried louder and shook. Frightened, Pamela looked around to find what the pony was seeing. There was nothing but the bird floating down the street. She twisted her head every which way to see what was happening as the pony kicked the carriage wagon.

Pamela looked again at the bird in flight. At first sight, it had seemed to be a bird, or maybe even a fish, floating in the air. As it came closer, Pamela saw it was a green-winged hummingbird streaked with white—Miss Jones called them doctor birds. In the fading afternoon light, it hovered mid-flight right before Pamela and transformed into a large, gnarled woman. A witch! She cast her terrible great eyes on Pamela and pointed her bent finger.

Miss Jones's shouts reverberated as she ran out from the store. "No, no you don't! You git away from my girl!"

The fierce eyes of the witch turned to ash as Miss Jones charged across the sidewalk, an errand boy carrying boxes close behind. A silvery metallic sound rang out, and the witch doubled over. The spirit slipped out of her body, her skin crumpling and falling to the ground like a discarded snakeskin, and floated above them.

The outline of the witch cried out to Miss Jones. "Kin, you no know me?"

"Duppy, you no kin of mine. Away!"

The witch's silhouette shimmered and then evaporated. On the ground, her blue-black skin shriveled into a small, blackened pile.

Miss Jones yelled at the boy to put the boxes on the wagon and climbed in the back to rifle through one of them. Pamela hung onto the side of her seat and looked backwards to see what she was doing. The pony continued to dance and fuss as the errand boy soothed him. Miss Jones finally found a tin of pepper. She raced to the front of the carriage and poured a stream of powdered pepper over the now iridescent pile of the witch.

The errand boy stood staring at them both and then tore back into the market.

Miss Jones unhitched the pony from the post and pitched herself into the driver's seat, barely giving the reins a shake before the pony took off with a jolt. After racing past people for two blocks, she got him back under control and maintained a steady pace as they headed back to St. Andrew.

Pamela wound her arms tightly around her protector's waist as she drove. "Miss Jones, did you kill the witch?"

She burst out laughing, then put her pipe between her lips. With one hand still grasping the reins, she lit her pipe and eyed Pamela.

"That was a duppy, not a witch. And you don't wanna kill them. But should you have to, you kill fire with fire. Remember that."

Pamela clung to Miss Jones as the carriage swayed from side to side in the late afternoon light. It was a lesson she would never forget.

CHAPTER THIRTEEN

The Golden Dawn Commences

D r. Westcott looked over the half a dozen people studying in the library at Mark Masons' Hall. The smell of lemon oil and wax from the cleaned floors wafted over him as he sat in the most comfortable chair in the room, his right as "Chief." Maps lay unfurled on desks, books were propped open, pencils scratched on paper. Months of negotiations had finally led to this official headquarters for his community of magic enthusiasts. It gave him a sturdy satisfaction that so many quality people, people of respectability and renown, were interested in this newly formed Golden Dawn group. The only fly in the ointment was that they had to admit women, which was not in his initial plan.

The women recruits had furnished the headquarters, creating an atmosphere that was almost too cozy. The leather chairs had elaborately designed hooked rugs underneath them, while the books were sorted into categories and arranged alphabetically on the shelves. Several large artist's tables were arranged, their large tops tilted at different angles to hold atlases. Westcott wondered if they were going to be able to afford this headquarters much longer. Women paid more in dues than the men; but the dues barely covered the rent.

Samuel Mathers opened the door and gave a cursory nod. His umbrella dripped water all over the entrance, and he fumbled with his overcoat as he hung it up.

Mathers was an enthusiastic member, but it was questionable whether he was truly an asset to the new order. His knowledge of many languages helped with translations, and he was very good with codes and ritual understandings. But he was an idiot when it came to social niceties and decorum. He stuttered and stammered and had a deplorable habit of standing too close and lecturing someone too intensely about his recent obscure findings.

"No letter from Count Apponyi?" Mathers asked as he came close to Westcott.

Apponyi was a magician who led a Golden Dawn chapter in Hungary and had been in contact with the group. During a recent conjuring at Westcott's office, a collection of the writings of Count Apponyi had materialized. The magicians determined that it was a collection of spells written down from the Hungarian magician. They nicknamed these spells the "Hungarian Papers." Unfortunately, the papers had been impossible to decipher, and they had written the Count to ask for a translation and rights to the spells.

This supposed Count seemed pleased to be asked for permission to use the spells, but as his letter said: *Clearly you want to experiment with the contents; otherwise you would not be writing to me to ask about the steps of instruction that are only available to Golden Dawn members. For further instructions to proceed, contact Fraulein Sprengel, German Rosicrucian adept, address enclosed.*

"So far, he has not given us permission to start an official offshoot of the Golden Dawn," Westcott growled. "This German Fraulein Sprengel is to process our application."

"Oh, b-b-bother," Mathers answered.

"Well, go into the vault-room; we have a new Hungarian dictionary. See if you can't decipher one of the spells," Westcott said. "If other magicians are threatened by our group, we'll need defensive conjuring. The last thing we need is an astral attack from whoever had first put Count Apponyi's spells together."

"I don't think I'll be able to translate those spells, but I'll try," Mathers mumbled.

Westcott handed Mathers a key and the dictionary, and he shuffled off to the vault. Perhaps Mathers could conjure a spell to bring in wealthy members to this group.

There was a lot of concern about the order's ability to attract the right people with money. Westcott realized they needed women with money to contribute, as most men would demand a title or such in return for their dues. He didn't want women rising up the ladder to the higher levels here. It was bad enough they allowed women in, unlike most men's clubs. There had to be a way to guarantee that Golden Dawn men would be magicians and women would be assigned their muses. Or helpers. At least, that was *his* concept for their Golden Dawn and the effect of the womanly touch.

The one room in which he would not tolerate the "womanly touch" was in the vault. The vault was a seven-sided chamber that was eight feet tall, with cabalistic, astrological, and alchemical symbols. The vault was to be the scientist's laboratory. He tolerated the cleaning and sprucing up, but drew the line at flowers or pillows on chairs next to the vault. It could only fit four people inside, and Westcott was determined to keep it uncluttered and sterile.

As a coroner, Westcott saw many astounding things that could not be explained by pure science. He steadied his mind by experimenting with magical spells that defied the physical laws governing the universe. Certainly, practicing the spell where he handled lightning was a thrilling experience, and he plotted ways to gain more special powers. He had tried unsuccessfully to reenact the magical creation of that bolt of lightning. He hoped it was not a once in a lifetime experience. He dreamed about the lightning traveling from his arm out into the night sky.

Mina Bergson, a petite and comely young woman, came in, bundled up from the winter's cold. After hanging up her coat next to Mathers's and securing the box of her artist's supplies, she approached Westcott.

"Good day, Dr. Westcott," she said. "I'm here to work on the vault. Is it open?"

"Yes, Miss Bergson, Mathers is in there now. Let me know if you need any more supplies."

"Just a ladder, if one isn't in there," she replied. "I'll have Mr. Mathers fetch it."

Westcott watched her neat figure retreat to the vault room. Not bad if you liked that sort of thing. Recruited for her ability to paint, she was in charge of the designs on the vault. She was talented in languages too, and Mathers was absolutely smitten with him. He was often found near her with two or three obscure reference books, volunteering to translate a word or look up a symbol she was researching. But how many levels would she pass? What title would she be given and by whom? She'd probably want to be known as Adept Mina, a title they used in Hungary.

It irked Westcott that secret and private magical instructions were becoming common and available. It was becoming clear to him that a second level of instruction would be necessary in the group, a level beyond astrology and alchemy, a level where true, exclusive magicians could practice.

There were many groups that were starting: Masons, Freemasons (of which he was a member), Rosicrucians, Theosophical Societies, Heretics Societies, Cabalists. He knew that Waite, Felkin, and Mathers had their own ideas about starting up this order. This founding group to study magic and the occult should remain at the top of the hierarchy of their Golden Dawn chapter. The method of study must be controlled from the setup. If he could get permission from Fraulein Sprengel, they would all begin at the Neophyte level, in accordance with the Golden Dawn levels she presided over.

Each member was to create their own motto as they took on a Golden Dawn identity. Westcott even knew what his motto would be: *Dare to be wise.* At the Neophyte level, there was to be grading of learned skills, and he wanted each level to be exact and precise so there were no mistakes. Here there would be no sloppy magicians creating havoc. There was enough of that on the streets of London.

Just today he had had to determine the cause of death of a young girl, her neck slashed spectacularly from side to side. Rumors of a murderer, a "Leather Apron" type butcher running the streets at night and killing helpless women, were starting to make the rounds.

Woodman was, thankfully, out of the picture (even if he did have a little help on the way out with the aid of liquid cocaine) and his will had left the money that rented this headquarters. There was also a fund for Mathers to interpret the Hungarian papers. But it was running out.

Waite entered, slamming the door. Even at a distance, Westcott could see he was bristling with energy.

"Where are the others?" Waite asked.

"Well, hello to you too, Mr. Waite," Westcott said, remaining seated.

Edward Waite was ambitious and socially capable. His smooth good looks and well-formed vocabulary were assets for his long lectures, and he was especially good at talking to the young women with money. He intuited who was either bored with university and the limited curriculum available to them, or those with time and energy to spare outside their family obligations. As a married man and father, Waite appeared to be a solid family man.

The lanky Dr. Felkin entered and Waite clapped his hands. After Felkin sorted his belongings out, he approached them, and Waite slowly pulled a letter from his jacket pocket. The three men stared at the envelope where the name *Fraulein Sprengel* was written.

Westcott stood. "The vault, now!"

The three men scurried to the vault.

When they opened the door, Mina was seated on a ladder before the eight-foot-tall black structure. A wooden temple built to enclose magicians during conjuring, it had been constructed by directions discovered in a French grimoire. Above the little entrance door, a series of astrological symbols were painted.

"Mina," Dr. Westcott said. "Would you give us a moment's privacy here? An important issue has come up."

She looked at the three men and with an ounce of defiance made her way down the ladder, Mathers holding her hand the entire time.

When she left the room, Westcott turned to Waite. "What do you have there, and why do you have it?"

"Gentlemen," Waite said, his buttons almost bursting from his shirt. "I started a private correspondence with Fraulein Sprengel discussing a possible tarot card curriculum for our Golden Dawn affiliate."

"You do not have the authority to discuss that—" Westcott started.

"Now, now," Dr. Felkin said. "Let's hear what Sprengel has to say first."

Waite's blocky mustache quivered as he opened the letter.

"'Dear Gentlemen, Count Apponyi vouches for your character.'" Waite raced ahead in the letter, his finger following the handwriting. "Ah, here it is: 'There is a new world order starting. If you sign on to the edicts of the Golden Dawn, you will be expected to be obedient and lead in the new order according to our rules. You have my solemn permission to form a branch of *Die Godlene Dammerung*—The Golden Dawn.'"

Waite looked up from the letter at Westcott, Felkin, and Mathers. "Gentlemen, we have our order of the Golden Dawn."

An hour later, Dr. Westcott, Dr. Felkin, Waite, and Mathers had all declared themselves the four visible "chiefs" of this order because they had already worked their way through five spells. The second order of spells would be coming from Fraulein Sprengel, and then a third level, a secret, more exclusive sphere of magicians and occult artists would assemble—separate from the hubris of the first. Oh, the plans for this Level Three. The plans!

Waite looked at the jumble of notes made before them. "Fine, gentlemen, fine! Now we just need money to fund the Golden Dawn's tarot deck! This deck will be a simple teaching tool for our group's mission."

"I should b-b-be in charge of this," Mathers said. "No one understands language and symbols like I do."

"You two are fools not to realize how powerful this deck could be," Dr. Felkin snapped.

"More than that," Dr. Westcott said, taking up Fraulein Sprengel's letter. "If we are to be the new scientists and scholars, holding the keys to the future, our real challenge will be to keep this tarot deck to ourselves."

CHAPTER FOURTEEN

Auditioning for Magic

In 1899, the Star Theatre in New York City stood at Thirteenth Street and Broadway, in the German neighborhood. The red-bricked theatre seated almost 1,700 people, and at center stage stood Pamela Colman Smith. She wore a red tunic with a dark green skirt, and on her head was a sort of crow feather band. Pamela was now nineteen and seemed like an old child. She was auditioning for three people assembled to judge her at the side of the stage as company members watched from the house.

Ellen Terry sat in the center of the trio of auditors. Her daughter, Edy Craig, stood behind her, with Bram Stoker leaning on the proscenium nearby. Ellen was at the height of her career, touring the United States as part of the Lyceum Theatre Company with her lover and leading man, Henry Irving. Ellen, attired in a beautiful coat dress, her hair in the Gibson Girl style of the day, was a vision. Even though she was under constant observation from the public, she maintained a sweet disposition and a regal air that belied her childlike spontaneity. She watched Pamela auditioning with a merry face.

Not so merry was the face of Edy Craig, only in her early twenties, but blunt and forthright. Called a spinster or a sister, she was punctual and loyal, not given to flights of fancy, and today looked most displeased that the company had to watch a new actress audition. Edy's intimidating demeanor was amplified by her current garb. She was dressed in a papal robe as a hierophant, a high church official, her costume for the production of *The Corsican Brothers*.

Bram Stoker, still leaning against the proscenium of the theatre stage, watched his latest discovery with a neutral face. What Bram was thinking was hard to tell. He had spent his life being of service, handling the Lyceum Theatre and following the dictates of Henry Irving, theatre manager and star. It was very hard to get a spontaneous reaction from Mr. Bram Stoker unless his Irish temper was lit, and then everyone knew to follow his commands unquestioned.

Pamela took a deep breath onstage and thought back to Miss Jones telling folktales on the beach in St. Andrew. Using the Jamaican accent of her caretaker, she began. "In a long before time, before Queen Victoria came to reign over us, there lived three sisters—Isadora, Florinda, and Laurita. The eldest were very cross and spiteful to Laurita; they always went to parties and teas, and they would never take Laurita with them. She was so kind and pretty, and they were so ugly, in thought and deed."

Edy cupped her hands to her mother's ear and whispered, "I don't care what that witch outside your carriage foretold—this is not your second daughter."

Ellen teasingly swatted her hands away and continued to listen to Pamela.

"An old Obeah woman asked Laurita, 'what was the matter?' and Laurita told her all about her misery. Then, the old Obeah woman took out of her pocket a lot of little sticks, and an old iron and built a fire."

Henry Irving entered from the other side of the stage but stopped at the sight of the audition, standing just out of sight. He was carrying his mahogany walking stick with its most unusual handle: a piece of ebony tektite that had fallen out of the sky. His demeanor was old-fashioned, serious and unsmiling.

Pamela continued with the story, unaware the great actor was nearby. "The old woman said a great many funny, Obeah words and out of the pot came a lovely frock!" Pamela mimed holding up the dress and putting it on. "And there was a wreath of silver flowers, a gold necklace, beads, and shoes of real gold!" As she finished the show of dressing for the ball, Pamela continued. "The Obeah woman took a gourd and put it in the pot. Out came a big coach, horses and a coachman!" Pamela whirled about the stage, whirling her way into an imaginary carriage. "Laurita got in the coach and goes to the ball at the king's house. Everyone wonders who she is until finally the king sees her and asks to dance with her." Pamela bowed to an imaginary king and stopped mid-bow as she spotted Henry offstage.

Ellen ended the audition by lightly clapping her hands and laughing. "Brava, well done Miss Smith! I love the accent." She noticed Henry and waved him over. Henry took long strides and reached the center of the stage in moments. Pamela was speechless as Mr. Irving moved toward her like a locomotive. He took in the entire group.

"Well, unless we can use this pot of magic to liven up *The Corsican Brothers*, Miss Terry, you are requested at rehearsal."

Ellen rose from her stage throne and took Henry's hand playfully. "Oh, Mr. Irving, you must meet my latest discovery! This is Pamela Colman Smith, William Gillette's cousin. She's the artist, the orphan who draws, the one I told you about? She created the tour brochure of our Shakespearean characters that you liked."

At this introduction, Pamela felt laughter bubble up inside

her, and she rushed over to Mr. Irving and the group. She touched Bram's sleeve and he turned to her, pride shining in his eyes.

Bram ushered her into the circle around Miss Ellen's throne, his Irish brogue now somewhat tamed. "Now, Miss Terry, you can't be claiming that Miss Pamela is your discovery. You know right well I found her last year, when I hired her to design our theatre brochure. Mr. Irving, this is Miss Pamela Colman Smith, *my* discovery."

Mr. Irving executed a stiff little bow, and Pamela extended her hand. He seemed unprepared for this, but shook her hand anyway.

"Oh! Oh! Oh! So pleased to meet you, Mr. Irving. I saw your electrical sparks and steam in *Faust* three years ago, so magnetic!"

The entire stage and audience of company members laughed; even Edy put her hand over her mouth to stifle her laughter. Praise for special effects over the legendary Irving acting was taboo in the theatre company. Mr. Irving straightened himself up and scrutinized Pamela to see if she was being genuine.

Pamela felt his intense gaze and smiled, trying to win him over. "Did I say something offensive?"

Ellen seated Pamela on the throne. She examined her crow feather band, and then her assortment of necklaces, and finally the bangles on Pamela's arms. Bram and Mr. Irving talked in hushed tones, apart from the group.

Pamela felt a slight tug at her heart. It was Miss Jones's story that made them interested in her. Miss Jones was the one who had given her the crow feather band in her hair, along with the story of the King discovering Laurita and her pot of magic. She had imagined Miss Jones was here, watching over her as she recited the folktale, floating high above them. Their nightly ritual of her guardian telling her Annancy stories was now alive in the stage light of a theatre in New York City. And how her mother would swell with pride to know that she was auditioning for Henry Irving. The memory of when they had been extras in *The Corsican Brothers*, on the night the mirror fell, came rushing back to her.

Edy looked at Pamela and hissed, "How old are you?"

"Almost twenty," Pamela whispered back. "How old are you?"

Edy leaned back, saying nothing, and Ellen laughed, patting her daughter's cheeks. "Oh, Edy, if she's not going to fawn over Henry, she's not going to be fawning over us!"

Edy finally smiled at Pamela and sat next to her on the throne. "Yes, interesting that you would praise his scenic design before his talents." Though with her lisp it sounded like "hith thenic dethign before hith talenth."

A speech impediment in a young actress? Pamela thought. *How interesting that she has a lisp.*

Mr. Irving and Bram suddenly appeared before Pamela and Edy, and Mr. Irving clapped his hands behind his back. "Why did you like *Faust* so much? Was it only for the sparks and steam? Not the acting?"

Pamela rose and looked straight into his eyes. "Oh, I'm so sorry, Mr. Irving. I thought you knew you were a genius."

Pamela heard several sharp inhales as Mr. Irving studied her. "I hear Jamaica and Manchester in your voice. Were you born in England?"

"Born in London, lived in Chislehurst, Manchester, Paris, Jamaica, Brooklyn, and now, Manhattan."

"You are an orphan? What is your age?"

"My mother passed away four years ago, and my excellent father just passed this December." Pamela's voice hitched, and she paused. Taking a deep breath, she continued. "I'm nineteen, and a published illustrator. I have fallen in love with your theatre, your Coriolanus, and your cycloramas."

Ellen, Edy, and Bram laughed softly. Mr. Irving turned his head, saw them laughing, and started to chuckle too. "My cycloramas?"

"The world-famous Lyceum Theatre scenic design by Hawes Craven, T.W. Hall, Perkins, and Carey . . ."

"You certainly know of our great set painters . . ."

". . . W. Hann and J. Harker . . . My family took me to see the canvases being painted in the Covent Garden Opera House paint rooms."

Mr. Irving turned to Bram and nodded. He started to head offstage when he stopped and addressed Pamela again. "Why the theatre?"

"My mother was a painter, a stage actress, and a fortune teller."

"A fortune teller? What did she foresee?"

"That one day I would be part of the calcium lights on stage. Mr. Irving, I have one question."

"What is it?"

"We saw you in *The Corsican Brothers*. I was ten. We were part of the masked ball scene that night, the night the mirror broke. And there was snow. How did you do the snow? You started the duel and kicked snow out of the way, and it didn't melt on stage."

Henry Irving looked perturbed when she mentioned the mirror. He finally cracked a genuine smile and gave a bark of a laugh. Giving his attention to Bram, he said, "Bram, it seems that we have found the replacement for the small roles for the remainder of our Lyceum Tour. Mr. Stoker will sort out the details. Miss Terry, five minutes, in rehearsal." Henry Irving started to leave, but then he returned to whisper only to Pamela: "Salt. Coarse rock salt."

The rest of the company was unable to hear what he had whispered and strained forward to be included. Mr. Irving gave them a teasing look, held his hand to his ear, and strode offstage. As he passed Ellen, he saw her beaming at him, a sweet, unguarded smile. Only when he thought he was visible to her alone did he tap his right hand twice over his heart. But Pamela saw his gesture and knew instinctively that this must be his signal for *My heart beats only for you.*

Ellen pivoted her head, blushing as he disappeared from the stage. Pamela knew now would be the time to take the floor.

"I'm so thrilled to be part of the Lyceum family," she said, turning to Bram as he applauded, the company in the house following his lead. Pamela started a short, happy little dance and Ellen got up to join her. Ellen performed a short do-si-do with Pamela, and Bram came over and patted them both on the back. Edy turned away and sulked. In her hierophant costume, she looked like a sad sack pope who didn't like the offering of the day.

Bram exulted, "Well now, I didn't think it would go as well as all that. The Great Man usually doesn't give much attention to the young people auditioning to be part of the company, but you certainly won him over."

"Thank you, Mr. Stoker! I can never thank you enough! My father would have—"

At the mention of her father, a swirl of color and sound seized up her brain. It had been only a month since his funeral in Brooklyn; the sickness he had in Jamaica had gotten worse until he passed away at his brother's house. Her relationship with her uncles was fraught; only Uncle Teddy thought she should be auditioning. But now that both parents were gone, none of the family in New York wanted her.

"Well, since I promised your father I would look after you, I'll be Uncle Brammy to ya. But you must be punctual and reliable. We set no store by wastrels here. Edy, you'll be her first handler."

With that, Edy groaned as Ellen teasingly whipped her hand, saying, "Edy, all I've ever heard from you is that you wanted a sister. Well, here she is!"

Bram pulled himself up and patted Edy on the back. "Well, Edy, she's your headache now; enjoy her. She might bring some fun onboard." He hurried backstage.

Ellen continued to fuss over Pamela's costume until she heard Bram's offstage voice. "Miss Terry, rehearsal right now, if you don't mind. In the sitting room."

As Ellen started off, she took Pamela by the arm. "What a pixie you are! There, you have a new name for the tour—Pixie! And what a fascinating wreath you're wearing."

"My obeah ooman gave it to me."

Edy intruded between the two of them and looked at the feather band. "Your who?"

"Miss Jones, my protector, who practiced witchcraft."

"Edy, wouldn't it become me? If Henry saw this on me, he'd want me to wear it in *Coriolanus*. Oh, and Edy, Sydney Valentine's wife just arrived. Do see that she has a seat for tonight? Front row?"

Offstage, Bram boomed, "Miss Terry! You are . . . !"

"Right there, Mr. Stoker." Ellen dashed backstage. The company members in the auditorium tittered as they made their way to the downstairs rehearsal room. The minute Ellen was offstage, they heard her singsong "Goodbye" to them.

Pamela asked, "And Mr. Sydney Valentine is?"

"The married actor in the company Mother is trying to keep away."

"From herself?"

"From me. All right, Pixie, by way of Manchester, Jamaica, and Brooklyn—let's get you sorted out here. You'll go backstage and you'll see which of the many, many small roles you will be filling."

On hearing Edy's lisp, Pamela understood that the great Ellen Terry's daughter was not destined to follow in her mother's footsteps.

They made their way backstage, past the many rows of ropes and weights, potted plants, vases, and ornate chairs placed around a table. On the table a large notebook lay open where lists of plays, roles, and actors were set out in a grid. Edy threw herself into one of the chairs and proceeded to go through the lists.

"All right, Pixie, since you aren't here to fill the role of a great genius—that's Mr. Irving—or beautiful actress—that's my mother—or useful actress—myself when not designing costumes—what are your talents?"

"I hear music, see Sidhe, the invisible children of Dana, make 'Opal Hush'—that's claret and fizzy lemonade—have a fairy for a sister, and have sold four of my watercolors at the William Macbeth Gallery here in New York! Oh, and my Annancy stories are to be published with my illustrations this year."

"Very well then, Pixie, goddaughter to a witch and sister to a fairy, you will oversee the costumes and the prompt book," Edy said. She motioned to a long sheet of paper on the wall with rows of plays and performers' names penciled in, mirroring the one in the book. Gesturing to the bottom row, she added, "These four roles are yours. I take it Mr. Stoker previously explained the low pay and long hours—or is it now 'Uncle Brammy' to you?"

"Yes, and he said he's a writer too! He's working on a story about vampires."

"Yes. Did he tell you he's fashioning the main vampire after Mr. Irving?"

Pamela's great laugh burst forth and Edy joined in. After a hearty moment, the two girls looked at one another.

"Is William Terriss still part of the acting company?" Pamela asked, trying to keep her heart from beating too loudly.

"Not on this tour, he's off trying to bring Asian sheep to Scotland, from what I hear. All right, Pixie, let's get your accommodations set. I have a feeling I have a new roommate."

Edy was picking up material from the desk when Pamela's attention was caught by a rolled-up script on the prop table; it was fashioned after a Torah. She picked it up, looked around, and snapped up a hand to Edy as though to caution her to be quiet. Very seriously, she handed Edy the Torah prop. As Edy held it questioningly, Pamela found an odd-shaped vase and put it on Edy's head as a crown. Pamela murmured, "The perfect high priestess."

Edy looked at her and tilted her head. "Pixie, costume design another day?"

Pamela grinned and removed the improvised crown from her newly found friend's head.

"Time to show you your very small dressing room assignment," Edy said, heading up a flight of stairs to the second floor.

Pamela glanced back at the throne. The strange music that happened only when a new situation presented itself began to play. Pamela had heard this phrase before, but could not place where or when.

She concentrated on finding the pulse of white light, a light that seemed to come from inside her rib cage, a practice that she had learned from Miss Jones. The light that illuminated the visions and visitors that weren't there. When she found it, she willed it to flutter out into the room. The orb of light landed on a coat rack where dozens of swords hung by their hilts. The orb settled on one particular sword she recognized—Mr. Irving's sword from *The Corsican Brothers*. She crossed to the rack and lifted the weapon with both hands to look at it. It lit up in a spectacular way; the light came from *inside* the sword.

"Pixie!" Edy called from above.

Pamela strained to see more of the magic in the sword but the light had disappeared, so she replaced the prop. She turned and ran to find Edy.

"Here I come!"

CHAPTER FIFTEEN

WATKINS BOOKS

⏤⏥⏤

Arthur Edward Waite entered Watkins Books with the intent to find more of Eliphas Lévi's volumes. He was obsessed with Lévi, a Frenchman who had studied to be a priest but found the study of magic more to his calling. He loved Lévi's illustrations, but one of Lévi's tenets bothered him: "To practice magic is to be a quack; to know magic is to be a sage." Practicing magic was the most thrilling event of Waite's life. Dr. Westcott had let slip a long-ago mishap involving an incantation manifesting bricks. He had almost been sealed up by the bricks which could have proved fatal. If only they had allowed Waite to be there, he could have possibly prevented the entire mishap.

By day, Waite was a clerk; by night, a misunderstood mystic. He had published one of the best-known books on the study of black magic, *Book of Black Magic and of Pacts,* and Waite was enormously proud of it. His next project was to translate Lévi's book *Transcendental Magic, Its Doctrine and Ritual.*

He would soon complete his collection of the Lévi books! Usually he had to check them out from the library of the British

Museum. It was these books that had made Waite the expert on the Templars' well-organized, comprehensive plans for the future. Dr. Westcott, the most aggressive leader of their chapter of the Golden Dawn, believed that the faith, practice, and secrecy executed by the Templars was a good model for their chapter. The Warrior Templar knights had at one time owned the land on Chancery Lane where Waite was now living with his wife, Lucasta, and child, Sybil, and he took that as a good sign.

After he bid hello to John Watkins, he strolled down the aisle of religious studies to the shelf where Lévi's books would be stocked, stroking his fine walrus mustache in anticipation. But someone was already there, leaning against the bookcase. He was a young man of about twenty, clean-shaven and well-dressed. Even worse, he was thumbing through *La Clef des Grands Mystères*, one of Waite's favorites, a manuscript with beautiful illustrations that Lévi had done of Baphomet, the horned goat devil the Templars worshiped.

The young man looked up and casually said, "Hello there."

"Yes, hello," Waite coughed back.

Waite scoured the shelves to see where the other Lévi books were. His blood started to boil—they were all gone! Every single copy! It was as if someone had punched him in the stomach; he had considered this his private stash, and no one had ever expressed interest in the Lévi books before. He had felt that they would always be there for him to purchase whenever he could afford them. Who else would buy an obscure series of French books seen as pagan and blasphemous?

He hurried to the front desk. "John, where are all your Lévi books? Have you moved them?"

"No sir, it seems you started a movement," John said cheerily. "Why, that gentleman back there purchased most of them last week."

With a dry mouth, Waite turned around and saw the grinning man standing next to him. "Hello again, I'm Aleister Crowley."

Waite and Aleister sat across from one another in the pub, the copy of *La Clef des Grands Mystères* lying between them. Waite looked at this stylish Aleister, so posh with his Cambridge accent, now stoking his pipe. *Of course, the Golden Dawn is becoming the plaything of the leisure class.*

Waite had a somewhat posh accent himself, having attended St. Charles College in Bayswater, but the origins of his birth were strictly secret, as he was illegitimate. Born in Brooklyn to a captain in the American Merchant Marine and to an English mother, he still had traces of an American accent. When he was quite young, his father died at sea, leaving his widowed mother who was pregnant again to come home to her English parents. When it was discovered that Waite's parents never married, his mother's parents disowned her, leaving her to bring up Edward and his sister in the Catholic faith and on charity. Brought up by a single mother who adored him, Waite became a devoted researcher and Roman Catholic, at least for a while, until his sister died. He still respected the Catholic faith but was not a great follower and had become an ever more zealous researcher. Ten years ago, when he married Lucasta, they had both been enthusiastic followers of the mystic movement; even now she was studying to be a Neophyte with the Golden Dawn, one of the few women. However, with a nine-year-old daughter to attend to, Lucasta's interest waned, especially since she could see the disrespect for her husband among the top chiefs.

Aleister ordered a whiskey, Waite an ale. They sat in silence until the drinks arrived, eyeing one another.

"Well, Mr. Crowley," Waite said after his first sip, "your name reminds me of a beer I enjoyed back in the day. Let's drink to the Crowley."

Waite looked into Aleister's eyes. *Yes, I know you are the heir to the Crowley Brewery.*

Aleister lifted his glass. "To the immortal health of both our fathers." They both took a hearty swig. "Well, Mr. Waite," Aleister continued, "I see you are interested in my recent acquisitions from Watkins."

"Yes, very interested, as the Lévi books are a particular expertise of mine."

"Oh, and of mine also. I have a very keen mind for the world of the occult."

And stalemate. "All right then, what would it take for me to buy some of your newly acquired books?"

"Oh, Mr. Waite, I'm not interested in selling them. I'd be interested in sharing them with a fellow Golden Dawn member. Your group is looking for new recruits, is it not?"

"Well, Mr. Crowley, the main requirement of the group is that you have a talent to offer."

"Obviously. I read French; I could do some translating."

"And why would you want to be a part of our group?"

"There is only one reason, Mr. Waite, the same as you, I would think: magic. And access to it."

Waite sighed and looked away. "The book you really ought to be reading is Karl von Eckartshausen's *The Cloud upon the Sanctuary*."

"Really? And why is that?"

"In order to recruit within our group, one must recognize that we are dealing with a Christian society. He veils Christian mysticism in hermetic code."

"Of course, this von Eckartshausen's work is in German?" Aleister asked, his voice going up an octave.

"But of course. You read German?"

"No."

Waite stifled a smile. "Isabelle de Steiger has done an excellent translation; I'll get it for you."

"Now, why would I be reading Eckartshausen before Lévi?"

Waite drew himself up. Now was his chance to show his expertise.

"Mr. Crowley, Eckartshausen was a member of the Bavarian Illuminati and left this world mentioning a 'society of the Elect' which originates from the beginning of time. It is known as 'the invisible celestial Church.' It was, according to him, 'the society that will be the Regent Mother of the whole World.'"

"The Regent Mother of the whole World! That's a tall order." Aleister took two fingers and saluted Waite.

Pompous and insulting.

Aleister took a deep drink and slyly looked at Waite. "You know, I read your book."

"To which book are you referring?" Waite answered with a flat tone.

"*Black Magic and of Pacts.*"

"And?"

"Better than Mathers's *The Kabbalah Unveiled.*"

Waite waited a moment and almost smiled. "Well, there's that."

Aleister exhaled. "So, where are we, Mr. Waite? Am I to be admitted into the hallowed halls of the Golden Dawn?"

Waite could feel the disdain rolling off him. *Just what I don't need, one more disrespectful person judging me.* Looking out the window, he very carefully said, "I'll petition the group, Mr. Crowley. You know, we need to keep control of how many people we let in."

"Yes. A 'society of the Elect,' as it were. Well, here is my card; I live near here on Chancery Lane."

Waite's blood froze to think that he would be seeing him in his neighborhood. He slowly picked up the calling card. *Did he know where I live all along?*

"Excellent. I will let you know."

Aleister picked up the Lévi book. "I'll be loaning you this when I next see you at the Golden Dawn meeting."

And with that, Waite watched the arrogant young man stride out of the pub. *If I could seal you up with bricks, I would.*

❧

Aleister made his way back to his flat on Chancery Lane.

What Waite didn't know was that Aleister was secretly studying the demonic system of Abra-Melin magic with a fellow Golden Dawn member, Allan Bennett. Allan was an acclaimed magician and chemist who was currently staying at Aleister's plushy apartment. Allan and he had even built two "temples" or "vaults" in his apartment to consecrate magic in, one devoted to white magic, the other to black magic. The use of hallucinogenic drugs was also introduced during the incantations, tapping into the ability to move bodies and foreign objects and to conjure bad energies to expel worse energies, going back to Aleister's earliest learnings of Paracelsus, experimenting with the idea of "evil expelling evil." Allan had tried through Mathers to petition for Aleister to no avail, so now his chances lay with Arthur Waite.

Allan was sitting cross-legged in the parlor, in the middle of a small pyramid crudely constructed from sheets and clothespins, known to them as the temple of white magic, his eyes closed. Allan was an attractive young man with a huge head, "a horse's head" according to some, large soulful eyes, and prominent eyebrows. He was also a trained scientist, specializing in chemistry and electricity, so his knowledge of drugs and their effects was just what Aleister needed. Allan was also a devoted student of Hinduism and Buddhism, interesting side ventures to Aleister but not as essential as his knowledge of drugs.

Aleister made himself a pot of tea, hoping to rouse Allan from his trance. He wanted to give him an update on his acceptance into the Golden Dawn, but an hour ticked by and still Allan made no sound from the tent. Finally, Aleister went and plopped himself right outside the white-magic temple and sighed.

"Yes, what is it?"

"Waite detests me and won't lift a finger to help."

Allan opened an eye and saw Aleister splayed out in front of him. "How do you know he detests you?"

"Because I detest him and his petty bureaucratic ways."

"Well then." With that Allan sighed and came out, shaking himself out of his reverie. "Let's look at this from a scientific point of view. He has a set of energy that is impeding your progression toward the light."

"True, he is a dark cloud, that is certain."

"In the realm of learning and enlightenment, there is only one goal: Let there be light."

"So, what am I to do? I need to make him suffer until he realizes they need me."

"I do not approve of this black magic suffering, even if Waite himself wrote the book. Try to bend your mind around to the light."

Aleister jumped up and began pacing. "How can I do that? How can I bend myself to his limits? How will that help me?"

Allan took Aleister by the shoulder. "I will teach you the evocation of the Spirit of Taphthartharath, but this must be for the intent of good."

Aleister's eyes grew round. "It will be for good, I swear." *Good for me.*

Allan was a practitioner of white magic and decried any attempts to conjure the Devil. This Spirit of Taphthartharath is the spirit of Mercury, who was his spiritual adviser. Allan was asthmatic and chaste, never dallying with sexual partners, a contrast to Aleister's continual parade of conquests whom he would bring to the flat for one evening, never to be seen again. Usually, Allan would keep to himself in his room or the white temple, going to work as an analytical chemist for his former teacher at university on an as-needed basis. He was barely making a living, and he had been living in a room with six other people before Aleister invited him to stay with him in exchange for magic lessons.

Allan went to his room and came back with a simple white shift and handed it to him. "Put this on." Like many of his contemporaries, Allan was a former Roman Catholic, and although he no longer believed in the Mother Church, he was an ardent enthusiast for ceremony and ritual. As Aleister took off his outerwear, Allan went inside the white-magic temple and came out with a small vial.

"What is that?"

"Caapi, a mind-bending drug from Africa. We will be using it during the ceremony."

"And the Spirit of Taphthartharath will be in the room?"

"He will, but he will need some of your blood."

Allan passed into his bedroom, rummaged around for items, and then was heard in the kitchen. He came back with salt, oil, milk, and wine. He put everything between them, and they sat facing one another cross-legged. He reached into the white temple and retrieved a small crystal dagger and candle and put them on the floor with the caapi. He lit the candle and placed it to the side.

"Now we must empty our mind and heart of desire and be present. When the flame of the candle turns blue, he will be here."

Aleister leaned forward; Allan opened the vial, motioned Aleister to open his mouth, and took the dropper and placed two drops on his tongue. Allan lifted both hands upwards, breathing deeply. Aleister was mesmerized by the proceedings and started to feel his heart beat faster.

"Magic is the divinity of man conquered by science in union with faith; the true Magi are Men-Gods, in virtue of their intimate union with the divine principle."

Immediately the candle flame turned blue.

"On this day we are assembled together for the purpose of evoking unto visible appearance the Spirit of Taphthartharath. And before we can proceed further in an operation of so great danger, it is necessary that we should invoke that divine Aid and

Assistance, without which our work would indeed be futile and of no avail. Let us kneel and pray. From Thy hands, O Lord, cometh all good!"

They both knelt, then prostrated themselves on the floor, their hands stretched out before them.

"O thou Great Potent Spirit Taphthartharath, I do command and very potently conjure thee by the Majesty of Thoth, the Great God, Lord of Amena, King and Lord Eternal of the Magic of Light."

They both lifted their heads up. Something sliced Aleister's face. He touched his temple, and a drip of blood trickled down.

"He is here," Allan whispered.

A pool of water surrounded them. Could this be a pool of magic? The minute Aleister reached his bloody hand to touch the magic water, it disappeared.

CHAPTER SIXTEEN

Lyceum Electricity

Spying through a crack in the castle scenery, Pamela concentrated on Ellen and Mr. Irving. They were lit by the soft glow of limelight in the center of the stage of the Lyceum Theatre, the audience rapt during this climactic scene in *Macbeth*. Even from the side view of the stage, Pamela could see Ellen's famous beetle dress, the thousands of iridescent beetle wings shimmering in the globed light of the stage. Mr. Irving wore a very ornate crown and a tartan tunic with a belt shaped like an ouroboros, a snake biting its own tail. He held Ellen's hands as though they were praying, both standing stock-still as they listened to the sound effects of thunder.

Standing next to Edy, Pamela couldn't help but notice that her own armor was wider and at least a foot shorter. They were queued up with the rest of the extras lined up next to a primitive electrical light unit, waiting for their entrance. Pamela was the closest to the light and ran her finger over the socket, a blue current running up and down the chain mail of her costume.

Macbeth was the first show they had been cast in together since the Lyceum troupe had returned to London after touring for almost two months. Things had changed a lot since they had come back from being on the road. Edy's younger brother, Gordon, now lived with Ellen, making Pamela feel more like a trespasser while she stayed with her. The sheer size of the theatre company had grown, and Pamela no longer felt the intimacy she'd felt with Bram, Edy, or Ellen. Some cast and crew didn't even know who William Terriss was, that he was the next in line to play leading men, after Mr. Irving, of course. And now that Pamela lived in London without her parents she hadn't even heard from her distant Colman or Smith cousins in Pimlico, where she was born. The only member of her family she still communicated with regularly was her Grandmother Colman, in America, and Uncle Samuel, a painter taking a world tour, whom she had never met in person.

During the tour, Pamela and Edy had been roommates and best of companions, with Ellen acting as a sort of mother to Pamela. Edy was loathe to dine out using her mother's name, so she went by the name Edy Craig, Craig being the name of her father, whom she rarely saw, even though Ellen was friendly with all her former lovers, much to Henry Irving's dismay. But Edy seemed to be disappearing inside herself lately. Maybe it was the pressure of all the different jobs she and Pamela had to juggle to earn rent money: designing costumes, printing menus and illustrating books, performing for parties and soirees. But even with all these activities, they did not earn much more than their small salaries with the Lyceum Theatre.

Edy noticed Pamela playing with the socket's blue flame as it raced over her costume. She whispered, "Pixie, doesn't that hurt?"

Pamela, engrossed by the small blue flame, barely moved. "No, Edy, watch. If you touch this metal part, you can see. Blue flames mean a ghost is near."

"Pixie, that can't be good for you!"

"Try it, it only burns a little. Here, I'll show you," Pamela said, reaching once more for the blue flame. She bumped into a principal actor standing in the wings waiting to go on in the lane marked for major actors. He turned to look at her.

Satish Monroe, Mr. Irving's latest find, was a very handsome Negro. Beautiful and impressive, with a booming voice, he was magnetic. His parents, from the West Indies, had escaped from America during the Civil War and brought him up to study Shakespeare in London. He was dressed as Banquo, wearing an elaborate crown, a beautiful doublet, and an earring. He steadied Pamela as she almost fell.

"Did you feel a jolt of electricity, little one?" Satish asked quietly.

"I . . . think . . . I'm . . ."

Edy and Pamela had watched him during the rehearsals and were eager to know more about him. It wasn't every day that a Black actor performed at the Lyceum, much less one playing a major scene with Henry Irving. They'd heard Mr. Irving say that not since Edwin Booth had he seen such a talent.

Edy pinched Pamela under her arm, one of the few places the armor didn't cover. "I think she's feeling electricity now," Edy said dryly.

Satish smiled at the two girls and whispered to them, "This new electricity is nothing to play with. You'd best beware. There's enough magic here tonight, what with this play."

Pamela came closer to him. "Are you Jamaican?"

Satish smiled broadly. "Ah, little girl, more class than that. Close. Tobago. How is it you know Jamaica?"

Pamela looked at him, suddenly homesick, missing the warm smiles and big laughs from Miss Jones.

"I lived there with my mother and father."

"Do you remember anything about it?" Satish asked.

Pamela suddenly remembered a Jamaican singsong:

Once on a time in Slingo Town
Each child was born a poet
Dashed were his wings when older got
Alas! He didn't know it
And so we glided o'er the sea.

Satish's smile lit up. "You are a little star," he murmured.

Pamela leaned forward, her armor plates scraping against one another with a grinding sound. "Pardon?"

"I haven't heard that poem in many years." He looked down at her. Finding the chain underneath his doublet, he pulled it over his head and showed her the pendant that rested in his hand. It was a large five-pointed yellow star set in Mali garnet, outlined in black.

"This is of the air, little one. It will protect you."

He poured the chain and pendant into her hand as her eyes grew wide. She mouthed the words, *Thank you.*

Satish winked at her and went onstage for his entrance. She picked up the chain and placed it inside her left glove, clutching it tightly.

Mr. Lovejoy, the stage manager, suddenly raised the checkered flag, the cue for the extras to make their entrance. Edy and Pamela stood in the compressed line of soldiers, lowered the visors on their helmets, and joined the formation of the troops shuffling onstage. They made their promenade silently as the other actors shouted out their lines. Five minutes later, they scampered backstage for the next scene, another promenade after the battle. Done with their crossovers, Pamela rushed to the side of the stage and watched the end of the scene, Mr. Irving's monologue about remorse.

Edy left to go to her mother's dressing room, and Pamela flattened herself against the wall. Her next entrance wasn't for another fifteen minutes.

She watched Mr. Irving exit the stage, his chest puffed out and head held back, his Macbeth fierce and full of energy. The minute he and Ellen came offstage, he dashed to his quick-change room. Pamela could see him throw himself in the chair from her perch. The quick-change room was a small chamber along the backstage wall and was fitted out with an oval rug, a mirror, and a vanity. A dresser escorted Mr. Irving's fox terrier, Fussie, from down the hall into the chamber, and it scampered to Mr. Irving and jumped on his lap. He scratched the little dog's head while his tail twirled. Ellen and Bram made their way over to Mr. Irving's room and petted the little dog in concert. Pamela giggled watching Fussie become the touchstone for everyone near Mr. Irving.

They all took a moment to bathe the dog in caresses. Mr. Irving sighed and looked at his dearest companions.

"Ah, Fussie, ready for the battle scene?" Mr. Irving asked as he was handed a cup of tea by the dresser. "Miss Terry, the cuts for the last scene worked the best, don't you think, m'dear? Mr. Stoker, will Mr. Lovejoy have those limelights ready to be tested after the show tonight?"

Bram looked reassuringly at Mr. Irving. "Yes, Lovejoy will be prompt this time with the cue. And we will rehearse again when the curtain comes down."

Bram walked out to where the technicians were readying the limelight. Ellen leaned against the chair nuzzling Fussie. Pamela strained to catch what Ellen was saying.

"How can you rehearse tonight after the show?" Ellen asked. "You look like a great famished wolf as it is."

Mr. Irving put his tea down, the lines around his mouth deepening. "You are not like anyone else; you see things with such lightning quickness." He looked around and then quickly kissed her hand. "I'm only confused by one thing and disturbed by another, that is all."

Ellen straightened his crown, which tilted to the side. He looked up at her with a slight, sad smile. She laid her hand on his. "There, my Lord. Your crown, although heavy, is now straight."

Ellen and Mr. Irving almost embraced, but Fussie started to whine, jealous. Mr. Irving saw a signal outside the room from the stage managers and rose to make his next entrance. Pamela could see by the lamp in the room that Ellen had tears in her eyes.

Standing behind the curtain, Mr. Irving readied himself for his entrance. In a whisper he asked, "Mr. Stoker, all set?" Seeing Fussie still seated in his room, he motioned across the expanse of the backstage, "Go on, Fussie, exit!"

Fussie scampered off down the hall to his dressing room unescorted. Ellen left his quick-change room, wiping her eyes, Pamela making herself smaller so that Ellen didn't see her spying on them.

The curtain parted and Mr. Irving strode energetically to center stage, addressing an unseen spirit downstage. Ellen, Edy, and Pamela watched him from upstage center, peeking out from behind the upstage curtain.

Mr. Irving as Macbeth watched the spirit float by in front of him. He then spun around, with his back to the audience, and saw it materialize before him. It was Satish, dressed as Banquo, flying on a harness above him.

In his deep rumbling voice, Mr. Irving railed at the specter:

O, treachery!—Fly, good Fleance, fly, fly, fly!
Thou mayst revenge.—O slave!

With those words, he then charged at Satish, who started to fly upwards, the unseen cables pulled and weighted from backstage. Satish flew up and out of sight, then rested on the catwalk. As Harvey went to unharness him, he gave a thumbs-up to Lovejoy at the deck level. Then he saluted Pamela and Edy, who stood watching his every move.

On stage, Mr. Irving planted himself with one hand raised, the other down.

Avaunt! And quit my sight! Let the earth hide thee!
Thy bones are marrowless, thy blood is cold;
Thou hast no speculation in those eyes
Which thou dost glare with.

As she watched Mr. Irving's scene, Pamela's gloved hand lifted toward the stage. She felt a strange warm sensation streaming through her palm. She was clenching Satish's pendant inside her glove. *Was the star necklace heating up?*

Looking to the stage, Mr. Irving rose, his black mustache framing his mouth, his ornate eight-pound crown gleaming, his large eyes dark and flashing. He was a perfect demon/god—the sum of roles he loved to play, the fallen angel. Then all at once, he was floating. He was frozen and yet moving in the gaslight. The gas from the lights made his image undulate until he was a wavering mirage. Pamela alone saw that he was floating as she had been floating with Maud, listening to the tale of Nera. An actor from onstage suddenly ran by her and handed her Henry's helmet. She looked back to Mr. Irving, now standing on the stage, not floating.

She remembered her task, to run to Mr. Irving's quick-change room and preset the helmet for the next act. His dresser was busy on the other side of the offstage area with the end-of-show preparations. As she bent over the table with the helmet, her foot gave out beneath her, and she felt herself pitch backward, falling and hitting the wall of the little room. Sitting on the floor, she shook her head, and then tried to stand in her confining armor. Then she noticed something different against the wall. It was a hidden compartment with a door popped open. She must have hit the latch when she fell.

She came closer. It was like a little altar with offerings. Pamela recognized most of the items: a burnt ebony wand, the Bertrand sword, and a stage prop chalice from *The Cup*. All of these things were familiar to her from her time on tour with the

Lyceum: the wand, the sword, the cup. But why were they all together on this hidden shelf? Maybe they were there to protect Mr. Irving? But there was something missing—Pamela could feel it. She needed to add the star pendant Satish had given her. She pulled off her glove and poured out the necklace onto the little altar.

Listening to the music of the scene on stage, and seeing she had time, she quickly made her way out to the prop table, grabbed her sketchbook, and ran back. She sat cross-legged on the floor and started to draw the symbols Mr. Irving had taught her, the Egyptian signs of protection: a pelican, a pair of walking legs, and a circle with a dot in the center.

She would add this drawing to the altar's collection, so in addition to the wand, sword, and cup, there would be a star. All the symbols together would protect Mr. Irving.

Bram passed by and saw her sitting on the floor in her armor, her gloves off, drawing on a sketch pad. Quietly he stood next to her, looking at her artwork. Egyptian drawings. Then he noticed the sapphire star next to the wand, sword and cup already on the altar; the magician's suite all assembled. Bram knew immediately: It was time for her to meet the Golden Dawn.

CHAPTER SEVENTEEN

Three Witches

In her bedroom, Pamela took care to dress in a more subdued manner. Tonight, there were no coral beads threaded in her hair, orange blouses or purple shawls, only a simple lilac dress with a cerulean-blue sash. Ellen insisted that she wear this borrowed outfit to help advertise Edy's new business, a costume rental shop. When Pamela joined Ellen and Edy downstairs to catch the cab, she realized her dress coordinated with their blue and purple gowns.

Bram met them at the entrance to Ada Leverson's parlor. "Good, you're on time, Miss Terry, Miss Craig." Taking Pamela aside as they walked, Bram lowered his voice. "I'll bring up the position with the Golden Dawn later. First, let's make a good impression." He shepherded the women to the open door.

Ada was surrounded by four men, none of whom seemed to be her husband. Pamela vaguely remembered meeting this quartet at Watkins Books after her Annancy Tales performance.

"Mrs. Leverson, may I present Miss Ellen Terry," Bram said as Ada and Ellen shook hands. The men lined up to kiss Ellen's hand.

"So pleased you've come to this recital, Miss Terry," Ada said, fanning herself. "Here are your devoted fans, Dr. William Felkin, Mr. Edward Waite, Mr. Samuel Mathers, and Dr. Westcott."

The four men excitedly attended to Ellen, who was gracious and gay, almost flirtatious, while Ada turned her attention to Edy and Pamela.

Bram brought both girls forward. "May I present Miss Edy Craig, Miss Terry's daughter, and Miss Pamela Colman Smith, Miss Terry's protégé."

The men stopped fawning over Ellen for a minute and took in Edy and Pamela.

Pamela cocked her head and smiled. "Dr. Felkin, Dr. Westcott, Mr. Waite, Mr. Mathers. Happy to see you again." Pamela noticed Mathers bit his lip; both Felkin and Waite wore glasses, and none seemed particularly happy to meet her.

The men politely bowed, and Ada's attention went to guests at the door.

"Gentlemen, perhaps you will escort these beautiful ladies to their seats?" Ada said, more a command than a question as she pivoted to her new arrivals.

Bram walked Edy in with Dr. Westcott and Ellen threaded her arms between Felkin's and Mathers's, leaving Pamela to walk in with Waite. Edward Waite was a short man with sandy-colored hair and blue eyes that watered behind round glasses. He reminded Pamela of her old postal clerk in Jamaica. He gestured for her to walk beside him, and Pamela took in a deep breath of the heady scent of flowers, cologne, and musky oil lamps as they entered the parlor. Ada's receiving room had been set up with five rows of seats, and a grand piano on a small stage was awash with lilies and lit candelabras.

The group sat themselves down in two rows, Ellen and her male admirers in one row; Pamela, Bram, and Edy in another. At least she was seated with Bram and Edy.

Pamela picked up a program off her seat before sitting. "Well, Mr. Waite, I've heard this singer, Miss Strong, is divine."

"'Divine' is a burdensome word, Miss Smith," Waite said, turning around in his seat, with a condescending tone. "I would apply it sparingly."

A clicking sound started off in her head. *What is this? Did Waite set this off?* The clicking grew louder. Pamela took off her gloves and rubbed her forehead.

In the row ahead of them, Mathers turned around in his seat and laughed in great snorts. "Divine? Ha! Divinity! Ahhhh . . ." He managed to stop his hacking laugh and took a deep breath. Looking at Edy's startled look, he continued, "Yes, yes, you are right, I am not accustomed to s-s-speaking in society."

Felkin, his hair gleaming like a polished stone to match his exquisitely groomed beard, leaned over to Mathers.

"That's all right, Mathers, speaking in general isn't your forte," Felkin said.

Pamela caught Edy's eye and arched an eyebrow. Edy gave a slight harrumph in response, and the two girls studied the program for tonight's recital. If this was the group Bram wanted Pamela to work with, so far they seemed fairly unpleasant.

"Edward," Bram said, "Miss Smith is the artist I was telling you about. The one who understands symbols and Egyptian writing."

Waite finally looked at Pamela with interest. "Really?"

"Yes, I am a novice," Pamela said, her interior sounds now recognizable as typewriter keys striking. "But I am an enthusiastic student of Egyptian hieroglyphics. Symbols from all great cultures intrigue me."

"Where did you study?" Waite asked quickly.

"Pratt Institute in Brooklyn, with Arthur Wesley Dow."

Waite grunted. "And you say you understand the Egyptian symbols? Our group is just now studying them."

She tried not to blink each time Waite spoke, but the typing noise grew louder on each word.

Ellen turned around and noticed Pamela's strained expression and reached out to pat her hand. "Mr. Waite, what exactly is your group about? Bram has not been entirely clear on its purpose."

The men stared at Ellen and shifted slightly, an uncomfortable air of calculation hanging between them.

Dr. Westcott finally smiled and replied, "Phenomena. The world of the unknown."

Waite started to relax and joined in. "Yes, metaphysical studies."

Pamela saw Waite jerk in his chair as someone approached. The typing sounds stopped.

A tall, dark-haired young man with glowering brown eyes approached the end of the aisle and stared at Westcott and Felkin.

"Aleister Crowley," Bram said, standing. "Let me introduce you to Miss Smith here. You will have many subjects in common with—"

"Magic!" he said loudly to the men. "I want access to the magic rituals you are exploring."

Pamela laughed her loud laugh, which disconcerted the others, all except Bram and Ellen. The clinking noise in her head was now gone. Perhaps it was due to the energy overtaken by this overdressed young man. He was handsome and animated, stirring up energy as he assessed Ellen, looking her over intensely.

"Mr. Crowley, let me introduce you to Ellen Terry," Bram said dryly.

Aleister performed an elegant bow, a dip at the waist, and came up to take her hand and kiss it.

"The famous Miss Ellen Terry, I am honored," Aleister said, looking into her eyes as she remained seated.

"Mr. Crowley, pleased to make your acquaintance," Ellen replied, without her usual effervescence, motioning to Edy and

Pamela. "This is my daughter, Edy Craig, and my discovery, Miss Smith."

"*Your* discovery, Miss Ellen?" Bram teased. "I thought I brought her to you?"

Before Ellen or Pamela could say something in return, Ada walked to the front of the room with an older woman who walked with a cane. The cane caught Pamela's eye; it had a dragon's head with rubies for eyes.

"Who is that?" Pamela asked.

"That is Annie Horniman, richest woman in England," Bram whispered. "And, if I have my way, she is going to fund your project with the Golden Dawn."

Before Pamela could ask any more questions about the project, the men rose from their seats and dashed to Ada's side.

While Ellen and Edy huddled together, Aleister approached, trying to get Ellen's attention.

He finally looked down at Pamela. "So, you're a Smith, are you? Fairly common name, isn't it?"

"More universal than common, I think," Pamela replied cheerfully.

Aleister's head whipped up as he spotted the empty chair next to Miss Annie Horniman and he bolted to her side. Pamela watched Aleister introduce himself to Miss Horniman and sit down next to her as Bram looked on with crossed arms.

The last stragglers came in, and Ada sent the men back to their seats and stood in front of the stage. In plummy tones, she announced, "Welcome, ladies and gentlemen. I am pleased to introduce our American star, Miss Susan Strong!"

Susan Strong entered the room and stood on the stage next to the piano. A woman in her late twenties of considerable girth, she wore a loose gown, her flowing blonde hair reaching her waist, like a Roman goddess. An accompanist, an older woman, followed and arranged the sheet music at the piano as Miss Strong closed her eyes and breathed heavily. Pamela glanced at the program: Venus's aria from Tannhäuser was first. Pamela watched Miss Strong open her eyes, so calm and confident. With a wave of her hand, she gestured for the music to start.

As the first notes sailed, all fanning and rustling ceased. The room stilled, mesmerized by her trills and runs. Two more arias from Wagner followed. When the last note ebbed away, there was a moment of silence. Miss Strong bowed her head, and the room exploded in applause.

Aleister jumped from his seat and extended his arm, leading the soprano down the steps to the now standing crowd. "Here is my next Venus," he said, holding up her hand in triumph.

Ellen turned back and gave a look to Pamela and Edy. "Missed my chance," she whispered to the two girls and they giggled.

Miss Strong continued to acknowledge the room until Ada approached and kissed both cheeks. She dislodged Miss Strong's hand from Aleister and presented it to a dapper man with a handlebar mustache.

"Who is that?" Pamela asked Ellen.

"The composer, Giacomo Puccini," Ellen answered.

Ada gave a short round of applause for Puccini, motioning for her guests to follow her lead. After a few moments, she cut it off, like a conductor leading an orchestra.

"Ah, Susan, so few missed notes!" Ada said loud enough for all the room to hear. "Such tone! Such bravado! And now, ladies and gentlemen, let us move to the dining room for our buffet supper."

Pamela and her companions stood to join the exodus to leave the room when Miss Horniman appeared next to her. Bram was about to introduce her when Aleister popped up. "Miss Horniman, may I escort you to supper?"

Miss Horniman gave a resigned look to Bram and pointedly peered at Pamela as she took his arm and walked on with the rest. Aleister escorted Miss Horniman with his elbows jutting out to make sure no one else came near. He looked back at

Dr. Westcott and gave him a haughty smile. The three other men looked at him with amusement and derision.

Pamela watched Westcott turn to the other men and mouth, "Ass."

After the buffet supper, Ellen was busy talking to almost every woman in attendance. They all had daughters and nieces who wanted to make a career on the stage. They fawned over her, asking her where she got her clothes. She answered, "Isn't this a charming frock? Edy Craig Clothes, she's the cleverest proprietor of a costume rental business." Only then did she reach into her purse and hand out Edy's calling cards.

As for Edy, she and Pamela hid near the servants' entrance to the dining room, obscured by the heavy drapes. They were both nursing a second glass of wine and smiled at one another in their private corner.

Familiar voices were heard on the other side of the curtains: the dreary men from Watkins Books. Pamela and Edy stationed themselves in the folds of the curtains so as not to be seen.

Pamela could tell it was Felkin, the very tall man with the shiny hair who was speaking first.

"Now, if the three witches would only open their moneybags."

Pamela and Edy looked at one another wide-eyed.

"Really, Dr. Felkin! Witches?" Waite's thin voice replied.

"Come on, man," Felkin answered. "What else would they spend their money on? A Jewess, a spinster tea heiress, and an American would-be society singer? They need us more than we need them."

It hadn't occurred to Pamela that Ada was Jewish, or that Miss Horniman's money came from Horniman's Tea, or that Miss Strong was a would-be society singer.

"The G-g-golden Dawn would be a good investment for them," Mathers added.

They drifted away still talking amongst themselves.

"Witches?" Pamela asked Edy. "Do they mean real witches?"

"Nonsense," answered Edy, taking a healthy sip of wine. "That is what men call women when they have things men want. Shall we rescue Mother?"

They stepped out from behind the curtains to almost bump into Ada with her performer, Miss Strong, and Miss Horniman, flanked by Bram and Aleister. Bram motioned Pamela over as Edy made a quick jog to join her mother.

Miss Horniman extended her hand to Pamela. "Miss Smith, I've heard such excellent things about you from Mr. Stoker. We have an opportunity with our Golden Dawn group that we are setting up that we would love to discuss with you."

"We? Who is the 'we' in this Golden Dawn?" Felkin asked, as he and his compatriots drifted up to the group.

Aleister licked his lips and smiled. "Why, it's a magical group that will evolve from your fumbled beginnings. This will be an official group of Aleister Crowley's Golden Dawn."

Waite stomped his feet in exasperation and Mathers gurgled.

Ada inserted herself in the center of the group and looked at Aleister. "That's not what we agreed to, Mr. Crowley."

"I should think not," Waite said, his rheumy eyes darting amongst the group. "Could there be anything worse than a Golden Dawn according to Mr. Crowley and his obsession with magical sources? Disastrous!"

Aleister stood next to Ada. "Mrs. Leverson, I thought I was to be one of the founding fathers. With my classical training at Cambridge in Latin, physics, and languages, I will bring high academic standards with me."

Waite and Westcott started talking over Ada, and Mathers and Felkin argued between themselves while Bram patted Pamela on the back.

"What would I be doing with these people?" Pamela asked Bram through gritted teeth.

"You'll see," Bram answered back tersely.

Mathers repeated, "W-w-why . . . W-w-what . . . ?" over and over until finally Ada clapped her hands to restore order.

"Now, Aleister," Miss Horniman said, holding up her dragon cane. "Your role will not exactly be as founding father."

Aleister's eyes widened, and he opened his mouth in protest.

"Mr. Crowley, we think your proposition of a magical research group an interesting one," Ada said. "The three of us, Miss Horniman, Miss Strong and myself, would be willing to subsidize the headquarters and research for your team in the manner that you have suggested for the trial term of one year."

The Golden Dawn Chiefs exhaled and smiled. Dr. Westcott leaned over to shake Ada's hand. "Oh, Mrs. Leverson, that is so generous of—"

Ada cut him off with a wave of her gloved hand. "The condition we require is that one of us three, Miss Horniman, Miss Strong, or myself, will be in training with you to be part of the 'founding mothers,' as it were."

Miss Horniman stepped forward and energetically added, "I will be a most generous founding mother."

Sputtering, Dr. Westcott replied, "You know, Annie, really, there are other ways that we can incorporate your participation than—"

"The curriculum for the study of the Golden Dawn," Miss Horniman replied, "will be set by Golden Chiefs, which would be one of the three of us. Oh and you, Dr. Westcott, with your fellow teammates, Dr. Felkin, Waite, and Mr. Crowley."

Dr. Westcott rumbled a growl.

"This is our money and these are our terms, Dr. Westcott," Miss Horniman said coolly. "Or shall I be calling you by your nickname, Wynn?"

Miss Horniman held his gaze until he looked away. After a tense moment, with only Ada's fan moving, he finally laughed. "Mrs. Leverson, Miss Horniman, Miss Strong, we accept your conditions with gratitude and enthusiasm."

The ladies congratulated the men with handshakes and smiles. Miss Strong started singing the aria from "Ride of the Valkyries" as Bram squeezed Pamela's elbow, steering her next to Miss Horniman.

"But Miss Horniman, what would be our titles?" Waite asked. "And what projects are you funding?"

"Well, our first project will be a school with a curriculum based on the esoteric," she answered, looking straight into Pamela's eyes. "We'll have degrees of study for every subject. And our first project from this combined knowledge will be under the guidance of Miss Terry's protégé, Miss Smith. Mr. Stoker has been telling us about her gift of second sight and her understanding of symbols."

Aleister coughed violently and turned to Ada. "Bring her on as what? Miss Fairy Tales?"

Bram stood even straighter. "Miss Smith will be in line to be groomed for the position of a Golden Dawn Chief."

Pamela stared at Bram. *How long has he been planning this? Why didn't he tell me?*

"What?!" The men exploded in head shaking and jaw waggling.

Miss Horniman stood next to Bram and put an arm around him. "Yes, gentlemen, stage blood is thicker than water, and I've been working with Mr. Stoker on his *Undead* play. And my financial contribution to your group is earmarked for the creation of a tarot deck by Miss Pamela Colman Smith and Mr. Waite. We will discuss the details later."

Mr. Waite blushed beet red. Pamela couldn't tell if this was in pleasure or fury.

Aleister stood open-mouthed and stared at Pamela. She lifted her wine glass in a simple cheer to him, and he turned and stomped away. Pamela had never seen grown men succumb to a challenge from women this way.

Ellen and Edy drifted over, and Pamela felt Ellen's reassuring arms around her waist.

"Bram said an opportunity would be presented to you tonight," Ellen whispered. "Are you pleased?"

Pamela looked over to see Bram placating all the outraged men.

Ada stood nearby with the warmest expression Pamela had seen all evening. She looked absolutely smug.

"Miss Terry, we're so happy to be sponsoring Miss Smith, your discovery," Ada said. "We understand she is quite the empath to unseen vibrations. But first, I must tell you what a wonder it was to see your *Merchant of Venice* the other night," she continued in lingering tones. "Your Mr. Irving plays Shylock at the Lyceum like no other. I'm not sure it is a credit to my people, but I most enjoyed your Portia."

Ellen laughed. "Yes, my Portia! The loudest Portia in a trial scene ever witnessed. Mr. Irving's portrayal consists of the most quiet and dignified opponent. That left me to bellow my lines or our scenes would be nothing but breathless whispers."

"Yes, I could barely hear him," Ada said, her eyes alight with laughter. "But what an interesting Shylock—a victim and not some hated moneylender. He gave us a Jew devoted to his sacred tribe and ancient law."

Pamela asked Ada, "Do you think that people will understand that interpretation?"

Ada looked at Pamela. "To my family, this interpretation is magical. We learn by example that his Shylock is most vulnerable. It may restore the reputation of my people. As an empath, you understand how important symbols are?"

"Yes, my Pixie has been studying Egyptian symbols with Henry Irving for as long as I've known her," Ellen answered. "On the train in America, Henry would grill Pixie for hours on end."

Miss Strong looked up from her conversation with Miss Horniman and came closer. "You're American, like me?" she asked Pamela.

"I was born here in London, Miss Strong, although my parents and grandparents were American, from Brooklyn, actually. My grandfather, Cyrus Smith, was mayor of Brooklyn. Before the Civil War, of course."

Miss Strong started to laugh and clap her hands. "I thought you looked familiar. What are the odds of that! My father was Congressman Dennis Strong, also a mayor of Brooklyn."

Pamela embraced Susan. She was American like her parents and Brooklyn family! Ellen and Ada smiled at each other as the girls babbled about Brooklyn trains and Manhattan ferries.

Just as she was about to ask Miss Strong where her family lived, a low rumbling started shaking her. It started with tremors at her feet, and soon her hands were fluttering. Glancing at the others, she could tell none of them were feeling the waves convulsing her. *Am I having a fit?*

She turned away from the group, and a dark shot of pain pressed in on her head. She gulped as her throat closed up. Trying not to panic, she scanned the room for Bram, Ellen, Edy— someone. They were all far away. The noise in the room continued, but she was suspended in place, a web of agony and paralysis. The noise dimmed. It was hard to breathe; something was constricting her lungs, and her rib cage struggled to expand. She tried to open her mouth, but it was not responding; her hand wouldn't lift from her side. It was a nightmare from which she couldn't wake. The clacking sounds of typewriters moved within her again.

Suddenly, Mr. Waite was by her side. She perceived that he was standing between herself and Aleister. The clicking was now back, building to a loud roar. She could barely see, but a stack of bricks emerged midair in her sightline. They surrounded Aleister, encasing him as if he were in a brick cocoon. Pamela could see Waite's hand directing the position of the bricks, the sound of clicking growing louder.

All at once, the pressure on Pamela's head and throat vanished. She gasped and almost toppled over. Mathers, the stuttering one, was by her side holding her up. The bricks were now like a fixed dome around Aleister, the rest of the room seemingly oblivious to it. A rustling sound crinkled behind her, and she swiveled to see Dr. Westcott throw a ball of light from his hand to the dome. The bricks crumbled. Aleister came stumbling out of the pile, his face full of fury.

Mathers stood in front of Pamela and held his hand out to Aleister. His squeaky voice was now the rumbling sound from earlier. Aleister was thrown into the air and shaken like a rat being throttled by a cat. He was dropped, very roughly. He picked himself up from the floor and dusted himself off. Turning to see if the rest of the room noticed, he realized that this too went unmarked by the crowd. After smoothing his hair, he sauntered to a tray of drinks.

Mathers turned to Pamela and grinned slyly. "M-m-meow."

Pamela's jaw dropped open as she scanned the room. People were laughing, drinking, and carrying on as if nothing had happened. They were totally unaware of the magic that had just occurred. Pamela relaxed, looking into the faces of the four Golden Dawn members flanking her. A little dot of light burned within her brain. On impulse, she sent her light to them, thanking them, the strange men who had just saved her. All four nodded to her when the pulse of light reached them.

Their lips did not move, but she could hear a voice say very distinctly: "Tell no one!" Then, calmly, they turned and walked away, back to the group of laughing ladies. Bram, in conversation with Annie Horniman, caught her eye and lifted his finger. She was to be silent about what just happened.

From the sideboard, Aleister, furious and panting, clutched his wine glass. He downed his drink in one gulp and glared at Pamela. She looked straight back at him. In spite of his best attempts to intimidate her, she *would* create this tarot deck. Pamela had never seen anyone look at her with such undisguised malice.

PART III

TAROT
INCARNATIONS

CHAPTER EIGHTEEN

SECRETS OF THE VAULT

Aleister walked with a swagger up to Mark Masons' Hall on Euston Road, his back only mildly twinging from his mishap at Ada's. It was right before Lent, and the damp, fertile scent of bulbs and blooms wrestled with the earth's festering essence. Right now, he was waging the same war, trying to grow beyond the decay that surrounded him. Just as he had to fight against his mother's repressive morality, and struggle at Cambridge against the old guard and their outdated ideas, here his skirmishes were with these older occultists with their limited vision.

He took the stairs in giant strides. Once in the headquarters' open room on the second floor, he reveled in light streaming in through the four large windows, tables stacked with books, boxes of pens, inkwells, pencils, a globe, and maps pinned to the wall. Coats and briefcases lay scattered about. It was as if his chums were about to burst through the doors at any minute and start arguing about the latest controversy in class.

Aleister peeled off his coat, threw down his large satchel of books, and spotted several newspapers on a table. Fleet Street rags filled with "Jack The Ripper" headlines. *Butcher Apron Killer on the Loose,* one read. Another had a sketch of a victim on the cover. Aleister picked it up. He recognized Martha Tabram, his mother's former kitchen maid. The one who gave him cinnamon rolls and a decent half hour in bed. As he read the article, he felt totally unaffected, as if a mangy cat was the killer's victim and not the woman who fed him and made love with him. She was just an animal, a subpar example of a life who didn't understand how to live. She was merely a creature grubbing out a meager existence, dependent on others.

Laughter and music from an adjoining room startled him. For a moment he was furious that there could be levity during these thoughts of his.

But he called out, "Horniman?"

He walked to a door at the opposite end of the room and opened it. Inside lay the eight-foot-tall vault, a wooden chamber built according to a magical formula. A ladder along one side held Annie Horniman, perched with one foot planted on the bottom rung, smoking a cigar. She wore a red silk gown with silver threaded flowers. Before her sat three bullies from the mischief night at Ada's: Waite, Mathers, and Felkin. They looked up from their cigars, the smoke curling in lazy loops in the air. A woman with her hair tied up, Grecian style, wore the suffragette uniform of a blouse and skirt, and sat on a chair playing a loose tune on a hand harp. Everyone turned their attention from a beautiful woman on the ladder above Annie Horniman, painting symbols on the vault. Two attractive women in the group—this beat third-year metrics class by a yard.

Stepping down from the ladder, Annie took Aleister by the elbow and guided him to stand in front of the smirking men, still seated. "Mr. Crowley, you remember Mr. Waite, Mr. Mathers, Dr. Felkin."

The men eyed him coldly and muttered hellos while Aleister stared at the beautiful girl on the ladder.

"Oh, and Mr. Crowley, this is Mina Bergson painting away," Annie said with a wave. "We were at art school together. I was talented, although not as talented as our Miss Mina."

Mina was applying Egyptian hieroglyphics with a careful, steady hand. Mina was delicate and tiny, with curly, light brown hair and bright blue eyes. She wore a beige painter's muslin smock, smeared with bright colors. Giving him a cursory look and nod, she went back to painting immediately.

The harpist stopped playing her annoying tune and rose to greet him. She was tall and stunning in a more robust way, shaking his hand with decided firmness.

"Hello, I'm Florence Farr and I will be your tutor," Florence said, her voice husky and thrilling.

Ah, Florence Farr. She had recently recruited Aleister's roommate, the Adept Allan Bennett, and he had been able to invoke a spirit in the vault. According to Allan, this was the first successful attempt by a Golden Dawn member to conjure magic. Before that, there had been a lot of fruitless activity there by the three Level Two adepts, the Neophyte idiots sitting on the floor. Word was that they would emerge from the vault with bruises, black eyes, and cut hands but no magical manifestations.

"When was Mr. Crowley's tutor decided?" Felkin asked, scowling.

"It was decided, Dr. Felkin, by me, your patron," Annie replied. "It will be Florence's responsibility to teach you, Aleister, what you will need to know to pass the Neophyte level."

It seems this Annie would try to dominate any social setting. At least with Ada Leverson, Aleister could use his beautiful manners and learned Cambridge accent to charm her.

Aleister sputtered and crossed his arms, staring intensely at Annie.

"As a recent graduate of Cambridge," Aleister said, giving a strained smile, "I am accustomed to being tutored, but never by a woman. If anything, I should be tutoring her in languages!"

Florence smiled. "Ah, Mr. Crowley, how many languages do you speak?"

Somehow this devil had perceived this was a sore subject. He had been unable to learn the four languages Cambridge required in order to qualify for diplomatic service positions. That was the career he saw for himself. Even though he'd hired younger students to translate his Greek assignments, he was hopeless if he alone had to translate text. His French, German, or Italian consisted of what food he would like to order and what was the wine like.

"I know the three languages of the poets," Aleister said, as the men snorted.

"Ah, which three?"

"Miss Farr, I'm a poet, and I like my lies the way my mother used to make them."

Waite and Felkin laughed, but Mathers frowned and shook his head.

"N-n-not impressive," Mathers said.

Florence smiled, her large, expressive eyes luminous and her smile putting Aleister at ease.

Florence coaxed Aleister, "Mr. Crowley, as a poet, surely you know French. I will test you on the Egyptian language so that you can understand the magic the vault holds."

Felkin chimed in, "Florence, how many languages did that fan who followed you here speak? That fellow from Ceylon?"

"Oh, Dr. Lucien de Zilwa?" Florence asked, putting away her harp. "We also spoke French and German together, but he is also fluent in Tamil and Sinhala."

"Tamil! Sinhala! Languages you travel the world to hear," Aleister directed to Waite. "These will be the languages I will use conjuring inside the vault."

Waite crossed over to Aleister and looked up at him, his weak chin wavering. "Mr. Crowley, I'm sure if you pass your first level, you might be able to discover the secrets of the vault. Until then, it is off-limits. We have a set criteria for you to master first."

"Oh, and what is it you think I'll be studying?" Aleister said. "What languages will you be putting into those tarot cards? I suppose that vulgar Smith girl will put in some Jamaican nonsense?"

Mathers mumbled, "N-n-none of this is applicable to our studies."

Annie stood. "No, truly not. Speaking of which, we should get back to our list of new recruits, gentlemen, and what their donations to the new order of the Golden Dawn will be. Florence, could you break down the materials Mr. Crowley will be needing to study at Degree One, Neophyte level?"

Aleister's shirt collar seemed to grow tight as his heart pounded harder. Annie, Felkin, and Waite left the room. Mathers dithered around the vault, picking up the painting rags Mina had discarded.

Fine. I'll learn your drivel in a week or two and then be on to Level Two in the vault.

Florence placed her hand on his arm and led him to one of the empty chairs. In her throaty voice, she said, "Mr. Crowley, there is a first time for everything. Shall we get started?" She sat, motioning for him to sit beside her as she opened a box filled with pamphlets and books.

Collecting himself and lowering his eyes as if he were casually seeing it for the first time, he motioned to the vault.

"What is this structure here all about, really?" Aleister asked. He was damned if Allan was going to be the only one who experienced transcendent magic here.

"It will be restricted access for you until you pass your course, Crowley," Mathers said plainly.

Mina came down the ladder, and Mathers rushed over to help her. She thanked him with a smile and went out the door with her brushes and paints, Mathers following her like a hungry dog.

Once they were gone, Aleister stood up. "Restricted access? What is this vault all about? And what would this structure be used for? It seems large enough for several people."

In the silence, Florence fetched several books, then placed

them on his empty chair.

"Perhaps that is something you will be privy to once you pass Level One, Mr. Crowley."

Aleister stood closer to the painted symbols Mina had just finished.

"It is extraordinary," Aleister said to himself. "They seem to combine converged energies."

"The first step after passing the levels, which has four grades," Florence said, "is the signing of the pledge, which commits you to silence on your knowledge of the Golden Dawn." Aleister started to wander further into the vault as Florence called out to him, "You will be asked to select a motto in Latin."

"What was Miss Bergson's motto?" Aleister asked, tracing the dry paint of a falcon.

"Mina's?" Florence asked curtly. "'I never retrace my steps.'"

"Ah, a wise saying. What is your motto, Miss Florence?"

"I study Thoth, the god of wisdom and magic. Mine is 'Wisdom is given to the wise as a gift.'"

He slowly responded, "Wisdom is a gift? Not earned? And Thoth! Are you aspiring to have intercourse with the gods?"

Florence stared at Aleister and stood. "Your studies will include Sephiroth, the twenty-two paths in accordance with the Hebrew alphabet, astronomy, geomancy, and astrology." Aleister stepped away from the vault and began to walk very slowly up to Florence. "We will begin your journey from darkness into light. I am willing to take you on as a student, Mr. Crowley, but you must behave with decorum."

Aleister stood very close to Florence. He toyed with the collar of her blouse. She did not flinch away from him. "Perhaps, Miss Florence, I will take you on as my student, in your journey from light to darkness."

"Really, Mr. Crowley," Florence said.

"I've already prepared my motto. It will be 'Do what thou

wilt.' Or 'I will endure.' I can't decide; it's early days." Aleister draped his arms around Florence's neck.

"'I will endure'" seems more appropriate here," Florence said, picking up his hands and removing them.

"Oh, I have a feeling I will be doing what I will."

He held up his hand, trying to mesmerize her, but she put her hand on his and lowered it. He felt the effect of her power; it was very firm. He tried to resist, but her hand emitted a curious strength. So much so that after a few seconds he was repelled with such force that he was sprawling on the ground as she headed out the door.

CHAPTER NINETEEN

BOHEMIAN NIGHTS

The studio on the second floor of the three-story building was becoming a well-known bohemian meeting place. Edy and Pamela had arrived at the studio an hour earlier to set up. Nona Stewart, a tall dark-haired Scottish friend of Edy's, played the out-of-tune grand piano, while Edy and Pamela set up the refreshments. Pamela wore her orange duster over a green skirt, with black tassels and frills on a red turban. Edy wore what Pamela called the wallpaper dress, a dress with an obnoxious floral print, with an elaborate apron that came from the costume rack at the Lyceum Theatre.

"So, Chris is now to be Christopher, and you are not to refer to her as Miss," Edy said, setting out cheese on mismatched plates.

Pamela stared at Edy. "And so now she will answer only to Christopher?"

"Yes," she said, but it sounded more like "yeth."

Edy's lisp had only worsened with time, and Pamela saw behind her silence that something else was behind Edy's words—or lack of them. Then Pamela saw what it was.

"Edy, are you living with Christopher now?" Pamela asked, lining up the rows of wine glasses on the counter.

"Yes."

"I suppose I can no longer call her Miss Moonbeams. And Martin Shaw is now out as well? I thought you two were engaged."

"We were engaged. My mother pointed out a marriage to him would be a long period of starving along."

"Just because he's a composer?" Pamela asked, uncorking a bottle of wine.

"Just because he's a musician whose music comes first."

"Ah, but Edy, here we are trying to make money as artists too," Pamela said, reaching for another bottle. "Look at *The Green Sheaf*. That magazine isn't making money, nor are my bookplates, nor your costume renderings, nor our posters, scenic designs, or cards. And with you and Gordon starting the Pioneer Players, it seems none of us will ever be making money. But that doesn't make us less lovable."

"It's not about money, Pamela. It's about the freedom to fulfill my potential too, not just his."

Nona stopped playing and in her Scottish accent loudly called, "Do you need music for your 'Six Baked Eggs' tonight, Pixie?"

"Nona, it's 'Six Poached Eggs,' not 'Six Baked Eggs,' and the answer is no music."

"Why are you reciting your Annancy stories tonight?" Edy asked, picking up a wine glass and polishing it with her apron. "I thought you had said you weren't going to perform your Jamaican folktales any longer."

"What I said was I hoped to end my days hiring myself out as 'Gelukiezanger,' the West Indies storyteller. But I haven't been able to send money to St. Andrew for Miss Jones in over three months."

"Isn't she working there as a nanny for another family?" Edy asked.

Before Pamela could answer, a knock on the front door called.

"And don't expect me to call you Pixie tonight," Edy said, still polishing a glass. "That's my mother's nickname for you."

Poised outside the door were two young men in their twenties, both wearing glasses: Yoshio Markino, a Japanese dandy, and William Butler Yeats. Pamela recognized them both—Yoshio was an old hand at making the social rounds, while William had been at her recital of Annancy Tales at the bookstore last month. Pamela shrieked and embraced Yoshio and dragged him into the room as Nona pounded out more piano music.

"Pixie, William Butler Yeats. William, Pixie Colman Smith," Yoshio said.

"William, we met at Watkins Books," Pamela said, looking at the arrogant tilt of the young man's chin.

William started, "Miss Pamela, I enjoyed your performance—"

"Call her Pixie," Yoshio said. "None of her friends ever call her anything else."

Pamela kept her mouth straight as she took their coats.

Edy called from the kitchen, "Is it the Birds?"

Pamela called back to her, "No, it's Yoshio." She saw William. "And a William." Turning to both, she demanded, "What are you drinking?"

"Opal Hush, of course," Yoshio said, adjusting his glasses.

Edy came out of the kitchen carrying two glasses and handed them to William and Yoshio.

Yoshio took an enormous drink, then looked Edy up and down. "Miss Edy, whatever are you wearing?"

Edy gave him a slight chuck under the chin. "Yoshio. Pamela is wearing orange, green, and red—a jacket, pants, and a hat—and you are asking *me* what I'm wearing? I am wearing a dress."

"Ah, but Pixie dresses just like an English woman. You dress like a lady."

Pamela laughed. "And just how does an English woman dress?"

"English women spend all their money to wear everything—metal, stones, animal skins, dead leaves, dead birds. I would not be surprised if she picked up a dead snake in the field and wore that on herself."

There was another knock, and Pamela dashed off while Edy handed a glass to William.

A cacophony of shrieks and laughter came from the front door as well as kissing and teasing. More guests entered: Satish and Bram, Annie Horniman, Arthur Conan Doyle, and a host of other people Pamela didn't recognize. She took their coats and made them sign the guest book, and turned at the sound of another knock. Pamela opened the door and just stared at the tall figure in the hall for a moment, unable to place them. Suddenly, Pamela cried out and threw herself into the figure's arms. It was Maud Gonne, all grown up. She hadn't seen her friend in person in almost nine years. The embrace between five-foot Pamela and six-foot Maud stilled the conversation in the room for barely three seconds before the roar of socializing ticked up again.

"Maud, it's been forever! You're still so tall! How are you?"

"Yes, my young friend, it has been forever. It does my heart good to see you."

Bram came up to Maud, and they embraced. He took her aside. "Pamela, Miss Maud and myself will be plotting for Ireland's home rule for the next ten minutes," he said. "We could use a drink."

Laughing and crying at the same time, Pamela ran to get another Opal Hush from Satish, pouring out drinks and trying not to splash his elegant evening dress. "You look far too grand for our gathering, sir!" she teased him.

Ever since Satish gave her the star pendant at the theatre, it seemed as though he had been avoiding her. She wondered if he knew she'd drawn a picture of it to safeguard Mr. Irving. How could he? It was locked in Mr. Irving's properties box at the theatre.

Satish's dark eyes twinkled and he pivoted his beautiful frame, posing so she could get the full impact of his outfit. "Darling girl, it wasn't just for you and your bohemians that I wore this tonight. Earlier, I recited some of my best Shakespeare for the Green Room Club."

"And you came here afterwards! You are at the right place." Moving with Satish to join Bram, she saw Yoshio trying to edge into a conversation between Debussy and Whistler.

Pamela took him by the hand. "Yoshio, let me introduce you to Mr. Debussy and Mr. Whistler."

Once they included Yoshio, Edy charged up to her and Satish. "Pamela, the Birds need a sword. We have one in here somewhere, don't we?"

"Yes, that two-sided one hanging behind the painting over the piano," Pamela answered. "On the wall, there."

"I'll help you with that," Satish said, setting off with Edy through the mash of people.

William was suddenly by Pamela's side. "Who are the Birds? Critics?"

"Painters."

"And they need a sword for?"

Pamela smiled. "Well, the Benns, or 'the Birds,' are recently married; he's a painter, and they work together. She works with clay, wax, and wire to set up models for his paintings. It will probably be an ancient knight looking ruefully at his sword."

"I see," William said. "I thought the sword might be used for some sort of magical ceremony."

"Ah, yes, Bram said you are part of the Golden Dawn," Pamela said. "What is your position with them?"

In his light Irish accent, William demurely said, "I was just named Imperator of the Outer Order of Isis—Urania Temple to the Hermetic Order of the Golden Dawn."

Bursting into laughter, Pamela patted his hand. "Whatever does that mean?"

William's eyes flashed. "I will be taking on an important role in the leadership division."

"Well, congratulations! Let me introduce you to this actress who just arrived from Ireland, Maud Gonne." William didn't seem keen on moving at first, but Pamela took his arm. "Come on, Imperial-whatever-you-are. Maud!"

Maud, in mid-conversation with Bram, turned and looked at William. Her beautiful dark hair, pale skin, and black silk gown with its tiny waist made her stand out from the brightly colored floral dresses of the other women. She shook his hand, but he stood frozen in place.

He stammered out, "Majestic, unearthly—a goddess."

Bram gave a slight snort, while Maud stood even taller.

"Charmed to meet another Irishman," Maud said. Bram downed the last of his drink and excused himself, wandering over to the painter Whistler on the settee.

Two women in elaborate evening dresses, Lady Cynthia Garfield and Emma Dorset, marched over to the refreshment table, coyly asking Yoshio to light their cigarettes. Lady Cynthia wore a stunning yellow silk dress, its bodice sparkling with beads and musical notes embroidered in the scalloped neckline, the gauze of the three-quarter sleeves dripping with beads and gemstones. Emma Dorset's contrasting emerald dress was velvet and had sparkling gemstones set into the intricate weavings of the bodice. Pamela perched behind them on a stool, out of direct sight of the debutantes as Yoshio waited on the ladies.

Lady Garfield scanned the room. "Mr. Markino, this is quite the mishmash of people. Will our hostess be performing this evening?"

"Ah, Lady Garfield, she might," Yoshio answered. "It all depends on her muse, the Gelukiezanger, appearing." He leaned forward and whispered to them, "But judging by her costume tonight, it seems possible."

Emma Dorset whispered back conspiratorially to Yoshio, "She's such a strange little person."

Yoshio stepped back. "She is an excellent mimic, that is all. It is my understanding she spent some of her childhood in Jamaica, where her folktale stories originate."

"Really?" Lady Cynthia exhaled a curling wisp of smoke beautifully. "Well, I'm sure I don't understand why she would want to perform Caribbean stories. I'm sure it's entertaining, but isn't it ridiculous to put on another person's affect? Why be a mimic?"

Pamela's stomach knotted up. Edy was suddenly beside her, her arm around her.

"This is what people think of me, I'm just an entertaining mimic?" Pamela grimaced. "I was taught these stories by Miss Jones. She told me to share them with the world."

Adjusting Pamela's turban, Edy handed her a glass of Opal Hush. "They are Bloomsbury debutantes, Pamela, nothing more. You mustn't be bothered by their ugliness. But perhaps calling yourself 'Gelukiezanger' doesn't suggest West Indies tales to an audience."

"Ow. Through ugliness, sometimes truth is found," Pamela answered. "Are you saying I shouldn't perform my childhood stories?"

Edy finished her Opal Hush. "Maybe it's time for new stories."

Satish made his way over to them, but as he was almost by their side, Lady Garfield and Emma Dorset pounced on him and insisted he sit next to them. His eyes found Pamela's and he beamed a sort of apology. She responded with a shrug, trying to battle the sinking feeling she was no one's first pick. More people entered and a small crush of people gathered around the kitchen area. Pamela picked up a fork and tapped the side of her glass, calling the room to order with its ring, the piano music finally fading away.

"Good evening, friends," Pamela began. "Now that we've mingled and met, it is time for our contributions. Make sure you sign our guest book. Let's thank Nona for her music."

Nona half rose from her bench, blushed, then sat down.

"I'll go first, as usual," Pamela said, noticing that her hands were shaking slightly.

The group found seats and settled down.

Despite her dry throat, Pamela announced, "Usually, when I perform one of my Annancy tales, I introduce myself as Gelukiezanger." The sounds of chuckling went around the room. "Tonight, I will not go by that name or by Pixie, but rather by Pamela. A Pamela, who was coached by her guardian and caretaker, Miss Jones, of St. Andrew Parish, Jamaica. I give you 'Six Poached Eggs.'"

She lit the candles she had set out earlier. Sitting cross-legged on the floor, she inhaled deeply. She conjured up the memory of Miss Jones, a gaggle of children sitting enthralled around her. In her best attempt to remember her voice, she began.

"Before Queen Victoria came to reign over us, a man was traveling from one town to another and he was very hungry. So, he stopped at a cook shop, and they brought him six poach eggs. He ate them, and said he didn't any money to pay for them, but would come back and pay when he had found his fortune.

"So, after twelve years, the man was riding along the road, on his way back to his own countryside, and he went back to the cook shop to pay him six pence for the eggs he had eaten twelve years earlier. And the keeper of the cook shop told him, not good enough, that if the man had not eaten the eggs, he would have grown-up chickens and the chickens would have been hens and the hens would lay more eggs and they would grow up to be chickens and that the six eggs would be more than sixty pounds, not six pence! And the man said, he would not pay more than six pence. And so, the cook shop keeper took the man to the judge and while the judge was thinking, a little boy came into the courthouse. And him had a bag under him arm, and the judge say, 'What you got?'

"And the boy said, 'Dried peas, sir!'

"'And what you going to do with it?'

"And the boy said, 'Plant it!'

"And the judge said, 'But dried peas won't grow!'

"And the boy said, 'And poach eggs won't hatch!'

"So, the judge laughed! And he never made the man pay anything. The man was so thankful to the boy, that he took him home with him, and when he grew up, he got all the man's money when he was taken away by Death."

The room broke into enthusiastic applause, Lady Cynthia and Emma clapping the loudest. When Pamela performed this for her children's parties, her usual audience, they didn't react this way. Children were usually intrigued but not ecstatic listening to "Six Poached Eggs". Maybe it was time to move on to other stories.

Edy came to the front of the room, motioning for Pamela to move to the place near her as Maud blew kisses and Bram applauded. Pamela felt a hot rush go through her. The last time she and Maud had been together, Pamela had flown. Tonight, she had flown in a different realm.

Pamela took a glass of Opal Hush from Yoshio as Edy rapped the table for the room's attention. "Tonight we have a guest poet here with us. Perhaps he will grace us with one of his poems?"

William glanced down, swirled his wine glass, and drained it.

Edy looked imploringly at him and reached out her arms to call him forward. "William Butler Yeats, will you answer the call?"

After some deliberation, he clumsily rose to his feet and went to the front of the room. He saw Maud standing at the back of the room. A smattering of applause politely started up and immediately died out.

William cleared his throat and began his poem about the hazel wood, a glimmering girl whose hand and lips he kissed. He ended the piece whispering about golden apples of the sun.

The room applauded enthusiastically; Maud looked at him with appreciation.

William sat down next to Pamela and whispered to her, "That was completely nerve-shattering. And I'm not of a mind that anyone here understood it."

Pamela patted his leg. "*Quod tibi id aliis.* 'What to yourself, that to others.'"

William finally started to loosen up and laughed, pushing his sliding glasses up his nose, looking around to see where Maud had gone. Pamela laughed with him, pouring him more wine. How charming he was! How adult and sophisticated this evening was shaping up to be!

He leaned into Pamela. "I've just met the woman I'm going to marry."

Pamela's heart leapt as she kept pouring his wine. Would this be an unexpected admirer? Her first beau?

"Really? And who would that be?"

"Maud. Maud Gonne."

Pamela looked at his sparkling eyes as he drank the last dregs of his glass and stood, smiling above Pamela. Seeing her slightly smiling face too, he made his way over to the tall, lissome Maud, now holding court with Bram and Mr. Doyle. Yeats looked as though he was going to float away, much to the annoyance of Bram and Doyle.

Pamela's heart tugged as though something weighed on it. Would she ever mean that much to anyone?

CHAPTER TWENTY

ALEISTER'S POSSESSION

The dark shadow formed in front of Aleister and touched his head. "What do you seek?" the shape intoned. A searing pain went through Aleister's brain. The being asked, "My mind?"

The spirit threw a veil of black essence over Aleister. He could see nothing and heard only the sounds of his labored breathing.

"I want access to your translucent spirit, Anwass, most revered of Egyptian gods, so that we might share the pools of magic."

Words snarled inside his head. "Share? You think you deserve to share the pools of magic?"

"Anwass, if you share your temple of astral magic, I will make your name known."

"And if I refuse?" the inner voice said.

"Why would you?"

The blackness enveloping him began to lift.

"You will have no control," the god said.

The words of Aleister's father came back to him. "And then?"

As his eyes gradually could see again, Aleister registered he was in a cavern with many pools of water. Out of the depths of one of them, a shadow lifted itself up and poured itself into Aleister. The last thing Aleister remembered was the suffocating weight of being possessed.

CHAPTER TWENTY-ONE

AHMED AND PAMELA

Westcott, Felkin, and Mathers hovered around Pamela at her sketch pad. Bram had moved several boxes off the desk so she could show them her latest drawings. For the past two weeks she had used this small desk in Ahmed Kamal's office at the British Museum to start her research for the cards she was hired to create. As she tried to concentrate, the men signaled their impatience by drumming their fingers and clearing their throats constantly. It reminded Pamela of her time at the Pratt Institute during her freehand sketch classes. There, as now, she was the only girl in the art class, surrounded by men who critiqued and criticized her. To keep her hand from the slightest tremor, she roughly sketched the outline of a mountainscape with bold strokes. She looked up to see Bram nodding at her.

"Gentlemen, an audience is not helpful in sketching out first ideas," Pamela said. "If I am to design these tarot cards, I will need solitude."

"Miss Smith," Dr. Westcott said, peering over her shoulder. "The ideas behind each one of these cards will be Mr. Waite's job. In this collaboration, your job will be to execute his concepts."

Pamela was about to explain that was not the way artists work when Bram lifted his hand. "Miss Horniman has said that

half of the eighty-pound fee for this project is to be paid to Miss
Smith now. Isn't that right, Dr. Felkin?"

Felkin smoothed his shiny hair and then reached into his
vest pocket and took out forty pounds. Pamela stood to fetch
her purse, wondering if she should sign a paper receipt for it.

As she put the money away, she asked, "And what is the
date we are to finish this project?"

"You're a w-woman, so we thought nine months would
make sense for you," Mathers said.

"There are many things women can create in less than nine
months and many that take more than nine months," Pamela
replied. She was about to say more when Ahmed Kamal opened
the door, carrying a tray.

At the beginning of her time here at the Museum, Ahmed
was one of the first people she met. She was to share his office,
an imposition she feared he would resent. But on that first day he
entered his work domain to find her sketching at the secretary desk
outside his office, he stopped in his tracks and bowed his head in a
respectful greeting. She almost blurted out how much she loved his
fez, but decided to get to know this Ahmed Kamal first before she
was that familiar with him. Drawing a boundary like this was a new
experience for Pamela, but she wanted to start off on the right foot.

"Miss Smith," Ahmed had said, hanging up his coat and
then turning to her.

"Mr. Kamal," Pamela replied, readying herself for their first
work-place pleasantries.

Ahmed had stood behind her and gazed at her sketches. "I
will be spending most of my time in my main office to give you
privacy." He pointed to the door at the other side of the room.
"Just knock there if you need anything."

"Would you happen to have any brilliant ideas for a tarot
deck?" Pamela said, tapping her pencil.

Ahmed came around and stood in front of her. "Miss
Smith, I understand that you are hired to create playing cards?"

"Yes, playing cards, tarot cards," she answered, picking up a pencil and drawing a demon that looked like the freakishly tall man, Dr. Felkin.

"You like and trust these gentlemen?" Ahmed asked.

"I'm a woman who will be paid forty pounds in advance of a job. I don't have that luxury," Pamela said sharply. "I'm sorry, Mr. Kamal. This is a complicated situation."

"Yes, it is," Ahmed answered as he sat before her. "Tell me why you want to do this job, since it seems you will be working here with me for a while?"

"I have always loved symbology and storytelling, and I have ability."

"Ability?" Ahmed said, his eyes alert.

"A natural ability to channel. When I draw things, they present themselves to me. I taste colors, hear objects sing, or the drawing makes music. It comes through from the other side. I don't say it is a skill. It's simply a talent or a gift, as I have practiced nothing to bring these things to me. They just come."

Pamela had never spoken of her ability in this way to anyone, and it surprised her that she felt so at ease with Mr. Kamal. He was like Mr. Irving in that he sat a little distance away from her with his head tilted sideways, sometimes not even looking at her.

In a soft voice, he said, "These cards will be used many times in the future. The magic in them will be quite powerful."

Pamela almost laughed and then, looking at Ahmed's serious face, caught herself. "These are to be playing cards, as you said, Mr. Kamal. Playing cards to be used for a hero's journey. I have seen these images all my life, and now I will be able to tell a story with them. Sometimes objects speak to me and tell me that they are meant to be seen in a different way."

Ahmed took in a breath of air and sighed. "I see now why you were picked for this task, Miss Smith."

"Why?"

"There is a tear in your reality where you see the seen and unseen come together. Languages are forbidden or lost, but images may stay long after the language is gone."

"Like your hieroglyphics here at the museum?"

"Exactly." Ahmed crossed his arms. "And what is the first step in this hero's journey?" he asked. "How does he start?"

Pamela looked at Ahmed. Was he testing her?

"He starts as an innocent, without values or judgment."

Ahmed smiled. "When you create your cards, be sure you start the same way, innocent, without judgment. The only value or judgment I will pass on you here is if you don't wear the museum's archive gloves when I bring you an artifact to study."

Pamela smiled at him. "I promise to wear them."

"If only I could get your employers to make the same promise. They manhandle everything I bring them and risk damaging very valuable artifacts," Ahmed said.

Pamela replied, "Next time they are here with us, we will make a show of wearing the gloves. Maybe that will help."

Today, when Ahmed gingerly walked to Pamela, he winked just before he set the tray down before her. It held an ancient box with lettering that looked like Italian scrawled across the top. The men stood back as he put on white gloves. Ahmed was not wearing the typical muslin protective garb he usually wore at the museum. Instead, he was wearing an embroidered tunic, the red vines matching his fez.

Bustling with pride, he opened the box and spread out some highly decorated black-and-white cards on the tray in a fan shape.

"Voilà," Ahmed said.

Westcott whistled in appreciation while the others jostled to get a closer look.

"It has taken me two weeks to get permission for you to view the cards," Ahmed said. "But I am very pleased to grant you a private audience to see these Sola-Busca tarot cards."

Pamela reached to pick up a card and Ahmed handed her muslin gloves as Bram watched closely.

"I'm sorry, this card is so powerful," Pamela said, putting the gloves on. "I forgot that I was to wear gloves to handle them."

"Yes, Miss Smith, gloves should be worn at all times," Ahmed said, his eyes twinkling. No one in the room knew that she and Ahmed had discussed this moment weeks before. Bram's eyebrows knit; he would know it was not like Pamela to take a suggestion like this so demurely. Pamela put the gloves on as she looked at Bram, trying not to look like the cat who stole the cream.

"These are fourteenth-century cards and should be handled as little as possible," Ahmed continued. "They have been in the Sola-Busca family for over five hundred years. The museum acquired them in 1845, and we hope in the next few years to use this new photography medium to capture them."

Bending over them with his hands clasped behind his back, Felkin muttered, "Speaking of capturing, how did the museum come to own these Sola-Busca cards?"

Putting the tray aside, Ahmed pointedly replied, "In the world of acquisitions, there are only two methods—payment or plunder. I believe possession of these cards came through payment."

Pamela sighed in delight as she stared at the cards. She focused on another card, a minstrel with a dog biting him. "They are wondrous!" She delicately picked the card up.

"That's right, Miss Pamela," Ahmed said. "The Sola-Busca cards were the first tarot cards used for divination, communication, and meditation."

Felkin lingered near Pamela's shoulders. "But not invocation or conjuring?"

Mathers sniffed, "As far as we know, these cards were not used in magic or fortune-telling."

Pamela put the card down and opened her sketchbook, flicking pages open. A study of the male figure opened, and Felkin stopped Pamela's hand.

"You've drawn unclothed men!" Dr. Westcott said, wide-eyed.

"And women!" Pamela cheerily replied, turning the page to find the page she wanted.

"How is that possible?" Dr. Felkin asked.

"At the Pratt Institute in Brooklyn," Pamela said, finding the page of hearts she had drawn. "The teachers there have no qualms about women drawing men and vice versa, although I suppose that has not been acceptable for these many centuries."

"Ah, Miss Pamela, more talk like that and they'll think you're a suffragette like Miss Florence," Bram said. "You'll be a good addition to the ranks of women in the Golden Dawn."

Pamela looked at him, his eyes dancing.

"If the Golden Dawn is ever to be a certified chapter," Felkin glowered, moving away. "Right now, we're only a subsidized group of magic enthusiasts."

Looking at Ahmed for permission, she moved her gloved hand to the Sola-Busca cards in front of her. Once he nodded, she picked up the Three of Swords, a large heart with three swords piercing it and a swagged wreath strung underneath. "Look at this beautiful heart. Three swords right through it. I understand."

Chuckling, Felkin looked at the tarot card. "What do you understand about the Three of Swords in this deck, Miss Smith?"

Pamela put her gloved hand over the card and felt it. "For a woman—the flight of her lover. For a man—a nun, a rupture, separation."

The men look amused and entertained, except for Ahmed.

Bram put a comforting hand on Pamela's shoulder. "Well, that was a pretty good guess. At least you didn't say the obvious, disruptions of the heart or such. Pamela, I know the creation of this new tarot deck will be in good hands if you undertake this project."

Pamela, stung a little, turned and smiled at him. "Thank you, Uncle Brammy."

Ever since the night at Ada Leverson's when Aleister had tried to paralyze her, she had been unable to confide in Uncle Brammy.

If Aleister had been confident enough to send her an astral attack in public, there seemed to be no limits to what he might do.

When the four Golden Dawn Chiefs had retaliated on her behalf, she wasn't sure Bram had been able to see what she was seeing. Was he gifted as they were? Was there a special ability that he had that he couldn't talk about either? Was she safe by herself around Aleister? She was always with Waite or Bram or Felkin whenever she ran into him at the headquarters. Was that planned? She looked up and saw Ahmed studying her very carefully and went back to looking at the cards.

Bram clapped his hand. "Well, gentlemen, Miss Smith needs to get to work and I must get back to the Lyceum. Mr. Irving is putting in a new leading actor today, William Terriss. He's been busy at other theatres and we've just hired him back. Waite should arrive here soon to begin supervising Miss Smith."

Pamela's face went hot, and she kept her head down as her heart raced. She tried to keep her composure at the news that Terriss was back and at the Lyceum. He wouldn't even recognize her all these years later.

Dr. Felkin cleared his throat. "Ah, how our late Dr. Woodman would have loved this."

"Waite should be here shortly to start the first card with you," Bram repeated. He gave her the two-fingered salute that was their greeting and ushered the men out, gently closing the door.

Pamela plunked herself down in her chair and groaned.

"Of course, I am no longer with the Lyceum Theatre just when Mr. Terriss is hired back," Pamela said.

After a brief commotion of the men greeting one another in the hall, Edward Waite opened the door, exclaiming, "Hello there! Let's get started, shall we?" He took off his coat and threw it to the floor, rushing over to the table to see the Sola-Busca cards. He put on his gloves and clapped his hands, rubbing them together. "They just told me in the hallway they were here—fantastic resource for you, Miss Smith."

Ahmed looked meaningfully at Pamela. "My inner office is just beyond that door if you need my assistance." Waite grunted in response and Ahmed continued, "And once again, I ask you to handle these Sola-Busca cards with the utmost care." Before leaving, he placed a folded piece of paper under Pamela's hand.

He left the room, and Pamela slid the note into her skirt pocket. Waite pulled up a chair next to her, focused only on the Sola-Busca until Pamela handed him a pair of gloves to wear. He grudgingly put them on.

He picked up the Fool card. The clicking sound in her head started up. Was this a warning the bricks would be conjured soon? It was a softer sound than the one at Mrs. Leverson's soiree. More like having a fly buzz around you or a piece of grit in your eye, annoying and persistent but not overwhelming, and eventually she was able to tune it out.

"Miss Smith, we will start with the Fool, the first character in our tarot deck. What does the Fool mean to you?"

"A foolish person, someone who acts without thought. Reckless."

"Very good. Now tell me what you see." He moved the Fool card from the Sola-Busca deck closer to her.

Pamela studied the card: a man wearing a ragged costume with a large headpiece drooping with feathers and leaves, playing the bagpipes with a crow on his shoulder. "We're starting the tarot deck with a Fool?"

"Yes, the Fool will be numbered zero, the number of unlimited potential or complete loss. The Fool will come at the beginning of the journey."

"How many cards am I to create?"

"We. We are to create twenty-two. They will be in a deck showing the hero's journey and they will be major cards, or as we will call them, the Major Arcana. Then, if you are skilled enough, we will go on to create fifty-six more."

"Twenty-two cards depicting a hero's journey starting with the Fool?" Pamela picked up the Sola-Busca Fool, turning it over in her hand. "I feel no connection with this Fool. A ragged man with a crow? Playing bagpipes is the only foolish thing about it."

"Bah! It is not necessary for you to feel a connection to it. You can use the disks, clubs, vases, or swords in the design of it. Most of these use heroes of Greek or Roman history . . . What is it, Miss Pamela? You don't seem . . . enthused?"

Pamela put down the Fool card and started to look through the other cards. "This bagpiped vagabond is wrong for the Fool."

"What?! Miss Smith, I don't think you understand the nature of this job."

Pamela turned and gazed at Waite. "What is the nature of this job? Why do you need these cards?"

Waite hemmed and hawed, the clicking got louder in her head, and then he examined the cards with her. "Well, our deck of cards does not need to be a replica of the Sola-Busca, only inspired by them."

"Good, Mr. Waite. What are the aspects of the Fool you are looking to represent?"

Waite stood and paced in front of her. "Extravagance, lack of discipline, enthusiasm, folly."

Pamela picked out the Five of Cups. "This is the Fool, a man walking along a rocky path, a small white dog at his side tugging at the slouching boots, a bundle over his shoulder, gazing up at the sky."

"The Fool gazing up at the sky?"

"Gazing up at the sky, he will be stepping off a cliff, with the little white dog at his side. This is the Fool."

Waite seemed stumped by her response, not convinced. He picked up the other cards and began to sort them. Pamela sketched some ideas in her notebook.

"Well, it is good to get started, but let's not rush to judgment here, Miss Pamela. Let me see if there is another prototype that might be more appropriate. I will give you room here, just to start some ideas." He removed the tray of cards, set it on another table, and started to examine them, separately.

Pamela turned to a new page in her sketchbook, the music inside her head starting in earnest, and she sketched with new vigor. A pulse started inside of her that sang along with her heartbeat and the music. Many forms automatically appeared on the page: a bird, a white dog, a wand with a backpack, a handsome blond man with a flowered tunic, a mountaintop. It was Nera from Maud's Irish folktale.

She remembered the first time she floated and the vision of him stepping off the cliff. The music ended; the sketch was complete.

She stood and showed her drawing to Waite. "This is the Fool."

He stood staring at her. "Why, this is the very thing! The very thing!" Sitting down next to her, the clicking growing louder and louder, he picked up the sketch in his own hands, then put it down and started making notes in the margins. "Yes, it will be a white rose for the Rosicrucians, the wand will be the stick the back sack is on, the bird denoting the holy calling . . . Oh! Very good. Very good. This is the first time I've seen your drawings, Miss Pamela! I wasn't sure if you were talented at all. Let me make some notes here in the corner."

When she was sure he was not looking, she took Ahmed's note out of her pocket. It was a chart with many illustrations, a figure eight on its side, a snake, a vulture, something that looked like a hockey stick, a man sitting next to a hawk, and a lion at the very end.

Under the images written in English at the bottom was a single line:

If you understand these symbols,
you will know what this note means.

She looked up, staring at Waite. The clicking stopped.

CHAPTER TWENTY-TWO

Eight-Pound Crown

~⟨∘⟩~

After the evening performance of *Macbeth*, Pamela wandered backstage waiting for Bram and company to make their way down from the dressing rooms. She drifted past the battle axes packed upright in wooden boxes and the rows of armor hung on special rotating racks. Glancing at the props table, Pamela's heart thumped. The prop master had yet to store away the new replacement crown that Pamela had made.

This crown was lighter. The previous crown was too heavy, and the many layers of tree branches and gems snagged netting, getting in Mr. Irving's way during the battle scene. His long, drooping mustache needed the right crown to set off his Viking look. The bowl of the new crown had two wings on top, and a band around the rim embedded with beetle gems to match Ellen's green beetle dress. Pamela fashioned the beetle gems to resemble the fairies who had come to visit her childhood home in Manchester all those years ago during All Hallow's Eve. Her first visitation from the other side would live on here with Mr. Irving after her departure.

Pamela had decided to leave the Lyceum Theatre; the tarot design job and her new ideas for printing a subscription newsletter needed too much of her time. Before she left, she made an improved crown as a parting gift for her employer. She had worked with Lovejoy and the props department for a month to create it. Mr. Irving was uncomfortable with gift giving in public, so she arranged for the crown be given to him privately post show. She picked up the crown from its position on the backstage table.

She poked her head in Mr. Irving's quick-change room. The locked box was still hidden behind the false wall, and it should have cheered her to think of the little wand, sword, and cup nestled together with her star necklace from Satish. The tokens hidden in there were some sort of magical talisman to protect the Great Man, that much she knew. But would he know she loved and admired him? Would he care? There were inner worlds and secrets backstage and on, but she knew she would never be in the inner circle of Mr. Irving, Ellen, or Edy.

She took herself along the back rail and looked up to see the many canvases hanging in the fly space above. Next to the wall, the last canvas was from *King Arthur*, a show that had been out of the rotation for years. She leaned her head back and saw a familiar sight. It was the scenery from Craven, the painter of castles and scenery for the Lyceum. She squinted.

My banner! She spotted the four symbols she'd painted over a decade ago on the *King Arthur* canvas. It was during the visit to the paint room with her family before they moved to Jamaica. There was her tetramorph, the very symbol she had painted earlier with Craven, before she even understood its meaning.

She walked out further onto the bare stage of the Lyceum and gazed up at all the empty tiers and box seats. All that was left on stage was the enormous throne and a lit gas lamp. She sat on the throne and closed her eyes, holding the crown in her hands. The sound of light clicking on the floor grew louder, and before she knew it, Fussie had leapt into her lap. Fussie was an affectionate and spoiled dog, living up to her name by refusing to sleep anywhere without Mr. Irving's scarf nearby. The animal sniffed the crown and then set to work licking Pamela's hand.

Pamela felt someone watching her, and she looked up to see Mr. Irving standing there. He looked more like a typical Victorian deacon than a sacred monster with his long hair, pince-nez glasses, and a long frock coat. With tears in her eyes, she put the dog on the floor and ran to embrace him. He kissed her on top of her head. She knew she was one of the few people outside of Ellen who could show her affection for the Great Man, although he would roll his eyes when others saw her bounce around him like a Labrador puppy.

Tenderly unwrapping her arms from around him, he chucked her under the chin. "Miss Smith, I understand this was your last day with us?"

A slight sniff from Pamela. "Yes, Mr. Irving."

She composed herself and said, "Mr. Irving. I wanted to see if the new crown I designed for you was lighter."

She shyly handed it to him. He held it up to the stage lamp, turning it around. As he took in her crown, she saw his gaunt face, the beaked nose, the ever-more-graying hair, the large brown eyes that could be cold hard magnets or burning embers. As the most famous actor-manager of his time, it was rumored he would be the first actor to be knighted. The Lyceum would be touring again in America this next year, but this time without Ellen. She would be in a new show that George Bernard Shaw had written for her.

Mr. Irving handed the crown back to Pamela.

"It needs one last fitting from its designer," Mr. Irving said, and sat on the throne. Fussie immediately jumped up onto his lap and curled up. Pamela crowned him and he turned his head from side to side to test its fit, smiling wryly.

"Uneasy lies the head that wears a crown," Mr. Irving said.

"Especially an eight-pound crown," Pamela replied, flushed to be so close to her mentor.

"Especially an eight-pound crown. This feels closer to five pounds. Excellent."

Removing the crown and holding it, he leaned back and gazed at Pamela. He noticed on the top of the crown, a pair of wings flanking the sides. "Wings, Miss Smith?"

"Yes, the demonic and the angelic have wings, Mr. Irving."

Returning the crown to her, a smile crossed his face and he looked away. "Has your theatre life been all you had hoped? Learning the ways of stage and magic?"

Pamela hesitated and busied herself with the crown, then started her large laugh. Mr. Irving joined in. "Miss Smith, no one here, not even your beloved Ellen and Edy, want you to squander your gifts. Creativity is magic, and you must put your name to it."

"You see, Mr. Irving, I've been offered a big job for little money. Designing cards. Using the knowledge of the Egyptian symbols too."

"So Mr. Stoker tells me. If it's a big job, you don't do it for money the first time. You do it for the experience."

"I start fully committed with them tomorrow."

"Ah, I see." With that he woke the now-sleeping little dog, rubbing her ears and setting her down, and rising to his great height, said, "Make magic, Miss Smith. You are still under my protection, don't forget that."

"Yes, Mr. Irving."

Pamela wanted to shout out that she still wanted more. More special consideration, more responsibility, more inclusion. Pamela had constantly asked Bram if she could design sets or costumes, but she was told she never drew proper sketches for show concepts. Edy had told her that as long as Mr. Irving hired trained scenic designers who had all gone to London art schools, he was never going to hire her as a stage or costume designer.

Pamela's assignments were more along the lines of posters and cards, while large-scale scenes had complex proportions to consider, and Mr. Irving was not convinced she could handle the job when there were so many skilled hands ready to do exactly as he bade them. While tutoring Pamela on tour, she knew he appreciated her quick mind and ability to draw, sketch, recite, and entertain. But was she just a noisy imp, getting into mischief with Edy at a moment's notice? And now there were his two sons clamoring to be actors with him, much to the furious reaction of their mother. It was said the eldest, Laurence, would go on tour with the Lyceum at the end of the season, and Harry was rumored to soon be in the business too.

"You taught me so much, sir. Goodbye."

"I'm sorry you'll miss our big night tomorrow," Mr. Irving said, putting his gloves on. "We'll drag *King Arthur* out of retirement, but with our new Lancelot, it should have some fresh blood. The Beefsteak Club supper afterwards will be the most taxing part of the evening. Maybe I'll wear your magical crown there."

This was the most informal and chatty Mr. Irving had ever been with her. "Is it true the Prince of Wales will be there?" Pamela said, wishing he would issue her an invitation.

"Yes, Baroness Burdett-Coutts will bring him."

The sixty-seven-year-old Baroness Burdett-Coutts was the major Lyceum Theatre patroness and one of the wealthiest women in England. She had been Mr. Irving's longtime advocate, but Pamela had heard the rumors that her new husband, the twenty-seven-year-old William Bartlett, was influencing her to invest elsewhere. He was pointing to hospitals and the Columbia Flower Market and humanitarian organizations, not a theatre with 350 staff members and a leading lady who was paid £200 a week, the highest stage salary in London.

Mr. Irving took her by the shoulders, looked at her, and tenderly embraced her. Pamela became teary-eyed but Mr. Irving held her at a short distance and held up a finger, moving his hand like a magician pretending to gather her tears and throw them away. Pamela laughed and collected herself, taking a deep breath.

He looked at her to make sure she was settled and then turned and started to leave. "Come on, Fussie, home to supper."

As he started out, a laugh stopped him. Ellen was coming out of her dressing room talking baby talk to someone unseen, and then she appeared on the opposite side of the stage in a beautiful violet dress holding a miniature version of Fussie, who was whining at being held and seeing the bigger dog. Mr. Irving stopped and turned around and saw Ellen across the stage. Pamela held her breath as she also stopped and gazed at him. They were both oblivious to Pamela, almost obscured by the tall throne.

The two stood immobile, each on one side of the vast Lyceum stage. She finally put her hand to her cheek as though caressing it, and then opened the hand and waved it toward Mr. Irving, as though sending him a caress through the air. With his free hand he pantomimed catching it and putting it in his pocket. He patted it as though to keep it safe and gave her a nod, then turned and disappeared.

Pamela knew her surrogate mother, Ellen, needed to have people around her constantly: children and admirers, people representing the causes she was currently supporting, young women wanting to be her. Mr. Irving lived a very simple life, in simple rooms near the theatre with simple food and an occasional cigar. Yes, there were the society women who fawned over him and sent him on cruises, like the Baroness. There were also the demands of attending dedications to fountains and schools in his name. In comparison, Fussie demanded the right amount of attention and gave total devotion.

Backstage, the word was that Mr. Irving's stage innovations were drying up, that he was caught in a cycle of staging the favorites with the same tricks, the same special effects with lights and salt, and the same attempts to make fog on stage without creating a toxic blend of charcoal and fanning. It was years since he'd been willing to gamble on new effects, as the established repertoire determined that people would come back to see the beautifully painted sets. Those two thousand painted sets and flats were now stored outdoors near a railway line, as there was no room at the theatre to keep them. Pamela actually cried when she heard the painted flats were being stored outside, exposed to the elements, but Bram told her that when decent and affordable warehouse space became available, they would be moved back indoors.

Even though Ellen coddled her and let her live with her, recently Pamela had been told that the housing situation was only temporary. Then, Bram told her that her new work did not fit in well with the demands of the Lyceum Theatre schedule. She needed to go somewhere to freely express herself without trying to fit into a classical world theatre repertoire.

Ellen and Pamela both watched Mr. Irving make his way out. Ellen then spotted Pamela and saw the crown in her hand. She and the little dog made their way to the throne. "Did he approve of your new crown?" The little dog in her arms started to yip with excitement and tried to nuzzle Pamela.

"Yes, I think he did," Pamela said as the little dog whimpered in Ellen's arms. "But who is this?"

More noise and chatter echoed down to the stage and William Terriss, Bram Stoker, Satish, and Edy came out from the wings in their formal street clothes.

"Pixie, this is Drummie, just a little version of Fussie. Henry got me this sweet little fox terrier. He knows I am so low because you are leaving us." Held in Ellen's arms, the fox terrier held out a paw, and the approaching group laughed.

Pamela looked over at the cunning little dog and clutched at her heart playfully. Satish approached them, teasing, "You've been replaced by a puppy!"

They all laughed again, Pamela included, and Ellen embraced her while still holding the dog. "No, darling Pixie, you can never be replaced, not even by Drummie! But enough about my dog. You must tell us everything about your new job! But first, here is one of our original company members come home, William Terriss—he's our new Lancelot."

William Terriss, an Adonis, stepped forward to meet Pamela. His beautiful profile and blonde hair were exactly as Pamela remembered. He was wearing an enormous coat, balancing a stage sword on his shoulder, and had the jolly energy of an American. He stopped before the group and music in her head started, a new melody she had never heard before. "Oh, wait until my Eskimo dog meets this new pup," he said to Ellen. He looked at Pamela curiously. "Hello. Have we met?"

She stammered, "You saved me."

He looked at her more closely and exclaimed, "The little girl from the bridge!"

There had been moments in Pamela's life when people, objects, motions burned themselves inside of her like Ezekiel's vision of burning coals of fire. This was one of those moments. Although William Terriss was standing there in front of her, another form of him seemed to step forward. It was Nera, the Irish explorer who was trapped in the *síd*, stepping off the cliff with the dog by his side, the wind blowing in his hair, the wand holding his back sack. He was the very image of the hero that Maud had told her about all those years ago.

He was exactly the image of her tarot Fool card.

Looking past him, Pamela saw the canvases hanging above, her banner flying over the castle of Camelot. Embedded in the artwork, her winged figures started to writhe, the tetramorph that she first created with the scenic painter, Craven, all crawling and wriggling.

Suddenly, the four creatures lit up and flew out from the very fabric of the canvas over her head, coming back to float above Terriss. Her winged cherub, the winged lion, winged ox and eagle were all buzzing and darting around him, inspecting him and then looking back at Pamela.

Are they attacking him?

The winged, small beasts circled around his head and then flew straight up into the fly space of the theatre. Two words popped into her head. "Beware Anwass." She didn't even know what that meant.

"Pixie? Pixie? Are you all right?" Ellen was shaking Pamela by the arm.

Bram came near her and looked up into the fly space, only seeing the catwalk that crossed over the stage above the proscenium arch.

He turned to her and inquisitively looked into her eyes, his bulky frame towering over her. "What were you seeing there, my girl?"

Gulping, Pamela choked out, "Flies. Flying."

Terriss smiled at her. "Yes. When we fell off the bridge, it was as though we flew."

Pamela blinked and laughed.

Lovejoy came out with a bottle of champagne, and Edy followed with a tray of glasses.

They didn't forget me.

Pamela embraced Ellen as Lovejoy opened and poured the champagne.

"To our Pixie," Ellen said, lifting her glass as the others followed her lead.

The dark creatures from her tetramorph swarmed above them, invisible to everyone but Pamela.

CHAPTER TWENTY-THREE

DEVIL INCARNATE

"Where is the key to the vault?" Aleister yelled, picking up a grimoire off the Level Two Studies shelf and threatening to lob it at Florence's head.

Aleister could barely see in his blind rage, but he could make out Florence right before him in a skirt and white blouse outfit, complete with a man's tie and chatelaine, a ring of the Golden Dawn collection of keys. Her attempt to look like a suffragette authoritarian infuriated him even more.

"Mr. Crowley, calm yourself," Annie Horniman called from the safety of the doorway of the Golden Dawn's reading room.

"You! Hornibags! You and your filthy money! You think that can buy you access to magic?" Aleister asked, throwing the grimoire down. "You dare to limit me when you hire that mutt and give her free access to the vault?"

"Mr. Crowley," Florence said with half-hooded eyes, holding a few ancient fragile books. "Until you have reached Level Two, access to the vault is off-limits."

Aleister turned to the bookcase and shoved a whole row of books onto the floor. He then ran to the row of desks, sweeping everything off them as well. Florence followed him, still carrying the treasured tomes next to her bosom, and picked up the items as quickly as she could; maps, dictionaries, and encyclopedias hit the floor at a quick pace. Miss Horniman continued to clutch the sides of the entryway, only now she squawked for help. It was late at night, and they seemed to be the only people in the headquarters, where his quick steps sounded like a hammer pounding.

He raced around a desk and doubled back to Florence, landing so close to her he was near enough to slap the books out of her hands.

"Denied!" he roared. "How dare you deny me access! I have been granted powers by Anwass!"

In a tight voice, she answered him, "Anwass would have no complicity with someone who has defied the rules of our Golden Dawn. We have had several complaints that you have tried to have inappropriate relations with members here."

Aleister stood straight up and growled, "Who? Who dared to complain about me?"

Slowly walking from the doorway, Miss Horniman approached them, holding her dragon cane out in front of her as though she were trying to stave off a mad dog. "The identity of those who have come forward must be protected. Mr. Crowley, we have warned you before about using the Golden Dawn as a playground for sexual seduction."

"Your former flatmate, Allan Bennett, informed us you have been channeling an entity to own the Golden Dawn's access to magic," Florence said. "This supposed Anwass could be any spirit who decided to possess you."

"It is not for you to decide which god speaks to me," Aleister said, coming closer to Florence.

"It *is* for me to decide that the knowledge from the vault will be allowed to the few who will do good with this access," Florence said, picking up the books at her feet.

Choking on a laugh, Aleister slammed his hands on a desk. "This knowledge is mine, do you hear me? I can use it however and on whomever I please. It is hard-won and hard-earned through dark nights of experimenting and courage."

Miss Horniman stood next to Florence. "Courage? Humiliating a conquest is courageous?"

"I have no problem announcing my triumphal discoveries with Sex Magick," Aleister said, standing still for the first time. "It's Elaine's mother, Alice, isn't it?" Aleister asked, pacing in front of the darkened windows. "She has this absurd idea that I visited her daughter in her bedroom in astral form. If you must know, Hornibags, it was the attractive footman from downstairs who rumpled her sheets."

The two women came closer to Aleister as he sat on a table. "Aleister," Miss Horniman said, "you were overheard boasting that your Sex Magick was making a number of our young students your slaves. Your amorous conquests won't be tolerated here."

"Of course not! You would never be open to Sex Magick in your lifetime! But others are open to its ability to transport the mindset. It's a potent magic for those who embrace it, and its time has come. I should not be restricted because I practice this human freedom!"

"In all the philosophies embraced by the Golden Dawn, Christianity included, the tenets of kindness, goodness, and the pursuit of all good karma are the goals—"

"To hell with your goals," Aleister exploded. "Christianity, rationalism, Buddhism—all the lumber of the centuries. I bring you a positive and primeval fact, Magick by name! With this I will build a new heaven and a new earth. I want none of your faint approval or dispraise; I want blasphemy, murder, rape, revolution, anything, bad or good, but strong!"

Miss Horniman left Florence's side and came within reach of Aleister. "That is quite enough, Mr. Crowley. Your focus on these matters and your intention to use the Golden Dawn's resources as means of seduction will not be tolerated."

He angrily replied, "No, not enough! It is *me* who won't tolerate you!"

Florence reached out to push his back to the door when he lurched forward and grabbed her tie. He yanked Florence's neck to him, strangling her as he dragged her to him. When she was close enough, he tried to grab the set of keys at her waist. All the while Miss Horniman screamed for help as he drew her forward like a yoked animal. He finally wrangled the chain of keys off her and threw her down. Miss Horniman rushed to help Florence as he disappeared into the hallway to the vault.

Aleister threw open the door. Inside the vault, Mathers was levitating, sphinxes on either side of him steadily raising him. Aleister's whoop of delight sent Mathers crashing to the floor, and the sphinxes disappeared.

Mathers dusted himself off, furious, and turned on Aleister. "You. You. You. No right! No right!"

Aleister pushed past him and started to throw out the notebooks, candles, and canvas bag Mathers had with him. "Out! Out, you idiot! I will be using this now!"

From behind the vault, Dr. Felkin, in his typical elegant attire, appeared. "Really! What is going on here? You don't have permission to be in here, Crowley!"

Sputtering, Mathers joined in, "This. Is. Not. T-t-t-tolerated! In the vault, when I was practicing!"

❧

In a back room of the Golden Dawn Headquarters, Pamela tried not to look at her watch. It should be time for curtain call at the Lyceum Theatre for *King Arthur*. Mr. Irving would be gesturing for Ellen to come downstage, Edy would be peeking through her helmet as an extra to see if the Prince of Wales and the Baroness were sitting in the box seats. The Beefsteak Club would be set up in the actors' greenroom, and William Terriss would be charming everyone who sat near him at the supper. Bram would be directing everyone to their assigned seat, but even the older women who fed the cats at the theatre would be lurking to see if they could catch a glimpse of "Bertie," the Prince of Wales.

Meanwhile, here she sat with morose old Waite, "grading" her drawings. These were her final sketches for the first two tarot cards, and he had been adamant that she was to draw what he envisioned. The typing sounds in her head that always accompanied Waite's presence were subdued but still clicking away. Looking around for distraction, Pamela stood and crossed to the room's only window, overlooking Euston Road's back alleyway. At this late hour, she could only see the flashing eyes of a tomcat scrounging in the trash cans.

"This magician," Waite said, looking at her magician drawing, "is very ambiguous looking. I can't tell if it is supposed to be Henry Irving or Ellen Terry's daughter, Edy. Why is he so young? Magicians are old, with knowledge acquired over the centuries."

Pamela turned and sighed. "I know most of those tarocchi cards you gave me to look at had old men as magicians, but they seemed so feeble."

"Miss Smith," Waite said, his eyebrows shooting up. "Yours is not to question what has been the archetype of magic for centuries, and that is of an older man who has given his life to study."

From a distance, Pamela could hear doors slamming and people shouting.

"Mr. Waite," Pamela said, "listen."

"Now is not the time to hear your excuses why you can't follow directions, Miss Smith."

"No, Mr. Waite, someone is calling for help."

Pamela bolted for the door, Mr. Waite behind her.

Down two flights of stairs, they found Miss Horniman out of breath in the reading room. It was hard to understand what Miss Horniman was saying, but eventually Pamela understood that Aleister was here and, somehow, he'd choked Florence in a struggle to get the Golden Dawn keys to the vault.

"But where is Miss Farr now?" Waite asked.

"She went to the room with the vault," Miss Horniman said. "Mr. Felkin, Westcott, and Mathers are there now. I'm sure Aleister will try to use the vault."

Pamela's hands instinctively went to her throat, remembering how Aleister had paralyzed her at Ada Leverson's concert. Then she remembered how the three chiefs, Waite, Felkin, and Mathers, had saved her.

"Come on, Mr. Waite," Pamela said. "We may need your help in this."

Miss Horniman used her cane and led them down the corridor as quickly as she could to a room with the door ajar. Shouts and oaths were coming from inside the room, and Pamela told herself she was with magicians who would be able to cast a spell if they had to.

A large black structure, almost like a wooden temple painted with symbols, was at one end of the room. Pamela's hand shook, and she realized she was still carrying her sketchbook from upstairs. The four Golden Dawn Chiefs, Westcott, Waite, Felkin, and Mathers, barred the entrance to the vault while Miss Horniman reached for Pamela's arm to steady herself.

Aleister turned around in a fury. When he saw Pamela, his eyes lit up.

"You, the Smith girl," Aleister brayed. "Of course, you're here and you have access." Aleister charged up to Pamela and slapped the sketch pad out of her hands. He whipped around to the Golden Dawn Chiefs in front of the vault. "You give the assignment of the creation of these tarot cards to this simple girl, when you have one of the greatest minds of this century before you!"

Dr. Felkin tried to steer Aleister away as Pamela reached down to get her fallen sketch pad. Mathers and Felkin each held one of his arms, and Waite planted himself in front of Aleister and shook his finger at him.

"Mr. Crowley, Miss Smith has an extraordinary ability to draw," Waite shakily said. "She has an extremely deep knowledge of symbols, both talents you do not possess."

Even Pamela knew this was not the way to treat an enraged person with magical powers, and for a brief moment she felt almost sorry for Aleister.

Miss Horniman added, "We have a very exact directive that we are following in creating these tarot cards, Mr. Crowley."

"Yes, C-c-crowley, you will never create a tarot deck," Mathers said. "I'll see to that."

"Are you threatening me, Mathers?" Aleister said, as Dr. Felkin and Mathers tightened their hold on him.

"You have no talent for birthing a new tarot deck," Waite added smugly. "No drawing skills as far as I know, and what do you know of universal symbols?"

"But you, Mr. Waite, a clerk with no formal training, do?" Aleister asked, shaking off Dr. Felkin and Mathers's grip. "You, who have put this project in her very ill-prepared, mundane hands! If you really understood Lévi's version of magic and tarot, you would see that even your understanding of the pentagram is incorrect! You don't understand that the pentagram reversed represents evil, not good. You are blind! You are all a molt of muddled middle-class mediocrities!"

Miss Horniman sidled up to Aleister and stood before him. "Aleister, besides your hot temper, you show no sense for pure magic; this is why you will not be graduating to the second level."

Pamela took a deep breath and approached him, trying to touch his arm, but he jerked his arm from her and moved away. She lifted her hand to let the others know she would be alright and walked a couple steps to him, his back turned to her. "Aleister, that's Irish for Edward, isn't it? Not your given name, is it?"

Seething, he placed himself directly in front of her. "Damn my given name. My real name is Beast 666."

Where was that white light that came to her when she needed it? She closed her eyes. She would try to send a pulse, a throb of healing magic from inside her. Pamela moved even closer to him as he heaved before her. "We are kindred spirits, Aleister."

"We are not! I long for illumination, for perfect purity of life, for mastery of the secret forces of nature. You are a child playing with fire."

Aleister lifted his left hand in front of Pamela's face. It began to glow. The group backed away from him. With a booming shout, he raced past them to the open door of the vault, slamming the door behind him.

The men tried to force the door open as Aleister wailed in a language Pamela could not make out. Florence came to one side of Pamela and Miss Horniman held on to the other.

The thudding sounds of someone or something kicking the inside walls of the vault rang out, and the blasts of wood being splintered broke through the air. A hole in the side of the vault was soon punched out, and a blazing arm thrust itself out. Instead of a human arm, it was the arm of a beast on fire.

As he stepped through the hole into the room, human Aleister was no more. This monster's face was a golden goat with large horns, his haunches like a satyr with cloven hooves. Sputtering and cursing, he was at least two feet taller, and the beast spun and pivoted around them, invoking an incantation that none of them understood. The thing writhed until his hooves pawed at the floor, digging up the floorboards. The three men tried to reach out to him, but his left hand was now a torch, threatening to burn anyone who came near.

Huge bat wings were attached to Aleister's shoulders, and he grew to fifteen feet tall. He towered over them, his eyes transformed into golden embers. Pamela cowered under his wings as she watched a pentagram etch itself on his forehead.

His voice was now unrecognizable. "You are all caught in your own chains of imprisonment and powerlessness. I leave you to them."

He hovered over Pamela, his flaming arm almost grazing her face. His eyes glittered at her.

"I will destroy you and your name."

He charged to the other side of the room and hurled himself through the bank of windows. The sound of broken glass was drowned out by a howling wind, spraying glass shards at them. Everyone flinched, then stood in shocked silence. Pamela looked at the members of the Golden Dawn and backed away.

CHAPTER TWENTY-FOUR

PCS Magic

The emergency meeting two hours later at Ada's seemed more of a social visit than an urgent call to arms against an enraged sorcerer. Dr. Westcott was before the hearth with Mrs. Ada Leverson as Dr. Felkin and Waite mumbled with Miss Horniman and Florence, and Mathers made the best use of his time in a love seat with Mina. None of the Golden Dawn people who'd witnessed Aleister's transformation seemed rattled; they were more disturbed by the vandalism to the vault. But then, none of them had been threatened by Aleister as Pamela had.

Pamela paced around Ada's parlor, very different from how it looked during the concert with Susan Strong. As she walked from painting to painting hanging on the walls, her mind still reeled from Aleister's conjuring in the vault. She was desperate to be with Edy and Ellen, for their comfort and concern. But how would she explain a demon manifesting in front of her? Pamela tried to calm herself by looking at Ada's scenes of the French countryside and wet Parisian boulevards.

The last few chimes of the clock rang out as the group remained huddled over teacups and whiskey glasses. There was a jangle of the doorbell and a flurry of movement from the butler, and soon Bram was ushered into the parlor.

Bram broke the silence as he strode up to the hostess. "Ah, Mrs. Leverson, midnight, the witchin' hour, how good you are to let us meet at such short notice. I want to hear all about this spell Aleister pulled at the headquarters."

Pamela ran to Bram's side and uncharacteristically took his hand. He didn't shake it off. Ada insisted on first being apprised of the attendance of the Prince of Wales at the Lyceum Theatre and if he had also gone to the private supper that Mr. Irving held.

Bram spent the next ten minutes detailing the evening's performance of *King Arthur* (a standing ovation from the audience), the inclusion of Baroness Burdett-Coutts with the Prince of Wales's company, and the spring menu's inclusion of lamb for the Beefsteak Club supper. As much as Pamela had wanted to hear every detail earlier, now it seemed ridiculous. A man had turned into a devil in front of her and threatened to destroy her, and they were talking about the engraved menus for the supper.

The horror show Aleister put on kept echoing in her mind. Where did he get the power to transform himself? In Jamaican voodoo magic, birds turned into duppies that cursed you. Jamaican evil ones could transform into witches stealing babies, and Death could hunt you down like an ant. But Aleister's form was huge and vicious, his hatred almost a palpable thing. Because she had been chosen to design the tarot cards, this had set off Aleister's hatred of her. Was it just jealousy? It seemed unlikely that this alone prompted him to despise her to such unimagined depths. Pamela felt an icy patch of fear inside her, not only for herself but also for her future hopes. She squeezed Bram's hand as he finished describing the oysters that were eaten.

"The supper ended but a few minutes ago, and Miss Terry and Miss Craig have been summoned by the Prince to have drinks at the Savoy in a private dining room. Since this was a royal command, they were obliged to go." He saw Pamela's crestfallen face. "But they will make their way here as soon as possible."

There was a moment of silence as Florence and Ada looked at one another. Pamela watched the concerned looks on the women's faces. A private room with the Prince of Wales was not a light matter.

"Henry Irving, William Terriss, and the Prince's sister are also at the Savoy gathering," Bram added.

"Ah," Dr. Felkin said. "Safety in numbers."

Dr. Felkin, studying his own fine profile in the reflection of his half-empty whiskey glass, was perched between Miss Horniman and Ada. Miss Horniman wore a green, tunic-like day dress, while Florence was in her white blouse and skirt, but it was Ada's resplendent evening dress that took all of Pamela's focus. The intricate bodice was constructed as a dragonfly, its wings encasing her bosom. How dowdy Pamela felt in her Indian cotton dress.

"I'll be talking to you privately in just a minute, Miss Smith," Bram whispered as he gave her hand a soothing shake. He went over to Ada, Florence, and Miss Horniman, and the four of them talked amongst themselves in low voices.

Waite came and stood complacently in front of her, holding a glass with a rather hefty serving of whiskey. Mathers and Mina were in deep conversation on a nearby settee. They looked more like lovers than comrades in their non-blinking concentration on one another.

"Well, that was an exciting exhibition by Crowley tonight, wasn't it?" Waite said, his bloodshot blue eyes fixed on his drink.

"Exhibition?" Pamela asked. "It was something more than that, I think."

"Oh, come now," Waite said. "Why do you think he had to go in the vault before he became Baphomet the Devil? He obviously had someone plant all the costumes and such in there to give us a good scare and had someone have a blanket or other for him outside the window to catch him."

Pamela stared at him. Waite didn't believe the transformation?

"I knew at first sight not to trust him!" Pamela heard Dr. Westcott exclaim.

Ada broke off from the group and called for the butler to pass out cigars, even in front of the ladies, and for everyone to sit.

Miss Horniman took the prominent chair, and Ada stood next to her. Pamela sat at Florence's feet, who draped an arm over her shoulders.

"Well," Ada said, looking around. "The telling of Mr. Crowley's turn is amazing and frightening. I knew he was talented in possibly magical ways, but what you are saying is truly astonishing. Are you sure you didn't all ingest a drug for a group ceremony and experience a hallucination?"

Pamela watched Bram down his glass of whiskey as protests went up.

"Ada. You know me," Miss Horniman said, bringing a teacup closer to her. "Mr. Crowley may be talented. But he is deeply troubled. Florence suspected his intent to achieve even the lowest Level One in the group was not to be trusted. It turns out she was right."

Dr. Felkin sat back in his chair, blowing smoke. "The dilemma now is that we need to limit his access to the vault and to its powers. He obviously has the talent for group hallucination. Or manifestation."

Mina and Mathers broke off talking, and Mathers stood.

"D-d-deeply skilled in ways we are not," Mathers said. "He has spent time in a vault somewhere and has learned h-h-how to invoke spirits."

Dr. Felkin frowned. "Who do you suppose has been teaching him how to call them forth? Certainly, none of us have been tutoring him."

There was silence. Pamela watched each face as jaws twitched and sidelong glances went around the circle. It seemed these Golden Dawn rituals were the most coveted secrets. Could someone try to seize control by forbidden magic?

Bram sighed. "Well, it's not Yeats. He's in Dublin with Maud Gonne doing his singsong theatre."

Dr. Felkin hit his head with his palm. "Bennett. Allan Bennett. He's been going through a bad time, and I heard he had stayed with Crowley for a while. He taught him who Anwass is."

Dr. Westcott almost choked on his drink. "Of course! Bennett's a Buddhist now, so it is said. I remember once he told Crowley he wouldn't charge him for any knowledge he shared since he was given free lodging with him. The condition for sharing was that he would use it for good. Well, we've all seen how that worked."

"Will you continue to develop the tarot cards?" Ada asked Miss Horniman.

"Yes. But I don't think it's a good idea to have Miss Smith work on them at the headquarters," Miss Horniman said.

Miss Horniman refused to meet Pamela's eye. Was it because it wasn't safe for her or because it wasn't safe for the furniture there?

"She's been using the British Museum for research already. Pamela could use the office there full-time," Florence said. "I can check in on her when I go in to visit the mummy exhibit."

"And Mr. Kamal will protect Pamela at the museum," Bram said.

He would.

Mr. Kamal did feel like a true companion when they were both studying in the artifacts room. Sometimes, when he asked her about understanding her drawings, she felt he was the only one who really was interested in her concept of the cards. When Waite would disappear, which he did quite regularly, Mr. Kamal would bring her esoteric manuscripts with symbols from all the great cultures and religions, and he would point out to her something that appeared in one image and reappeared centuries later in another. Sticks would become wands in some tarot cards only to become swords in others. Waite would drone on and on about the Lévi French illustrations, but it was the Swiss deck of Claude Burdel, the Italian Sola-Busca deck, and the French Marseille tarot deck that spoke more eloquently to her. She thought of the simplicity of meaning that she'd been taught at Pratt and how Mr. Dow, her teacher, would be over the moon to see some of the artifacts Mr. Kamal had let her handle.

The butler entered. "Miss Ellen Terry and Miss Edy Craig."

Ellen, carrying her dog, and Edy rushed into the room, and Pamela ran to embrace them, the dog licking Pamela's face. Bram ambled over and hugged them like a big bear. The four of them made their way to the others. Ellen still wore her stage makeup, but somehow it didn't look coarse or bizarre; it only heightened her features in the dimly lit room. The men were rapt with attention as she approached.

"Miss Terry, Miss Craig," said Ada, "thank you so much for coming on such short notice. Your Pixie has had a most trying day."

Ellen linked arms with Bram and squeezed Pamela's hand. "I understand. Not that I understand what's happened. I only hope she is all right."

Pamela laughed, but it was a pale imitation of her usual laugh. "Miss Terry, I am fine."

Dr. Felkin blithely interjected, "You see, she's fine, Miss Horniman. We didn't need to involve Miss Terry."

Edy grimaced and then demanded of Dr. Felkin, "What happened tonight? Was there an assault on Pamela?"

Dr. Felkin rose from his seat and elegantly posed in front of Edy. "We sent word for you because one of our members seems to have had a nervous fit and threatened Pixie."

Edy stood toe to toe with him. "A fit? Threatened?"

Ellen tried to defuse the standoff by coming to Edy's side. "Ah, Dr. Felkin, was it Mr. Crowley?"

Dr. Felkin went back to his whiskey. "Yes, he had some sort of mental delusion. It could very well be depression or some sort of temporary mania."

"But he threatened Pamela?" Ellen asked.

"He threatened all of us, but Pamela seems to be his focus."

"How will you thwart him? Do we need to notify the police?"

"NO! No. The police are not necessary at this point. If he does more than boast, then we will have grounds to contact the police." Dr. Felkin puffed furiously on his cigar.

Bram then attracted attention by swinging his large arms to bring back circulation and moving his head back and forth to loosen it as though he were ready to step into a boxing ring. He then sparred with an imaginary opponent for a few swings. The conversation in the room came to a halt as the others watched him go at it.

Seeing their reaction, he dropped his arms, gave a slight chuckle and said, "Sorry, ladies and gents, I was just thinking on how I would like to take that Cambridge dandy on. But here's the thing: he can't touch us when we put our minds and energies to it. I feel the responsibility for the safety of our Pixie, since I'm the one who brought 'er in. For the next few days, Miss Terry, perhaps she could continue to stay with you while we sort out what we need to do?"

Pamela gazed at Bram in a new light. *Not just Mr. Irving's call button. Interesting,* she thought.

Ellen put an arm around Pamela. "She shall be well looked after."

Dr. Felkin put his hands over Ellen's, in an attempt to touch the grand lady. "Very well, then. We shall send Mr. Stoker to retrieve her when this whole breakdown business of Mr. Crowley's has been addressed."

Ellen smiled and retrieved her hands. "Excellent. Send word. We shall be at my lodgings, Bram. Good night, all."

Pamela turned to the group as she started to leave. "Good night, all. I hope Mr. Crowley recovers himself." Pamela, Edy, and Ellen were starting out when Dr. Westcott came and took Pamela by the elbow.

Smiling, he leaned down to whisper to her. "Just a quick word, Miss Pamela. I'll send you out in just a moment."

Ellen and Edy nodded and made their exit. Pamela looked around to see Bram and the others sitting back down around Ada.

Dr. Westcott stood over Pamela. "Miss Smith, you have seen the depth of Crowley's power. You must keep what you've seen to yourself, if you care about Miss Terry and Miss Craig."

Pamela's mouth twisted as she tried to say that she would not tell them, but the words would not come out.

"Until we discern Crowley's condition, you must not tell them what you have just seen. Do you understand me, Miss Smith? It would only endanger them."

"You think he would harm Miss Terry and Edy? They have nothing to do with the Golden Dawn."

"We will devote all our talents to making sure that you are all protected. But we are dealing with a madman who obviously has great abilities. Don't be frightened; we will do our best. Now, go with your beloveds. In a few days, Bram will come by and fetch you and let you know where we are." He added, "And Miss Smith, when you go to the museum to study with Mr. Kamal, don't go there alone." He looked at her almost fondly. "Remember, not a word."

Pamela stared at Dr. Westcott as he stroked his velvet waistcoat, trying to read his energy. She only saw a blank wall. He smiled back at her with a weak smile.

"As you say." Slowly she turned and saw Bram mid-discussion with Waite. "Good night, everyone."

They rose and bade her good night, Dr. Westcott strolling back to the group with a decanter he picked up off the buffet.

At the door, she pivoted and glanced back at Waite. He stood out from the others in a strange light not emanating from the fireplace. In her mind, she felt the pulse of the clicking start up again. Waite gestured in mid-conversation as dark dots gathered above his head. Pamela could see from the doorway that they were letters from a typewriter. The click-clacking started to pound inside her like a drum as the letters swarmed around him. They seemed to fly and swirl like insects until they formed a small tornado. The mass swirled its way toward her. The noise in her head pounded, the throbbing beat growing louder as it grew closer and closer. Pamela took a step back.

Out of the cloud stepped a man. It was William Terriss, wearing the costume of the Fool she had been drawing. She gasped and put her hand out to touch his arm. He vanished. Three letters—*P C S*—swirled around her and then floated past her into the parlor's chimney and up the flue. She stood open-mouthed. The room stopped talking for a moment.

"Are you all right, Miss Smith?" Ada asked.

Pamela took a breath. "The light fooled me just now. I'm fine." She turned and fled.

CHAPTER TWENTY-FIVE

FINDING THE TOOLS

A hmed sat back in the chair in his new office and lowered the letter he had just read. The British Museum would promote him if he didn't make trouble for Lord Compton, as it was decided that the museum would "let" the statue of Sekhemka live in Northampton. He read the letter again: *Spencer Compton, second Marquis of Northampton, who took possession of the statue of Sekhemka in 1850, has left it to his son, Lord William Compton. Rather than return the statue to Egypt, Lord Compton has agreed to donate it to the Northampton Museum, an affiliate of the British Museum.*

What would the Egyptian ambassador receive in exchange for this? During this time of British occupation or the "veiled protectorate" in Egypt, there were many under-the-table negotiations. Ahmed's job was to come to England and track down and procure the "wandering" artifacts that left his country and secure them for the new museum that his ruler, Khedive Tawfiq, was building in Cairo. And Sekhemka was to be the focus of a major exhibit.

In pristine condition when "found," this magnificent two-and-a-half-foot sandstone statue from the fifth dynasty depicted the royal chief and judge Sekhemka with a scroll on his lap, and his wife, Sit-Merit, sitting at his side. The statue had been found near the Giza pyramids, at the archeological site where Ahmed had worked during his tenure at the Giza Museum. How this statue had made its way from Giza to Northampton—rather than to the museum in Giza where Ahmed worked—was a subject of much debate and some heartbreak, at least in Egyptian circles.

How would Sekhemka, royal chief and judge, rule on this case? Ahmed wondered. Would it be better that this statue live in a museum for the English public to see rather than in a private house as a rich man's plaything? The Westcar papyrus was in a museum in Berlin thousands of miles from the ancestors who created it. Or should these treasures be left in the unguarded vaults of his people in Egypt, possibly plundered by the next regime or impoverished workmen?

As he sat there wondering what his course of action should be or even could be, he saw Pamela wander down the hall, her diminutive frame barely seen over the glass window.

She is not your typical Englishwoman, he thought. *Not like Miss Farr.* Florence Farr made regular appointments to sit next to one of the mummies while Sir Ernest did his tours here. She played a small hand harp and claimed to be having silent communion with Mutemmenu, the mummy of a young student from Thebes.

It was so curious that these English people, with an army of saints to worship, found the mummies from his homeland a compelling source of devotion. Florence was knowledgeable about Egypt; she lectured on it and knew its history. It was only a real Egyptian person that seemed to confound her, as Ahmed had tried on several occasions to start a conversation with her, only to have her defer to Sir Ernest. He couldn't tell if she was being demure or polite to the older Englishman in acknowledging him over Ahmed, but he found it odd that she had not a single question for him about his homeland and traditions. "Here is Egypt!" he had almost said to her the last time she avoided asking him a question.

Pamela was different. She would look at him with widened eyes and ask repeatedly for stories, personal stories: how he came to speak English and French, if he took part in the excavations at Dayr al-Barsha and the Nile Valley. She was the only one who seemed impressed that he had written eight encyclopedias. She seemed less interested in his hopes to start schools and a council of his country's antiquities in Cairo.

These tarot cards she was commissioned to draw were troublesome to Ahmed. Her employers wanted her to pick the icons from different cards and cultures, the Sola-Busca, the Burdel deck from Switzerland, the Lévi Illustrations, and now Egyptian symbols. It was a tower of Babel, with none of these men understanding the cultural integrity of what these symbols represented or the context of the stories they came from.

Another curiosity about this English girl was that she was not willing to draw anything on the card to just please Waite, who seemed more interested in looking through the private, exclusive research materials than concentrating on what these tarot cards were to accomplish. And their purpose was something Ahmed had yet to draw out of any of these "Golden Dawn" people. But Pamela seemed to understand that uniting select symbols from across cultures might create a cohesive image and message. She seemed to intrinsically understand the relationships that would connect them. Ahmed approved of her ability to find the universal link in the images she drew.

He watched her drift up to the new office.

She hesitantly knocked and opened the door. As she stood in the doorway, she clutched her satchel in one hand, her drawing pad in another. "Oh, Mr. Kamal, I wasn't sure this was your new office," she said, dropping her satchel on the nearest chair. "This is much nicer than your old one."

She sat down and looked at Ahmed at the big desk. With his black coat instead of the usual muslin overcoat, he looked like a teacher instead of the archivist she was familiar with.

"Miss Smith, what is to be your inspiration today?" he asked, putting his letter away.

"My favorite story—Osiris," she answered, hanging her coat up. "I'm still trying to get him in my magician card."

Ahmed leaned forward. "Why don't you tell me the story as you draw, and I'll point out the inaccuracies?"

Pamela laughed. This was her favorite part of working alongside Ahmed. He actually wanted to hear her talk. If she couldn't have music on the gramophone playing while she drew, then talking about what she was seeing was the second-best way to be inspired. Pamela took out a folded piece of paper from her satchel and put it on the small table in front of Ahmed's desk.

"I was able to decipher the hieroglyphics in your note."

"And what does it say?"

Pamela gestured to the paper's bird, the sideways figure eight, and the lion. "'The genius of creative utterance needs protection from evil.'"

"Do you need my protection?"

"I mostly need your help," she replied, setting out her sketch pad and bundle of pencils. She opened her pad and began to sketch the rough figure of a robed man. "What is the saying about Osiris again? The one that sounds like our King Arthur story?"

"'Only through the return of the king can order be restored to Egypt,'" Ahmed said.

"Yes. So, we start with Osiris, the all-powerful king, murdered by the jealous god Set."

"And why did Set kill his brother?" Ahmed asked, the memories of teaching in Cairo coming back.

"Because Osiris slept with his brother's wife and made her pregnant with Anubis," Pamela replied as she drew a staff in the right hand of the robed figure.

"Correct," Ahmed said, glancing at her pad. "You might want to make that staff bigger. Most men appreciate a larger . . . weapon. And how did he kill him?"

Pamela giggled. Only Ahmed could make remarks like that without making her feel self-conscious. He was like the brother she never had. "He invited Osiris to a party and invited everybody to try out a coffin, then nailed him shut in it." On Pamela's sketch pad, the figure's left hand pointed down. "And threw the coffin with Osiris locked in it into the Nile."

"And the world was thrown into chaos," Ahmed said.

"Yes, the world was thrown into chaos. Like now," Pamela replied. She concentrated on the snake around the man's waist and a figure eight above his head. "The symbols of the eternal struggle, the ouroboros and lemniscate—waiting for magic to begin life again."

"Well, Miss Smith, the snake devouring itself, the ouroboros, is actually Egyptian," Ahmed explained, leaning over his desk to see. "However, the lemniscate, the figure eight, is Greek."

"Good, because I'm putting in symbols from all over the world," Pamela said, ignoring Ahmed's sigh. She felt he didn't approve of her using images from all the cultures she could. "And now my favorite part of the story. Isis finds her husband's body still in the coffin. She flies above him like a kite and conceives a child."

"The less said about this part of the story, the better," Ahmed said, putting his feet up on the ottoman near him.

Drawing a band on the figure's forehead, she continued. "She wanted her husband to have eternal life, but then the murderer, Set, found the coffin. He hacked up Osiris's body into fourteen different pieces and scattered them around."

"Fairly accurate so far," Ahmed said, looking out the window at the diminishing light.

"Isis found all his body parts—except his male member, that was never found—and reassembled them."

"Well, it is said she used magic to have it reconstituted," Ahmed murmured.

"What does that mean?" Pamela asked.

Ahmed half closed his eyes.

"I can see you don't want to tell me, but are you saying that she had a magic spell that put his penis back together?"

Ahmed blinked at her.

"You said one blink is for yes," Pamela said. Her face unexpectedly reddened. "Well, that's a new wrinkle to the Osiris story."

"Let's just say that Isis was the first to use precious tools to embalm someone." He glanced at her drawing pad. On the table a sword, cup, wand, and star lay before the magician.

"You can bring someone back from the dead by embalming them?" Pamela asked.

"Yes, Osiris was brought back to eternal life to rule over the dead, in the land of the deceased," Ahmed said, standing to look out at the garden below.

"And this was through magic?" Pamela asked, standing and joining him at the leaded glass window.

"Magic of the gods," Ahmed answered. "It is a dangerous magic not meant for mortals."

"I see," Pamela said, sitting on the windowsill.

"What's wrong, Miss Smith?" Ahmed asked. "Are you being pressured to put magical symbols into your tarot drawings?"

"The magic Waite wants in the tarot cards seems very confusing," Pamela answered, looking at Ahmed. "And it's the Golden Dawn Chiefs who really want some sort of magical formula in the cards."

Ahmed gently cleared his throat and asked, "Do you think your gentlemen from the Golden Dawn are playing with fire?"

"You could say that," Pamela said as she sat back down. She doodled a dragon on a blank piece of paper. "One of them . . . turned into or . . . rather, he . . . revealed himself to be . . . a demon. The Devil."

Ahmed stood near. "Ah. The Devil. What did he look like?"

She flipped several pages back in her sketch pad and took out Lévi's Devil card, the goat-faced demon with bat wings.

"The French cards you showed us here, Mr. Kamal, it was with the Lévi tarot cards," Pamela said. She handed him her sketch pad. "This was the demon that Aleister turned into in the vault."

"Aleister?" he asked. "Ah, so not one of the Golden Dawn Chiefs who have come here but someone else? Tell me the story of what happened, from the beginning."

Pamela crossed her arms and looked down, unsure of what she should tell him.

He leaned forward and gently said, "You will have no worries about me knowing, I promise you."

Pamela let out a long breath and began with the story of meeting Aleister at Mrs. Leverson's soiree, where he paralyzed her. Then the disastrous second meeting at the Golden Dawn was told, and sounds click-clacking in her head around Waite, and the vision of letters above Mr. Waite's head at Mrs. Leverson's house.

Ahmed paced back and forth as Pamela recounted every-thing that had happened to her. He stopped and looked at her. "You never had any magical happenings before meeting these people?"

Pamela squirmed. "Well, they don't seem magical to me. But I've always felt things differently. Colors have tastes, num-bers have substance, time has textures. I've never thought of it as magical. Oh, I did once fly when I was seven years old, but only for a brief time."

"That sounds like you possess your own magic, Miss Smith."

"I never considered it *my* magic. It's just magic that is avail-able in the world. I can't control it. Like those typewriter sounds when Mr. Waite is around."

"But those sounds and your initials appearing to you esca-lated once you agreed to illustrate the tarot cards?" Ahmed asked.

"Yes," Pamela said.

He only had a few more questions to ask her. "What was this vault?" "Who has been claiming to make magic?" "Have *you* done any incantations?"

Pamela was conflicted but remained silent.

Then came his final question, "Do you know why these gentlemen want you to design these cards?"

"Mr. Waite says it is for meditation on a hero's journey for a select group."

"Meditation! These are amateur magicians, the most dangerous kinds, Miss Smith! They have every intention of using whatever passage to the other side that your cards will provide."

Pamela's hand instinctually closed the cover of her sketch pad. "And they are not to be trusted?"

Ahmed took a moment and looked at her. "What do you think, Miss Smith?"

"I don't know."

"Exactly. That is why, if you allow me, we can safeguard some of the magic your tarot cards will create."

"Why does my magic need safeguarding?" Pamela asked. Was Ahmed trying to limit the magic she was almost touching? "I've always channeled it to come out as whatever it wants. Like when I flew."

"Miss Pamela, you do realize that on the other side, there are just as many spirits and energies as there are here? Would you present yourself to any common crowd and invite them to come home with you and live inside your head? Or mingle with an undead who does not realize they are dead and wants to attach itself to you? No, you must learn to discern which spirit has good intent. This Aleister may have invited a very evil spirit to live inside his vibrations."

Pamela stopped for a moment and heard music, its drumbeat growing steadily. "I think he has," she whispered. "Mr. Kamal, I think my Fool card has already come alive."

"What makes you say that?"

"Because he came to me at Mrs. Leverson's."

"How did he come to you, Miss Smith?" Ahmed asked, standing very still.

"A mass of typewriter keys swarmed around Mr. Waite's head until it looked like a cloud of insects. Then, I thought I saw Mr. Terriss step out of it looking like this—"

She motioned to her sketch pad, where the Fool wore a brightly colored tunic.

Ahmed's eyes grew wide. He took a satchel from the bottom desk drawer and said, "Bring the rest of your sketches!"

He hurried them out the door.

CHAPTER TWENTY-SIX

Saving the Fool

Pamela and Ahmed halted at the darkened entrance of the Egyptian Sanctuary's Monumental Room. This staging area had been off-limits to Pamela during her time at the museum. Ahmed took a candle from his satchel and lit it. As the weak light seeped into the room, they could see deep grooves scratched into the stone floor. The grooves led to an empty sarcophagus pushed up against the wall.

"Could a person push that stone coffin?" Pamela asked.

"Not a typical person," Ahmed replied, and set the candle down in the middle of the room. The sarcophagus had been pushed up against a sandstone mural lining the enclosure, a depiction of four winged creatures: a man, an ox, a lion, and an eagle.

Pamela ran to it and traced the figures with her finger. "My *King Arthur* banner," she murmured.

"This stela has spoken to you before?" Ahmed asked. Pamela nodded.

He removed a piece of cloth from the satchel and unrolled it, motioning for her to sit. He placed a small metal dish before Pamela. After he poured powdered incense onto it, he struck a match and held it to the pile of powder. It flamed and he blew on it until the pungent scent of sandalwood filled the air.

"Can you take out your Fool?" Ahmed asked.

She quickly found the drawing of the Fool in her sketch-book and tore it out. She placed it next to the burning incense, leaving her sketchbook on the ground.

Ahmed stood on the other side of the bowl of sandalwood smoke and made a short bow in four directions. He began with what Pamela assumed was north and continued until all four points on the compass were acknowledged. In a language Pamela didn't recognize, he filled the chamber with chanting, its hum echoing off the stone walls. Quickly, he finished his chant and sat down cross-legged opposite Pamela. He pressed his palms together. She watched him as he lifted both arms straight up. He looked at her and nodded at her to do the same.

"Go to your Fool in your mind's eye," Ahmed said.

Pamela closed her eyes and saw the stage of the Lyceum Theatre, the curtains drawn shut. There was a throng of activity onstage. It was the rehearsal for *King Arthur*. Ellen and Mr. Irving were dressed in their finery, and the entire cast was assembled before them. But they were all looking up. On a high, narrow bridge that spanned the set perched an actor dressed as Lancelot: William Terriss. In his floral tunic and boots, even at twenty-five feet up in the air, Pamela could recognize him. He was the very image of Pamela's Fool in the card she had drawn.

"Ask for guidance," Ahmed instructed.

"Help me?" Pamela said, her voice breaking.

Ahmed sighed. "For your Fool," he said patiently.

Did he think she knew magic? Confused, she picked up her Fool card. As she touched it, the dreaded clicking sound tapped in her head, growing in volume, and she quickly put the card back down. Ahmed closed his eyes and placed his hands over his ears. She imitated him and the typing stopped. The smoke from the incense tumbled and rolled over the Fool card. It started to form the shape of a person, expanding until she could make out the figure of a tall man. From within a plume of smoke, the fully formed image of William Terriss appeared before them, undulating between Ahmed and Pamela.

A burst of music brought back the image of the Lyceum stage. The *King Arthur* overture thrummed from the orchestra pit as Mr. Irving stomped out from backstage, throwing the curtain aside to address the conductor. He was carrying the staff that was rumored to have fallen out of the sky. Pamela could see the entire scene as though she were on a chandelier looking down.

Mr. Irving paused at the edge of the stage looking down at the full orchestra. "Sir Arthur, I thought we'd cut that phrase?"

The theatre company waiting in the wings groaned. To start the technical run-through with Mr. Irving in the full throttle of displeasure was an omen of a very long rehearsal ahead. The euphoria of last evening's performance was now completely gone. Lovejoy, as official stage manager, drew his hand across his throat to indicate to the acting company that they should settle down. Off-duty police officers and military men hired to be soldiers in the pageant scene slumped against the nearest backstage wall. In circumstances like this, Ellen would usually rally the troupe with a quick jig, or tease one of the older actors about his costume, but now she stood looking straight ahead, seemingly oblivious to the restlessness of the cast.

"Something's wrong," Pamela whispered to Ahmed.

Sir Arthur conducted the overture's first phrase again, and Mr. Irving barked, "Too many flourishes!"

Pamela could see Ellen looking around as she stood in place for her entrance. She was probably looking for Edy, who would run to her and make sure everything was sorted out, but Pamela knew Edy was not working on *King Arthur*. Edy was with Christopher St. John, starting their own theatre group, the Pioneer Players. Pamela could hear the sound of nails click-clacking on the wood floors. It was Trin, the Eskimo dog belonging to William Terriss, who had escaped the dressing room, rushing to Ellen's side.

"Excellent, Sir Arthur, just the right length," Mr. Irving announced. "All right, Mr. Lovejoy, let us set for the first entrance, top of show."

Mr. Irving took long strides to the closed-curtain backstage, putting his King Arthur helmet on as he walked. The backstage crew and cast stood at attention, and the great velvet curtains were swept to the side, revealing the house. The painted canvas, done by Craven, Harker, and Smith, shimmered with a painted castle and forest. Seeing the painting almost took Pamela out of the moment and back to her ten-year-old self, painting in front of Bram Stoker and the crew.

As the lights onstage came up, Mr. Irving led his army from the wings to center stage. The knight's promenade for the first scene had begun. Pamela was glad not to be an extra in this scene, wearing that heavy unbearable armor. A whistle from the stage crew notified everyone that it was "heads up" for all on stage. In the catwalk above, Terriss walked cautiously along the rails preparing for his entrance.

Terriss placed one tentative foot on the catwalk. Pamela's head jerked back. "He's crossing!" she cried, and opened her eyes.

"Crossing *what*?" Ahmed shot back. "A river? A mountain? To the other side?"

"A catwalk!"

"A *catwalk*? What is that?"

"A crossover ladder above the stage!"

"You are at a theatre?" Ahmed asked, his voice unusually gruff.

"Yes! I'm in the Lyceum Theatre fly space, looking down."

"This 'he' is the Fool? Your incarnate?" Ahmed asked.

"Yes. He is crossing over on the catwalk."

"What do you see now?" he asked.

"I'm above him," Pamela said. "He's got one foot on the ladder, and the other is in midair. He's swaying over the edge."

The smoky form of Terriss wavered between them. Pamela picked up her drawing with both hands and held it steady. Waite's typewriter clicking started up again, shifting to a faster rhythm. It became a roar, taking over the room. Ahmed pointed to the ceiling.

Small dots of light appeared above them. They flickered and spun until they formed the letters—P C S—and drifted down. Each letter swirled like a snowflake at the end of a storm and as they descended, intertwined, becoming one shape. The melded image floated in front of them and circled around the Fool drawing, still clutched in Pamela's hand. Like a humming-bird finding nectar, the letters darted into the Fool card, settling on the lower right-hand side. Next to the little white dog's feet on the cliff, the initials glowed like embers.

The cries of extras watching on the stage brought Pamela's focus back to Terriss. He put one foot in front of the other on the shaky catwalk as his Eskimo dog barked below. Startled, the actor looked down and began to lose his balance. He tried to grab the sides of the catwalk to steady himself but instead tumbled over and fell through the air.

Suddenly Pamela was no longer in the Sanctuary Room watching but was in the Lyceum Theatre fly space, falling with Terriss! The same sensation she felt years ago as she was falling from the Waterloo Bridge hit her in the stomach. Terriss had rescued her from the Thames then; she could save him now. Instinctively, she thought of her three initials still glowing on her Fool drawing and was instantly back on the floor of the stone chamber with Ahmed. In one hand she clutched her Fool card; with her other hand she reached out to catch the falling Fool in the smoke. It writhed and twisted, but the bobbing specter ceased its fall.

The sound of a deck of cards shuffling caught both Pamela and Ahmed's attention. Looking up, Pamela saw tarot cards placed like shingles on a ceiling. A flutter of them streamed down, like a deluge from rain clouds. Pamela and Ahmed flinched when the first cards reached them; they were sharp-edged and bit into their hands and face. They stood, and Ahmed tried to slap the barrage of cards away, the edges slicing into their skin. Despite the biting pain, Pamela kept a firm grip on her Fool card in her left hand, her right hand balancing Terriss the Fool, suspended in smoke.

The smoke around the Fool suddenly twisted into a vortex. The Fool twirled, and was thrown against the ceiling. A gray haze overcame the room, and a dull, ghastly sound vibrated from the floor. It was a dog moaning, then howling. Pamela realized now it was a violent wind carrying the cards and whipping both she and Ahmed. There were even more cards now, carving their ears, their hands, and faces.

From the dim haze of the smoke, there appeared a pair of golden eyes set in a monster's face. Squinting, Pamela could make out a set of ram's horns on its head; in place of its left hand, a lit torch; and finally, the cloven feet of the Devil.

It was Aleister, in his monstrous form that she had witnessed at the Golden Dawn.

He blew the cards every which way and lit them on fire with his torch. She and Ahmed cried out as the wind flung the razor-sharp cards at them. Pamela struggled to keep her Fool card and reached out to try to regain control of the image of the falling Terriss as he flailed against the ceiling.

Aleister levitated above Pamela and Ahmed, exhaling flames of orange and yellow from his gaping maw. This seemed to use some of his power because the wind died down and the cards' attack lessened. Ahmed grabbed a handful of powdered incense from his satchel, and as the Devil expelled a ball of fire toward them, Ahmed threw the incense around Pamela and himself. The incense ignited instantly, creating a protective bubble of flames that flared all around them. Aleister stood outside the orb, and the blaze consumed his volley of cards.

As Aleister attempted to penetrate their fiery sphere, sharp howls reverberated in the room. His fire turned against him; the singed fur of his satyr-like legs emitted an overpowering odor that almost made Pamela gag. His demonic shape was consumed by the inferno, turning from bright red to charred black. He howled and screamed. Ash fell from the outline of the beast, a gray snow of soot falling on the stone floor. Fire had consumed fire, as Miss Jones had told Pamela it would long ago.

With alarm, Pamela looked up. With Aleister's magic no longer keeping the Fool against the ceiling, the likeness of Terriss writhed midair. Pamela took a sharp intake of breath, and as she exhaled their sphere of fire was extinguished.

Pamela threw her Fool card up to the smoky, twisting form of Terriss with both hands, crying, "Fly, Fool!"

As the card careened up, Pamela was back at the theatre, watching Terriss slip from the catwalk.

Mr. Irving whipped off his new crown as Pamela's spirit flew near his ear.

"I need the Magician's tools!" she cried.

Without even looking for the source of the voice, Mr. Irving understood. He held up the wand in his right hand. In a heartbeat, it turned blood red. As if in a spell, the cast and crew were literally frozen in place.

In Mr. Irving's quick-change room, the altar latch opened, and out fell the prop box holding the sword, the cup, and the star necklace. Pamela's heart soared as she watched the three talismans fly out of the room toward the stage. They climbed upwards, to Terriss high in the rafters. The star necklace caught the actor by the feet and dangled him in midair. The sword sailed to the end of the catwalk and slit open a burlap sack. From the sack streamed a river of prop snow. As the snow fell from the sack, it was caught by the cup positioned below. The cup then piled the snow into a mound right beneath Terriss. As the snow piled up, Pamela could only watch from above.

"Where is your Fool?" Ahmed's voice rang out in her ear.

"Suspended in air," Pamela answered.

"Guide him down," Ahmed said.

Pamela whispered to Mr. Irving again. "Command your magic."

Mr. Irving, wand in hand, flicked his wrist. With the sword and cup floating around Terriss, the star necklace gently lowered him onto the pile of artificial snow. Once his body lay safely on the ground, Mr. Irving used the wand to signal the enchanted objects to vanish. They flew like ravens back to their nesting place in the quick-change room.

Pamela flitted down to Terriss, still collapsed on the stage floor. His face was contorted, his eyes closed, his arms crossed against his chest. The combined shape of her initials glowed on his earlobe.

She was ten years old again, back on the banks of the Thames, where he was comforting her after her fall from the Waterloo Bridge. "We're so alive," had said to her then. Pamela's eyes teared up as she whispered the same to the unconscious actor. "We're so alive."

His body jerked upwards, as though a rope had grabbed him by the midsection and lifted him. A great breath expanded his lungs, and he started to breathe. The same breath pushed Pamela upwards, and no matter how she struggled, she couldn't get closer to him. What magic was this that didn't let her stay with her Fool? She drifted in the fly space, watching Terriss below.

As Terriss started to come to, Pamela noticed that everyone else in the theatre had frozen in place. They were no witnesses to this moment.

All, that is, except Henry Irving, who cast his eyes up to the floating Pamela as if seeing her for the first time. He nodded at her and waved his staff over the stationary actors and crew, all standing in frozen poses. They shifted and gasped. The spell over them had been revoked. Pamela tried to reach out, but her essence was only a fume, haunting the catwalk.

The stage slowly shrugged back to life. Actors shook their

heads, and soldiers rubbed their legs as though they were feeling the prickly sensation of limbs that had fallen asleep. Then, as if on cue, the actors on stage were aware of Terriss struggling to raise himself from a pile of rock salt.

Mr. Irving crouched down to lift him. Lovejoy, Bram, and the other stagehands dashed in from offstage. The actors around them watched as Bram and Lovejoy lifted Terriss from the prop snow and stood him on his feet. The actors began to applaud and cheer, Terriss's dog barking madly, as cries of relief and amazement echoed through the house. Ellen was the first to embrace Terriss. Pamela felt her heart swell.

Mr. Irving turned to Terriss after the third embrace by yet another comely actress. "That was the foolhardiest thing I've ever seen. How you survived that fall, I have no idea."

Terriss laughed and shook himself. "Yes, I *am* a Fool."

Ellen inserted herself next to Terriss and brushed the remains of salt off him. "Oh, Henry, thank God that bag of rock salt fell at the same time!"

Bram said, "How on earth did that snow fall?"

Harvey, the prop master, came forward and examined the salt pile.

"When the catwalk broke, it must have sliced open the bag," Lovejoy said.

"Sure, the metal edges of the bridge must have torn it," Harvey said. "We always store the snow for *The Corsican Brothers* up there. Never been a problem!"

"Another thing fiddled with here," Lovejoy said. "Let's go see to that catwalk."

Lovejoy and Harvey went off, fighting among themselves as they raced one another to inspect the catwalk. Harvey insisted it must have been the "theatre ghosts." Ellen immediately went trotting after them.

"Ghosts! In our theatre?" Ellen asked. "We have a theatre ghost? Oh, Mr. Harvey, you must tell me!"

Pamela tried to shout out, but no sound came.

Bram stood very close to Mr. Irving and Terriss, speaking in a low voice so that no one else could hear.

"It was almost as if it happened by magic," Bram said.

Mr. Irving's large, dark eyes studied Bram. "Almost."

Bram asked, "You all right, Terriss?"

"Unbelievably, yes. Of all things, only my earlobe burns."

They looked at his right earlobe. It had a faint tattoo of a cross, formed from the letters *P, C,* and *S.* Mr. Irving instantly put his hand up to *his* right earlobe. Bram and Terriss looked at Mr. Irving: the same tattoo.

A warm feeling bubbled up inside of Pamela. These two men she so loved were the first incarnations for her Major Arcana.

Bram whistled and then chuckled. "Well, gentlemen, you're marked men."

In the blink of an eye, Pamela was back in the Sanctuary Room with Ahmed, sitting on the floor. Ahmed's forehead and nose had rivulets of blood streaming down his face. She looked at her hands; they had the same little cuts as on Ahmed's face. She touched her own forehead and looked at her fingers. They, too, were spotted with blood.

Standing, she realized their clothes had been sliced in places by Aleister's cards.

Aleister!

She looked around. Aleister was gone, nothing left of him but a pile of ashes. Smoldering black mounds of his burnt tarot cards glowed on the floor. She sighed a breath of relief. When she exhaled she was astounded by the force of her breath. It blew Aleister's ashes away, leaving only a wisp of smoke that curled and snaked under the door.

"Is Aleister dead?" Pamela asked, turning to Ahmed.

"This incarnation of him burned," Ahmed answered, wiping away a bloody smudge on his cheek. "That's all we can be sure of."

Her Fool card slowly drifted down from the ceiling and dangled between them. It spun like a globe there and grew larger and larger until it was life-sized. It stopped spinning. A whole scene appeared behind the Fool: mountains, a cliff, the sun, and the little dog. The Fool stepped off the cliff and into the room. The little dog also came to life, jumping off the card and barking excitedly. The three figures, Pamela, Ahmed and the Fool, stared at one another, the little dog dancing between them.

In the fabric of the Fool's tunic, ten circles spun, sending out rays of light. As the beams reached the wounds on Ahmed's and Pamela's faces and hands, they healed instantly.

The Fool and the dog stepped back into the life-sized card. It fell over onto the floor.

Pamela heard the pages of her sketchbook rustling. She ran to it, and the sketch of the Magician flew from the pages. It also spun in the air, and as with the Fool card before it, grew to life-size. Within this huge card, the four talismans appeared on a table, and the Magician himself appeared, holding a staff up in the air. With a flick of his wrist, the tarot card shrank in size and dropped next to the Fool card. A perfect pair.

Unfazed, Ahmed stood back and looked at her. "Miss Smith, your first battle is won." He picked up the two cards on the floor. "Your tarot cards are now coming to life. You've opened this Pandora's box, and they've found manifestations of their own. They've been here all along just waiting for a source to inhabit, one that you've created."

Pamela took the cards from Ahmed. "How did the cards come to life? How did Mr. Irving know how to save Terriss?"

Ahmed pointed to her Magician card. "Ah, Miss Smith, the Magician has access to other spirits. You helped him call in his tools."

On her Magician card, she looked at the four tools: the wand, cup, sword, and star.

"There's *The Corsican Brothers* sword, and the cup from the night the big mirror broke, the wand that Mr. Irving keeps in his altar, and the star from Satish's necklace. My Mr. Irving is my Magician!"

As she peered at her Magician, the initials *P C S* glowed in the corner of the card. She stared at the Magician and Fool cards, one in each hand.

On the Fool card, she recognized the tunic of Nera, the Fool held captive on the "other side." The one Maud had told her about during her childhood stories: his tunic decorated with ten stars, the little dog at his side.

"Are these magic cards?"

Ahmed came up next to her. "You have called in energies from the other side. They obviously know that they will be needed for some sort of grand battle coming up. It looks as if you will be in charge of the order in which they are to be created."

She looked at Ahmed, a new feeling creeping over her. What was it? Maternal? Resentful of responsibility? "I just wanted to draw magical cards. Why do I have to be responsible for the magic they pull?"

"You are only responsible for your journey, Miss Smith."

"And what is my journey, Mr. Kamal?" Pamela asked.

"Only you can answer that, Miss Smith," Ahmed replied, picking up the incense bowl and cloth. "Are you on a hero's journey or a fool's?"

Pamela laughed for the first time. "Do they have to be one or the other?" she asked.

Now it was Ahmed's turn to laugh. "Well," he said, gesturing to the cards in her hands. "There are your Magician and Fool. Who is next?"

Pamela looked at her cards. A shimmer of energy came to her. "It will be—a High Priestess."

Ahmed's smile spread across his face. "Yes, Miss Smith, a High Priestess. And then?"

Pamela saw a Major Arcana, like the suite of cards in the Sola-Busca deck she had seen in the museum. "Empress, Emperor . . ."

As she recalled as many Major Arcana cards as she could, the room filled with a bright white light. The piles of burnt tarot cards on the floor floated upwards. From the ashes, the ceiling filled with the glowing outlines of twenty-two cards.

Pamela called out their names. "Hierophant, Lovers, Chariot, Justice—"

The outlines swirled between Ahmed and Pamela, presenting themselves before them when the card was called.

"Hermit, Wheel of Fortune, Strength, the Hanged Man—"

The cards arranged themselves in an arc, floating above Ahmed and Pamela.

"Death, Temperance, Devil, the Tower—"

More transparent outlines of cards glided to complete the arc.

"Star, Moon, Sun, Judgment."

The last glowing skeleton of a card completed the lineup. "The World."

The full-color, completed Fool and Magician cards floated up from Pamela's hands to complete the arc.

Twenty luminous incomplete shapes of cards glistened above them. The two fully manifested tarot cards anchoring the deck.

Ahmed grazed his fingers lightly over the Magician and Fool cards.

"You have found your first incarnates of your cards, Miss Smith. It will be up to you to create a pathway to protect your muses and ensure that these cards do not fall into evil hands."

Pamela edged closer to her cards. Twenty Major Arcana tarot cards still awaited creation. In the foot of her Fool card, her initials glimmered. Her shimmering Magician almost hid her initials in the flora of his garden.

She touched the letters. They glowed. They felt as warm and gentle as the breath of a sleeping child.

"My initials. My name, my father's name, and my mother's name. *P C S.* Pamela Colman Smith."

Ahmed softly whispered, "They will be your legacy, Miss Smith. What do you have to say to them?"

Pamela heard Maud's voice from all those years ago.

With a catch in her voice, she called to her cards:

"Fly!"

Acknowledgments

Foremost thanks to Stuart Kaplan and Lynn Aruajo at US Games Systems, Inc., the publisher who first brought Pamela's tarot cards out for major printing in 19171, for their encouragement and access to Pamela Colman Smith's materials. I'd also like to express my gratitude to the family of Pamela Colman Smith for their interest and permission to view and research Pamela's art and artifacts. This labor of love, in all its incarnations, would not have been possible without Robert Petkoff and Cynthia Wands. Special thanks to Debbie and Larry Freundlich, Deb Brody, and editors Jennifer Pooley and Shelbie Myers for helping me in the initial stages of putting this book together. To my writing groups, Barbara Lucas, Laura Schofer, Gro Flather, Finola Austin, Catherine Siemann, Loretta Goldberg, Kate Gale, Sandy McDonald, and Ellen Rachlin, thank you for your feedback and perspectives. Finally, a special acknowledgment of my readers and champions: Sasha Graham, Lisa J. Yarde, Kent Meredith, Christina Burz, Gillian, Burz, Margaret Emory, Mary Micari, Krystal Kennedy, Karen McKendrick, Ryan Brown, Joel Jones, Seth Jones, Eve Luppert, Joel Patterson, Diana Bloom, Nikki Saunders, and Holly Webber.

ABOUT THE AUTHOR

S usan Wands is a writer, tarot reader, and actor. A graduate from the University of Washington, she has acted professionally across the United States and on Broadway. Her adaptation of *Pride and Prejudice* was produced at the Cornish Institute in Seattle and she has written plays, screenplays, and skits and produce several indie films. She was a company member in Rumble in the Red Room, an off-Broadway troupe, for four years. As a co-chair with the NYC Chapter of the Historical Novel Society, she helps produce monthly online book launches and author panels. Wands's writings have appeared in *Art in Fiction, Kindred Spirits* magazine, and The Irving Society journal *First Knight*. She lives in NYC with her husband, actor Robert Petkoff, and two cats, Flora and Flynn.

Author photo © Robert Petkoff

SELECTED TITLES FROM SPARKPRESS

SparkPress is an independent boutique publisher delivering high-quality, entertaining, and engaging content that enhances readers' lives, with a special focus on female-driven work. www.gosparkpress.com

Dovetails in the Tall Grass: A Novel, Samantha Specks, $16.95, 978-1-68463-093-6. In 1862, thirty-eight Dakota-Sioux men were hanged in the largest mass execution in US history. This is the story of two young women—one settler, one Dakota-Sioux—connected by the fate of the thirty-ninth man.

Cold Snap: A Novel, Codi Schneider, $16.95, 978-1-68463-101-8. When a murder shocks her peaceful mountain town, Bijou, a plucky house cat with a Viking spirit, must dive paws-first into solving the mystery before another life is taken—maybe even her own.

Indelible: A Sean McPherson Novel, Book 1, Laurie Buchanan, $16.95, 978-1-68463-071-4. Murder at a writing retreat in the Pacific Northwest, but this one isn't imaginary. Authors only kill with words. Or do they?

Gatekeeper: Book One in the Daemon Collecting Series, Alison Levy, $16.95, 978-1-68463-057-8. Rachel Wilde—sent from another dimension to bring defective daemons in for repair—needs to locate two people: a woman whose ancestors held a destructive daemon at bay and a criminal trying to break dimensional barriers. Helped by a homeless man with unusual powers, she uncovers a rising shadow organization that's changing her world forever.

The Sorting Room: A Novel, Michael Rose, $16.95, 978-1-68463-105-6. A girl coming of age during America's Great Depression, Eunice Ritter was born to uncaring alcoholic parents and destined for a life of low-wage toil—a difficult, lonely existence of scant choices. This epic novel—which spans decades—shows how hard work and the memory of a single friendship gave the indomitable Eunice the perseverance to pursue redemption and forgiveness for the grievous mistakes she made early in her life.